NAÏVE

A NOVEL
BY CHARLES ROYCE

Chutter Hill Publishing
Nashville, TN

This novel, *Naïve*, is the first book of a trilogy. The next book, *Transparent*, will offer another story from a different perspective, with some repeating characters and overlapping timelines, while the finale, *Synchronicity*, will bring both stories to a climactic end.

Excerpt regarding visible wavelength hyperspectral imaging (page 213) is paraphrased from an interview with Dr. Meez Izlam for the *Northern Echo*, October 29, 2013.

Names: Royce, Charles, author
Title: Naïve, a novel / by Charles Royce
ISBN: 978-1-7343357-0-5

This book contains an excerpt from the forthcoming book *Transparent* by Charles Royce. This excerpt has been written for this edition only, and may not reflect the final content of the upcoming edition.

For my mother,
who I miss every single day.

GRATEFUL
ACKNOWLEDGMENT TO:

My beautiful partner Chris, who, even though my writing is far from his genre, is never slow to give me insight and praise for accomplishing my goals. I love you and am so happy to share this life with you.

My mother-in-love, Carol Smith-Merkulov, whose experience in criminal law and devotion to this process has helped in ways I will cherish forever.

My editor Jamie Chavez. You, my longtime friend, are the real deal. Your humor, expertise, and attention to detail is just what I needed to push me further. I have learned so much and love working with you. Your talent and your fingerprints are all over this book.

My friends who took the time to read fledgling drafts of this novel—Matt, Ruben, Jennie, Jonathan, Chris and Carol—your encouragement and love are what keeps me going. I adore each one of you!

To Kelly Oechslin: I started creating this trilogy about ten years ago and put it down because it was too hard. Thanks to your inspired talent, I gained the courage to revisit this world and fell in love with it all over again. You showed me, all of us, how to be a bona fide author. Thank you.

To Pete Wilson: You spoke directly to my heart when you asked us all to remember our early passions, the ones we've had since we were children. For me, those passions were singing and writing. I cannot begin to tell you how much the truth of your words has manifested in me. Thank you.

To my family and friends who've seen me through it all, and loved me because of it. You know who you are.

CHAPTER 1

Ghost sits in front of his computer, counting his money as if it were the last on earth.

The room is dark, although it is mid-afternoon. He is huddled at a desk in front of a cracked, mustard-yellow wall interrupted only by a single tiny window, haphazardly covered by black velvet curtains. Light trickles in above and below, revealing only the slightest details of him and his workspace.

A sea of splotchy pigmentation drowns his body, leaving only tiny islands of light pink skin. Wiry white-blonde hair bursts from his scalp straight toward the sky, as if scrambling to escape its host. Thin freckled arms sneak past the openings of a dingy white tank top. A tattoo on his left shoulder blade looks like a childlike drawing of a skinny house with a pointed roof and a curved wavy base. The skinny house has been sloppily filled in with black ink, leaving what looks like two tiny circular windows where bright pink flesh peers from underneath. A thick horizontal line runs straight across the middle of the strange icon, giving nublike arms to what now resembles a ghost in the most minimal of ways. Underneath the illustration is a strange mix of Italian and French, incoherent, partially eaten away by a circular scar.

He lays a third stack of hundred-dollar bills on top of two others.

"Daddy!" A ten-year-old voice cries out in an all-too-familiar screech from down the hall.

Ghost mumbles under his breath, then jerks the top bill out from underneath its currency strap. He shoves it in his pocket and returns the remainder to the pile, making sure all corners meet perfectly. He wants to answer his son, but he knows he must log in to his email first. Part of the deal.

He turns to his laptop, an obsolete behemoth by worldly standards, an extravagant necessity by his own. The screen is blurred by filth and neglect, barely alive, yet manages to breathe an eerie glow, outlining Ghost's body from the waist up. He begins to type.

I-T-S D-O-N-E.

C H A P T E R   2

"No! NO! Don't you do this!" Micah screams, pounding on his husband's blood-soaked chest. "Don't, don't, please God, please!"

He is straddled over Lennox's naked, almost-lifeless body, screaming and pounding. Over and over.

"Baby, please! Don't. Please God help me, please God PLEASE!"

Micah rolls up his sleeves. He places his hands together and forces his weight onto Lennox. Lennox gurgles, but then his body goes limp. Sensing that what he's doing is working, Micah presses down with the disoriented strength of a madman, over and over. Over and over.

The day they first met.
The fight.
The wedding day.

Their life flashes before Micah's eyes as he continues the chest compressions over and over.

"No! NO!"

Over and over.

"Please, baby!

Over and over.

"Stay with me! Please God."

Micah continues to press. He is only five-feet-nine-inches, but with solid muscular density. He begins to feel his weight crushing Lennox.

He slows down. He stops and lets out a deep sigh, releasing the only breath he's taken for the last few moments. He unclenches his hands. Lennox does not move again.

Out of breath, Micah sits back and looks around his living room for his phone. He moves his legs in order to stand but slips in the crimson pool that has collected around them. He falls back onto Lennox.

He thinks about trying to get up again, to search for his phone, to call 9-1-1, to do *something*. but he's exhausted. He rests his head on Lennox's chest and pulls his husband's arm around his own. He closes his eyes. As he lies there on top of his partner, his frantic efforts shift to peaceful resolve.

> *The day they first met.*
> *The fight.*
> *The wedding day.*

A loud beep brings him back to his current situation. He opens his eyes just in time to see a series of three blinking red lights flashing from the corner of the room. But the flashing red lights do less to confuse Micah than snap him out of his trance. He jolts up, remembers his phone is in his back pocket, pulls it out and dials.

"9-1-1, what is your emergency?"

Micah is winded, trying to come up with the words. *My husband is dying*, or *My husband is dead*? The anger of his confusion and desperation boils and explodes in a frantic display.

"Please help me! My husband! Something's happened here! I tried to save him. He was alive. Oh God, please come, please! Maybe you can help him!"

"Sir, please slow down. Did you say something's happened to your husband?"

"Yes! I got home, and he was just lying there." He looks down and utters, "Blood." Micah stares at his hands and arms, his chest

4

and legs, all saturated. "Oh my God, I think he's dead! Please hurry!"

"Sir, what is your location?"

"142 Henry Street, #7, corner of Rutgers."

"We have an ambulance on the way, sir, and police are very close."

He unclenches his grip on the phone. Micah looks back at Lennox, lying in what is a river now. As the adrenaline subsides, reality sets in. Micah begins to wail.

"Oh God, how did this happen? I don't understand!" Micah hears himself talking out loud, but he's still on the phone.

"Now, I need you to calm down, okay? Is there anyone else in the house?"

Micah pauses in mid-breath. "What?"

"Sir, could the person who did this still be there?"

Throughout the ordeal, this is the first time the idea has even crossed his mind. *The killer could still be here.*

"Oh my God, I have no idea." Micah's voice is now softer.

He looks around their condo. *Lennox loves this place*, Micah remembers. The century-old brick walls that perfectly frame the twenty-two giant vertical windows on all four sides, the Manhattan skyline visible to the west and northwest, the two-hundred-year-old church with the bell tower (which they both had secretly wanted to climb) resting peacefully in the windows to the north, the fire-red brick apartment building to the east, and of course the magnificent views of the Manhattan Bridge over the East River to the south and southeast. Lennox had always wanted a full-story condo, with an elevator that opened right into the middle of his home. He was overjoyed when he found one in the Garfield Building, a little-known landmark from the 1800s on Manhattan's Lower East Side. Micah had come to love it, mostly because it had made Lennox so happy.

"Do you have a neighbor or a nearby friend you can go to right now, until help arrives?" The 9-1-1 operator, impatient for Micah's safety, interrupts his memories.

"I think I'm okay."

"Just to be safe, could you find a place to hide, maybe lock yourself in a bathroom, please sir?"

Micah thinks the idea atrocious. After all, he has just tried CPR on his dying husband, now he's supposed to hide? His friend Jenna lives just across the street, next to the church with the bell tower. *She could be on her way home by now*, he remembers, having just left her at the event they were both attending earlier in the evening.

"Yes, I have a friend who—"

The doorbell interrupts him. He looks toward the security system, a sleek metallic-chrome console, which is now reflecting the red-and-blue lights flickering through the front windows.

"I think they're here," Micah says to the operator.

He hangs up and rushes to the call box next to his elevator door. As usual, the video is not working, but the audio is. Micah presses, and by rote he mumbles, "Come on up."

Micah presses to listen, only to hear shards of the building's front door glass falling to the ground. Micah releases his finger from the buzzer, noticing his own bloody fingerprints wherever he touches. Seconds later a giant boom right next to him makes him jump.

They're trying to bust open the elevator.

He presses the elevator OPEN button so no more damage will be done to the place. Lennox will not be very happy.

Lennox.

Two police officers try to enter as the elevator opens, but only one makes it through first.

"He's right over there," Micah says, pointing to the far window behind the sofa. He places his finger in his mouth to bite the nail but is startled by the metallic taste. He closes his eyes in disbelief at what is happening. He tries to catch his breath. He feels like he's

6

suffocating. He wrestles his blood-soaked tuxedo jacket from his thick arms and throws it on the floor in front of him.

The first police officer, a heavyset woman, ignores Micah, steps over the jacket, and walks in the opposite direction of Lennox's body. She begins to secure the rest of the house, pushing Micah into the wall that houses the security mechanism and the light switches as she bulldozes by. She puts on her gloves, walks into the first bedroom and begins to check the closet, then under the bed. Micah leans forward to track her while keeping his vantage point from the elevator in the center of the room. After all, there's a possibility Lennox could still be alive.

The second policeman, Officer Mateo Palino, a burly six-foot-two Italian-looking fellow, reaches into his pocket and pulls out a set of blue rubber gloves. He walks past Micah toward Lennox, who is lying still on the floor. He turns around.

"Do you have a code that unlocks your private floor, sir? EMT is close, and I want them to be able to use the elevator with the stretcher."

"Yes." Micah turns around to press the key pad.

"Sir, wait," Officer Palino says. "We have to be careful here with fingerprints. Do you mind giving me the code?"

"It's 925411. I'll still have to let them in, but at least they'll be able to get the stretcher up here."

The officer's latex fingers punch in the code. He rushes back to Lennox.

Micah watches. As if in slow motion, the officer follows the river of blood toward Lennox, past the soaked black office chair that has clearly been moved from behind the desk to the far west corner of the living room. Bloody tracks end right beside the naked body. Lights from the ceiling beam down onto the scene, illuminating the dust still swirling about in a traumatized dance from the night's events. The rays are bathing Lennox in evening peace from the neck down. A cold shiver touches the very center of Micah's neck, causing a chill that undulates down his back.

This could be it, Micah thinks. *He could really be gone.*

Officer Palino pushes down on Lennox's neck with two fingers. Micah squints to see the officer's reaction.

Is he really dead? Did this really happen? Micah doesn't know what to think.

The elevator dings. Micah reaches down without looking and presses OPEN. An EMT team, complete with a stretcher, appears.

"Hold up." Officer Palino raises his palm. "Secure?" he yells to the large female officer who has just finished checking the condo.

"Secure," she answers.

"Okay then, come on through. Crime scene protocol. Wear your fucking gloves."

Micah walks toward the officer, who has relocated to the center of the living room. "Is he—"

"Dead? Yes. Well, I'm pretty sure. Waiting on confirmation."

"Oh God." Micah collapses onto the couch, streaking the blood starting to cake on his hands onto the sofa arm as he goes down. The officer notices.

"I wouldn't. Jesus. Stand up, please."

Micah stands up.

The officer takes off his gloves. "Sir, I'm Officer Mateo Palino from Seventh District Precinct. What is your name?"

"Micah. Micah Breuer."

"Mr. Breuer, can you tell me what happened here?"

Micah clears his throat. *Where do I begin?*

"Well, I was at an event," he says, "wondering where my husband was—"

"And that's your husband right there?" Officer Palino bobs his head in the direction of the body.

"Yes."

"Subject is confirmed dead." The head EMT takes off his gloves and motions his team to exit the premises.

"No, dear God!" Micah begins to move toward Lennox.

Officer Palino stops him with an upraised arm. "Sir, this is officially a murder scene. I'm gonna need you to stand still, please." He leans in and puts his hand on Micah's shoulder. "Now, I'm sorry for your loss, but I need to ask a few questions."

Micah nods.

"You were at an event, wondering where your husband was ..." Officer Palino continues, as the female officer moves into position beside him.

"Yes, I couldn't get ahold of him. I was worried. So I left and came home. I walked through the elevator, yelled for him. Nothing. That's when I heard something like someone clearing his throat. I walked into the living room and saw him on the floor. It was dark, I thought he'd collapsed from choking or something, so I ran over to him and started doing CPR."

"CPR, like breathing into his mouth?"

"No, like chest compressions, over and over. It was working at first, but then he just ... stopped ... breathing."

The elevator door dings again.

"I'll get that," says Officer Palino, who wants to keep his crime scene as pristine as possible. He presses the OPEN button. The elevator reveals a tall man in a buttoned-up black overcoat.

Detective Bronson Penance walks toward them as the elevator doors close. "Just came from Union Square, some hotshot from uptown gunned down in the street. Busy night."

Detective Penance is 44 years old with salt-and-pepper hair, medium length, slicked back. His crystal blue eyes reflecting the lights from the ceiling as they scan the room. He takes notes in a small black book he's pulled from his coat pocket, then walks with confidence toward Officer Palino, who motions with his head to join him elsewhere. They veer together to the opposite corner of the room, away from Micah and in a whispered hush, Officer Palino begins to share the information he has collected.

Micah looks down at his hands, which are beginning to crackle from the dried blood. He jiggles his wedding ring right-to-left with his thumb to release it from its crusted bondage. For a second, he thinks about going to the bathroom to wash his hands but remembers Officer Palino's reprimand from the last time he tried to do anything normal, like sit on his own sofa. Micah turns and looks at Lennox, his partner of four years, his husband of two.

>*The day they first met.*
>*The wedding.*
>*The last time he saw him alive.*

Micah begins to weep.

Detective Penance walks over to the dead man's body, past the desk, noting the bowl of half-eaten cereal still on the glass desktop. He continues past the green velvet sofa, situated behind the desk to signal the start of the living room, and onto the thick grey jute area rug, which is soaked in blood. Being careful not to touch anything, he bends down to examine Lennox. *Skinny man, but built*, he thinks. *Poor guy*. After only five or six seconds, he gets back up, nods to Officer Palino and walks toward Micah.

"You told Officer Palino here that it was dark when you first saw your husband on the floor?"

"Yes. I thought he was choking."

"You must've turned on these can lights above us here *after* you tried to save him?" He points to the ceiling.

"I—I guess so. I don't really remember."

The detective takes another step closer to Micah.

"Let me get this straight," he says, eyes down in his notebook, walking closer. "You walk into your house."

Closer.

"Your husband is lying on the floor in a pool of blood."

Closer.

"You hear him choking, possibly still alive."

Detective Penance is now face to face with Micah.

"He's got what could be over thirty stab wounds in his chest, throat, and abdomen. *Thirty*."

He cocks his head, piercing his eyes into Micah's.

"And your very first thought … is CPR?"

CHAPTER 3

"Let me out here, please."

Jenna has experienced a rather wretched night at the launch party for the September issue of her former company's most elite fashion magazine and wants to rid herself of the lingering unease. Despite the unexpectedly chilly August evening, she decided about two seconds ago that she wanted to walk the rest of the way home, and somehow a cigarette is already in her mouth.

The car screeches to a halt at Orchard and Grand. Jenna, put together in a timeless little Armani black dress, swipes her credit card through the cab's smudged and tilted machine, grabs her coat and purse, and exits. With an unlit Parliament Light in her mouth, she situates her Burberry trench over her left arm and her Chanel clutch under her right shoulder. The addition of trying to maneuver her Manolo Blahniks within the grooves of the cobblestone street proves too much for her tipsy condition, and she slams the taxi door like a sloppy sailor during Fleet Week.

"Oh my God, I'm drunk, girl." She laughs, noticing her French accent is thicker than normal. "I'm that girl, that girl who hobbles around the Lower East Side on a Friday night." Realizing she's mumbling out loud to herself makes her laugh even more. "Yep," she says, affirming what she just said to herself. Her heels manage to take refuge on the sidewalk, and Jenna stops to take in a deep breath.

It was one of those quintessential Manhattan nights … the crisp, cool air mixed with the smell of wine from restaurant patios, and the occasional whiff of the unknown. She is anxious. And because the evening has not turned out as she had planned, she congratulates herself on using the walk to clear her head.

A French-born, mostly American-raised thirty-four-year-old, Jenna Ancelet is a tall, stunning woman, graceful in appearance, but unaware of these qualities. She carries herself like a bull in a Waterford crystal shop, is the first to light up during a nice seven-course garden dinner with the company executives, and normally dresses in J. Crew sweaters and jeans. She believes her current ensemble is a bit too much for her. Timeless, sure, but comfortable? *Hell no.*

She jostles her left arm to resituate her trench and puts her Bic to the cigarette that's been hanging off the side of her mouth. As her mind turns to earlier in the evening, one thought begins to gnaw at the back of her mind: *Lennox.* She remembers how Micah had been anxious all night at the party trying to get his husband on the phone and still wonders why he'd left so abruptly.

She takes a huge drag and continues walking.

Jenna often finds herself worrying about Lennox. Still. She first met Lennox when she became his executive assistant three years ago. Having handled everything for him during that time, both personally and professionally, she still wonders how he's managing without her, how he ever could.

Despite leaving Lennox under precarious circumstances to work for his competitor, they have remained friends. He's a handful, very precise and businesslike, and not very intimate, which she has come to accept. She has grown to love him, not in spite of these qualities, but because of them. She feels safe with him, and with his husband Micah, too. They all plan dinners together, weekend jaunts to the Hamptons, and even housesit for each other.

She puts on her coat and continues walking, ruminating. *It's so cold and quiet and peacef—.*

She sees a tall man walking toward her and stops. She holds her clutch closer to her body. The young man pivots to the opposite side of street and disappears into a bar, the door opening and closing in staccato, unleashing a brief but loud interlude of music and lively patrons that echoes down Orchard Street. The subsequent silence helps to slow her heartbeat. She exhales.

Jenna continues walking, ruminating, swerving. Being intoxicated sometimes impairs Jenna's sense of judgment when it comes to being alone on the streets of New York. The longer she lives here, the more confident she feels, the more potential danger she ignores. *These streets are my 'hood, and the Lower East Side is not what is used to be*, she muses as she turns the corner at Orchard and Canal. After all, what was once semi-abandoned real estate filled with displaced immigrants, active druggies, and extremely active prostitutes is now a gentrified playground and a young New Yorker's dream come true.

She passes her favorite restaurant, PM, a relatively new high-end establishment. Around five or six in the morning, the restaurant changes to AM, and becomes a breakfast/brunch place, which Jenna thinks is brilliant. She's been wanting to catch them changing the "A" to a "P" on the sign outside, or at least the "P" to an "A," if she could get up that early.

"So cool," she says, as she laughs to herself. "AM, PM." She chuckles again. She's completely drunk. She turns the corner at Canal and Rutgers, one block from her apartment.
She sees red and blue lights flickering from behind the two-hundred-year-old church with the bell tower.

CHAPTER 4

"Thirty times?" Micah asks.

"Yeah. Somebody had a vendetta." Detective Penance wants to elicit a reaction.

"I had no idea. I mean, it looked like a lot of blood, but I didn't know where it was coming from."

Detective Penance leaves a moment of silence to see if Micah will continue. Of course, Penance has his suspicions. In his experience, he has found such displays of psychotic overindulgence to be crimes of passion. And who usually commits these types of murders? Someone extremely close to the victim. *New perp. Same old story.*

"What happened?" Micah breaks the silence. "Who could've done this to him?"

"That's the question, isn't it?" Detective Penance looks at Micah. "Mind if we talk downtown? I want to hear about your night from the beginning. Why don't you come with me, let them do their work?"

Micah recognizes the question as a command. "Of course."

Detective Penance nods to the police officers and to the crime scene team that has begun to document its findings. "Keep me posted."

He stands behind Micah, nudging him in the small of his back as they enter the elevator. They ride down in silence and exit the building through what's left of the front door. Glass crackles underneath their feet. Red and blue lights are now illuminating the entire city block, which is barricaded to through-traffic. A bevy of police cars begins to swarm the corner of Henry and Rutgers.

The odd evening chill rushes through Micah's wavy blond hair, and he realizes he is still wearing his white tux shirt, discolored to a blackened crimson. A short, auburn-haired woman Micah has never seen before is holding the door open to a black Lincoln MKZ, motioning for him to enter. Lights are flashing in his eyes. Entire news crews are also assembling, photographing and filming the worst night of his life. A familiar voice calls out from the crowd.

"Micah!"

He scans and spots his friend, who is waving, dressed in her trench with her clutch still in her hands.

"Jenna!" Micah yells with a mix of excitement and relief, knowing he now has a brief link to the outside world. He locks eyes with her and makes a phone call mime with his right thumb and pinkie. "Call Shawn!"

Jenna nods and watches Micah get into the car with Detective Penance. They drive away.

"Who's Shawn?" Detective Penance asks, turning around from the front passenger seat of the car as they make their way to the police station.

Micah, sitting in the middle of the back seat with his head down and his hands in his lap, never looks up.

"My lawyer."

CHAPTER 5

A flash of light. *((Buzzz.))* Another flash. *((Buzzz.))*

"Turn to the left, and lift up your left arm," says the female photographer, the same lady who'd opened the door to the Lincoln MKZ and driven Micah and Detective Penance to this place, a sticky little corner of Manhattan's Seventh Precinct police station's basement.

Her name is Lilith McGuire. She has been Detective Penance's right hand for less than five months. Her hope has been to be considered partner within the year, but her three-month evaluation contained Detective Penance's handwritten remark "hit or miss" underneath "Decision-Making," a setback that still haunts her. Standing at only five-foot-four, skinny, beautiful by any standard, with long, straight, dark auburn hair that she puts up in a ragged ponytail most of the time, she is inherently eager, which is both her biggest strength and greatest weakness. In all aspects of her life, she is the dominant one, and most often does as she pleases, which is why her last long-term relationship with a woman ended in an ugly divorce. She hates her name, and would prefer "Lil," but no one calls her that. Everyone who works with her loves the irony of calling her Lily. *It's like calling the Pope "Franny,"* they often joke.

Having only been an investigator for a short time, she takes advantage of any opportunity to prove herself worthy of partner status. But right now, she finds herself in charge of taking nude photos in the basement of the precinct.

"Now turn to the right, and lift up your right arm," Lily says to Micah, who is standing naked in front of her, covering his privates with whichever hand is available. "Thank you for consenting to these photos. We're almost done. Just a few more."

Micah's muscles tense as his body shivers. "Anything you need."

The computer screen in front of Lily flashes Micah's different body parts frame-by-frame while she continues to snap photos.

Micah's neck. *((Flash. Buzzz.))* His face. *((Flash. Buzzz.))* His hands. *((Flash. Buzzz.))*

◆

Lennox's mutilated chest. *((Flash. Buzzz.))* His punctured neck. *((Flash. Buzzz.))* The crime scene photographer stops, feeling nauseous at the site of the butchered body, one of the worst he's ever seen. He turns his head.

Just beside the photographer stands Officer Palino on the phone with Detective Penance, filling him in on everything they've found thus far.

"You got the password I sent you for the victim's phone, right?" asks Officer Palino.

"Yep, thanks, looking at it now. Shows texts to a Jenna, a couple of texts and voice mails from Micah, one unknown, and one that just says 'WORK' in all caps. Haven't listened to them yet of course. Got the suspect's bloody jacket. Got his bag too. We've also secured two laptops, looks like a work one and a personal one, and a huge iMac that has pictures of both the victim and the suspect floating on the screen saver, with a bunch of mail and papers sitting around addressed to Micah Breuer. You think the iMac uses the same password as the iPhone?"

"If not, he's being cooperative, so I'm sure we can get that one too. Mark 'em, bag 'em. We'll go through them and see what we can find. The suspect has also consented to photos and DNA sampling, so we will have some documentation on bruising, blood, signs of a struggle. Keep going, but I think we're in good shape."

"Wait, that's not all," Palino says. "I'm no detective or anything, but I'm noticing all this recovery literature on the bookshelves, and a couple of notes about sponsees and shit around one of the victim's laptops."

"Yeah, so this Lennox guy was probably a recovering drunk or drug addict, or both, and he sponsored people. So, what of it?"

"Well, one of my guys was searching through the closet in the back bedroom and found a box of old cards and letters addressed to Lennox, and at the bottom of the box were a couple of bags of what looks like heroin. One of 'em is half empty."

"Hmmm. Maybe this recovery thing has gone awry somehow."

"Yeah, that's what I was thinking, probably the dead guy fell off the wagon would be my guess."

"Nice work, Palino. Anything else?" asked Detective Penance, halfway to getting off the phone.

"Yeah yeah yeah, just one more thing. There's a sticker on each of these heroin baggies, with some sort of emblem on it. It's one I've never seen before."

"An emblem? What do you think it is?"
"It looks like some sort of ghost or something."

CHAPTER 6

Micah is sitting alone in a holding room on the second floor of the police station. His hands are folded, his head down, the exact position as he was in the car on the way over. He is defeated, forlorn, anxious, sad, terrified. From his perspective, the room seems to be encroaching ever so slowly upon him, as if preparing to consume him. The light gray walls with fake wainscoting painted halfway up, the two-way mirror across from him that he can't bear to look at, the camera with the flashing red light in the corner of the ceiling—all moving in, inch by inch.

With his tux and shoes in evidence, he is now wearing navy scrub pants and a white T-shirt, with flat white shoes peering from pant legs that are way too long. He is still partially caked in blood, around his face, his hands. He stares at his fingers and begins to pick at them.

Lily, waiting for her boss Detective Penance to arrive, sits in a cold aluminum chair across from Micah. She notices him deep in thought and allows herself to see him as the second victim of this tragic crime.

"How old are you, Micah?"

"Thirty-seven." His response is obligatory.

"We tried to find your parents but fell a little short there."

"Yeah. I'm all that's left."

Lily reaches for some empathy. She may be known as a bit cold-hearted, but she knows hurt when she sees it.

"I lost my mom a few years ago. Brain tumor." She remembers a long season of life-changing decision-making.

"Yeah?"

Lily recognizes the connection and lets the silence do its job.

"I'm sorry for your loss. Breast cancer for mine," Micah says, still picking at the dried blood. "Gosh, she was great. She mostly took care of me, like from ever since I can remember, to, well, always, really. Didn't have another job. She used to be a kindergarten teacher, but mostly she was a housewife. Painted sometimes. I like to think I got my creative side from her."

He relaxes his hands and places them on the stainless tabletop that separates them.

"Boy, she was strong, too," he says. "She'd seen her sister die after a long battle with cancer. Fucking cancer, right?"

"Fuckin' A," Lily says before she can rephrase.

"We think she knew something was wrong for quite some time before she went to the hospital," Micah says. "We think she just didn't want us to worry."

Lily scoots her chair forward. "Us? What about your dad?"

"Pssshht. That's a whole other story. Great man, yes, but more of a pastor than a father. I mean, you know the drill, right? Christian family, gay son. That was fun. He's the one who named me Micah. Stupid biblical name. Lenny always liked the name. But then again, he's a Republican." He pauses. "Was."

"How did you two meet?" Lily is practicing her psychological skills.

"We met at a meeting. In AA. I was getting coffee and this really hot guy started staring at me while he was swishing around his powdered creamer." Micah half-heartedly mimes a stirring motion with his hands. He laughs. "We smiled at each other across the room the whole night. Then a group of us went out after the meeting. We started talking. Figured out that we both worked for the same company. He was some bigwig finance guy at Élan Publishing, and I did freelance art direction for the same exact company. Can you believe that?"

"That's quite a connection."

"It is," he says, switching tenses as if he's in transition. "It's a classic introvert-extrovert, thinker-feeler thing, ya know? He was the thinker, which I loved. And I feel everything, like *everything*, which is what he loves about me. Well, most of the time."

He laughs, then stares at his reflection in the two-way mirror behind her. His smile turns downward.

Lily can tell he is about to clam up. "And how did your dad die?"

"It was pretty recent. Stage 4 kidney failure. Diabetes. He never took care of himself after Momma died." Micah jerks his head away, wanting to scream. He runs his fingers through his hair and leans back with an audible groan.

"Can we stop, please?" he says, his voice cracking. "I'm sorry. Just for a second."

Lily lets him be.

As Micah tries to relax, his teeth begin to grind. He begins to wonder where Shawn, his lawyer and his friend, could be. He hopes Jenna has found him. *Shawn was at the event tonight too,* he thinks. *Maybe he still is. Jesus Christ. This is going to be a really long night.*

Detective Penance enters. Lily stands.

"Micah, thank you for coming down here with us tonight. I know it's been a rough evening for you. You're free to go at any time, but I would love it if you'd answer a few questions for us. Is that okay?" Detective Penance asks.

"I have nothing to hide. I don't mind."

"There's quite a story unfolding in your home. Would you mind telling me how *your* story goes?" Detective Penance raises his eyebrows.

"You mean after Lennox told me good-bye and said he'd meet me at the event later?"

"Sure. Start there."

CHAPTER 7

Earlier that night, Micah had looked around in awe, marveling at the red-carpet frenzy and the magnificent crowd. He couldn't have dreamed of a more perfect New York evening. The mid-August air was alive with a rare pre-autumn chill, and the lights from the paparazzi added just the right touch to Manhattan's Midtown nightscape. Several news outlets had already coined it "THE LAUNCH PARTY OF THE DECADE," and Micah could definitely see why. He looked around at the bustling swarm of entertainment's elite and publishing's power player and felt jealousy bubbling to the surface.

Josh made all of this happen, Micah thought as he walked through the vast concrete and marble courtyard and ascended the majestic stairs leading into the foyer of the new Élan headquarters. Huge two-story banners rippled down both sides of the staircase, each displaying a different celebrity featured in the September issue of Élan.

Damn, this is good.

Fucking Josh.

Micah saw Josh from a distance, talking with the actress Jennifer Lawrence at the top of the stairs. Micah made a point to brush by him, bumping him with his shoulder, just to let him know he was there.

Micah kept walking and stopped at the triple-decker appetizer table. He grabbed a shrimp and was about to choose a sauce for dipping.

"Hello, Micah!"

Startled, Micah dropped the shrimp in the cocktail sauce. At first Micah thought it was Josh, but when he turned, he was face to face with James West, Élan Publishing's CEO, the man most often credited for the company's dramatic success.

James West was a tall, slender man with gray hair, and at forty-three considered very young for his position. He was a handsome Harvard Business School graduate who'd started the company from scratch at age twenty-eight—a mere fifteen years ago. He owned every room he entered, and he had the money to literally own it as well. His business philosophy was to hire youthful, passionate, driven people who knew what they were doing, guide them, and watch them make him look good. The "West Way," as his employees had coined it, was the main reason why he had hired Lennox. And that's also why he approved of Micah as a top freelancer for his burgeoning marketing department.

"Thanks for coming!" James West replied in a loud voice, overcompensating for the crowd noise echoing off the stark cement walls.

"I wouldn't have missed it." Micah's voice was at a normal level, hoping Mr. West would take the hint. "Quite the lobby, and quite the launch party."

"Wait till you see what Josh has in store for the grand opening party, where we let you into the rest of this magnificent place!" He was still screaming. "Where's your better half, by the way?"

"Well, sir, last time I saw Lennox, he said he should be here around …" Micah looked down at his phone and grimaced. "Any minute now."

"Please give him my best and have him find me. We have something to discuss."

"Will do, sir." Micah knew this was the extent of his time with Mr. West.

"Have a good night, then." James turned around. "Angelina!" He was already in another conversation.

Micah continued to look through the crowd. *Jenna's late. Typical.* He walked toward the celebrity meet-and-greet area, noticing how alone he felt. *I wish Lennox were here.*

He texted him.

> OH. MY. GOD. You said you'd be right
> here. Lemme know an ETA, baby.

Micah looked up from his phone and saw his friend Shawn and his wife Haylee, both gawking at Meryl Streep, who was talking with Goldie Hawn. Shawn and Haylee were standing less than three feet away, staring as if their stalking would be rewarded with a private conversation.

"Oh, wow, they actually think they're next in line to talk with her," Micah mumbled out loud.

"You know Meryl is just dying to meet them," said Jenna, sneaking up from behind.

"Haha, that's what I was just thinking," he said, kissing both sides of Jenna's face. He looked at her little black dress. "I thought you were gonna wear the red gown, the big Halston one with the flared sleeves?"

"I couldn't find it."

"Jesus, Jenna, you need constant supervision."

"Are we having fun?" she asked, in her signature coarse and crumbly voice, with a classic European upward lilt at the end of her inquiry.

"Sure! If you call 'fun' looking at this amazing event and the ridiculous people your boy Josh got to come here."

"Josh told me he, um, ran into you."

"That was fast."

"Well, I've been here just a little bit, walking around with him, enjoying everything he's done. I went to the bathroom, and when I came back, he told me I just missed you."

"You *still* love him, even after everything that happened," Micah said, looking for contradictory validation.

"I can't help it. And you can't help but like him too. Admit it." She nudged him a little too hard, but Micah did not move. "God! You two are in constant competition. So Josh didn't hire you for this event, who cares? You literally design everything else for this company."

"You know it's not about that, Jenna." He rarely used her name so sternly, and Jenna took note.

"Oh. Speaking of, where is that handsome man of yours?" she asked, emphasizing the word *yours*.

"He's so late. I was just about to call him again."

"Well, don't let me stop you. I've got some sleuthing to do." Jenna winked to let Micah know that she knew how weird it was for her to be here. She was the executive assistant to the competition's CEO, after all, and the only reason she was there was to be her best friend's date. Josh had pulled some strings.

Micah headed to a nearby alcove just outside the breezeway of the lobby, dialing Lennox as he made his way through the crowd. Lennox didn't answer, so Micah left another voice mail. "Hey, baby, where are you? I miss you. I can't tell you how many people are asking about you. Text me or call me, I have my phone. I hope everything's all right."

Over an hour had passed since Micah had arrived, and the party was moving from mingling and drinking to presentations and speeches. Micah saw that Jenna had relocated to the back of the crowd, which was transitioning into an audience, and made his way toward her.

"Lennox still isn't here, and I can't get ahold of him. Something doesn't feel right," he whispered to Jenna. He kissed her good-bye and left before she could say a word.

CHAPTER 8

"Then I took a cab, came home, opened the door, and I told you the rest."

Micah exits his dreamlike state of remembering the normalcy of the night ... how everything was beautiful and right, and then shattered in an instant. Of course, Micah has hit only the highlights outlining the evening aloud to Detective Penance. He doesn't feel the need to go into the details his mind tends to embellish.

"Can you think of anyone who would want to harm him?" the detective asks. "Maybe this Josh character. What's his full name, and who is he to you?"

Micah pauses, then answers.

"Josh Harrison. He had an affair with Lennox two years ago."

"Hmm." Detective Penance jots down the name.

"Josh is harmless and wouldn't hurt a fly. Besides, he was there at the party. He was in charge of the whole freaking event."

"Still. We'll check. How about the Élan CEO you mentioned? What was his name? Mr. James West?"

"James West, yes. I only barely know James," Micah answers. "Although he was *very* serious when he said he wanted to talk to Lennox. I still have no idea what that was about."

Lily leans forward and whispers something to Detective Penance, who then moves the conversation in another direction.

"That brings us back to you, then," the detective says. "There's no blood on the light switch. Can you explain that?"

"Excuse me?" Micah asks.

"You said it was dark. But Officer Palino was the first on the scene, and he says the lights in the living room were already on."

Detective Penance pauses for an answer. Nothing. He grows impatient and slightly raises his voice.

"There's blood everywhere you touched, but there's no blood on the light switches. Can you explain that, please?"

Again, Micah does not respond in the timely manner that Detective Penance would like, and the detective grows weary of what he takes to be consistent avoidance. He decides to shift his questioning to get Micah's attention and almost yells. "Why did you pound on your husband's mutilated body when you knew he was still alive?"

"Sir, I told you, I was freaking the fuck—" Micah stands up, but then he discards his momentary anger and pauses. He looks up at nothingness, then looks down.

"Geez, oh man, did I …?" Micah locks eyes with Detective Penance, then the two-way mirror, then Lily. They all become nameless, faceless people in the seeming blur that is this moment.

"Did … did I kill him?" Micah asks, to anyone who would answer. He places his hands around the temples of his forehead, slumping back in his chair. "Oh, dear God, I killed him myself."

The door to the holding room opens.

"Fellas, that's enough." A new face enters the room. "Shawn Connelly, I'm the lawyer for Mr. Breuer."

Detective Penance looks up, collects his belongings, and stands up.

"Yes, and he's gonna need you. He's just confessed to murdering his husband."

CHAPTER 9

A cockroach scurries in front of a heavily worn cardboard box, back and forth, back and forth, like a night watchman keeping guard over the contents inside.

A tiny hand slowly peels a small sticker from a dirty white sheet of paper, and places it on a small, sealed plastic bag of light brown powder.

"How's this?" the ten-year-old voice asks, proud of his clumsy sticker placement.

"Almost."

A larger hand takes the bag from the smaller hands, peels the sticker off, then centers it on the bag. Ghost throws the branded heroin into the cardboard box with the others. The cockroach scurries away.

The ten-year-old speaks again.

"Thanks, Daddy."

CHAPTER 10

"We need to find out what's going on with the drugs that were found. Any leads on what scumbag uses this ghost logo?" Detective Penance is in his office, already dissecting the evidence while Micah consults with his lawyer in another room.

The old-school clock plugged into the wall of Detective Penance's office reads 3:20am. The room is dark, with an overhead light bulb illuminating the paperwork on his desk. *This is tense, but electric, just like I like it,* he thinks.

"Nothing in the database on initial search, but we're still looking," Lily says, knowing that the "we" she is referring to is most likely only herself.

"I want this Josh character followed up on, and this CEO of the company they all work for as well," Detective Penance orders, prompting a nod from Lily. "Apparently, there've now been two murders in the same night, and both victims are from the same company. This one is within our jurisdiction, so let's get on it. The computers and phones found at the scene ... once they get to the station, make sure we get the passwords we don't have already, then make goddamn sure everything is in order, logged, and organized. I need to read and listen to these messages the suspect says he left on the victim's phone, I need transcripts and recordings of the 9-1-1 call, and I want any and all phone records of both the victim and the suspect. Plus anything else they find on this cold-blooded murderer."

◆

"They think you killed Lennox in cold blood?" Shawn asks Micah, as if it were the furthest thing from any earthly realm of expectation. He reaches out to touch Micah, who seems to flinch at first, but then accepts the gesture. Micah feels safe. After all, Shawn Connelly is here.

A balding straight man, short in stature, but tall in experience, Shawn is both the butt of his friends' jokes about ego-inflated lawyers and their unabashed cockiness and the defender of his friends' mistakes, especially when they need him most. He first met Lennox at Harvard Law School, before Lennox decided to switch from law to business. Since Lennox had always been drawn to outgoing extroverts, he and Shawn hit it off and had remained best friends despite their differing paths.

Shawn went on to become quite adept at criminal law, graduating second in his class, and had enjoyed his subsequent pick of New York City's elite defense firms. He'd finally settled on Lyte & Morgan, where he paid his dues and blossomed into one of the most sought-after up-and-coming criminal defense attorneys in the city.

Lennox chose finance, and was hand-picked by Élan Publishing, a startup at the time, right after graduation. He also chose drugs, which almost cost him his job and his friendship with Shawn until Lennox got clean.

Through weddings, promotions, drugs, sobriety, Shawn has seen the best of Lennox and the worst. Ever the hero, Shawn now stands in service before Micah, whom he'd always admired for keeping Lennox sober. Shawn has been through way too much with Lennox, his best friend, his best man, to stand by and let Lennox's husband be put away for something that he would never do.

"I didn't do it on purpose," Micah says, looking up at Shawn.

"I know." Shawn grabs his hand and sits down next to Micah.

Micah, feeling true empathy for the first time throughout this awful ordeal, lays his head on Shawn's shoulder and begins to weep. "What am I supposed to do now?"

Micah wipes his eyes on Shawn's shoulder. Practicing his skills of walking the delicate balance between friend and lawyer, Shawn lays his head on Micah's for a brief moment.

"Well, first of all, I need to know every detail about what happened tonight." Shawn lifts his head. Micah takes the cue and sits up. "And not just what you told the detective. I need to know everything, what you were wearing, hearing, seeing, thinking … Did you have a fight, was he cheating again, is there someone else in the picture, was he doing drugs, was he meeting with weird people again … All of it."

Micah nods. He thinks about how weary he is of talking and processing this horrible evening. He flashes back to seeing Lennox, hearing his gurgles, pounding on his chest, hearing the weird beeping sound, wondering about the flashing lights from the corner of the room. He wants to talk to Shawn but is fighting to keep his eyes open.

Shawn reads the situation.

"Maybe we should do this tomorrow. Let's get you a hotel room for the night." Shawn looks down at his watch, which reads 3:50am. "Jesus."

◆

"Christ!" Detective Penance is on a phone call with the crime scene. "I'm sorry, one more time. Slowly."

Lily looks on, shrugging her shoulders as if to ask, *What the fuck are they saying?*

"Ok, thanks." He hangs up the phone.

"What?" asks Lily.

"Sit down." Detective Penance smiles. Lily was already sitting. "There was a wireless camera in the corner of that room."

"Come again?"

"The battery was dead, but the camera was still warm."

"Wait. What? How? What? Wireless?"

"Yes!" Detective Penance exclaims. "A tiny camera, hidden in an African-looking wooden box, all hand-carved and shit, with a hole in the front. Coulda recorded everything."

"Fuck me."

"Yep. Now we just have to find where it recorded *to*."

C H A P T E R   1 1

Josh Harrison is waiting at AM, the brunch place where he is supposed to meet Jenna. Late August is once again pounding the city with its sweltering heat, and he wonders if sitting outside is the best idea, despite it being the only open table.

Jenna is late. Sunday morning is a busy time for the NYC hot spot of the moment, and Josh is thinking of succumbing to the passive aggressive pressure from the waitress with the rolling eyes.

He has chosen the best spot for people-viewing, right below the two huge restaurant sign letters that read "AM." He sits at one of three black metal curbside tables, reading the *New York Times* Sunday edition on his iPhone. He scrolls through a raving review of his launch party and smiles. Then he reads an in-depth story on Lennox's murder.

Lennox.

He stops on a color photo of the murder suspect, a man who vaguely resembles himself, with the same hair, same defined features.

"Fucking Micah," he says out loud. He runs his fingers through his sweat drenched, wavy blond locks. *Lennox had a type. That's all. Stupid to think I was ever anything more.*

43

Despite his feelings about Lennox and Micah, Josh wants to continue enjoying his weekend, continue basking in his success. But he can't seem to settle his thoughts.

Relaxing is supposed to be one of the perks of having a big budget. He thinks of the janitorial crew he hired, mostly likely still cleaning up after the event. *So why can't I sit back and be proud of what I've done?*

He checks the time on his phone.

Waiting on Jenna, he thinks.

Sounds like a romantic comedy. Or a fucking frustrating film about ...

"I'm so sorry." Jenna appears from behind on his left, a full twenty minutes past her planned arrival. She kisses him on both sides of his face. "You wouldn't believe it if you tried."

"Jenna, lovely Jenna, right on time." Josh tries to mask his frustration with sarcasm, a language he knows she will understand. "Where have you been? And don't tell me you've been home, because you never are. You barely even sleep there."

"Stop. You know I nanny in Soho on Friday nights, but since I had your event that night, I told her I could do Saturday instead. Just got done."

Jenna, dressed in seersucker shorts and a yellow v-neck, crosses Josh and seats herself in the chair opposite him. She looks up at the sign above Josh's head and smiles.

"Dammit, I missed it again," she says.

"You and that sign."

"My dear sweet Josh, are you okay?" Jenna reaches in her purse for a cigarette. "I'm sorry I haven't called, it's all been a bit too much."

"You're talking about Lennox, right?" Josh tries to act like the fact that his ex-lover was murdered shouldn't faze him one bit. "I'm in shock, I think. Mind if we ease into talking about that?"

Jenna lifts the mood by raising her voice a half-octave.

44

"Okay, where do I start?" Jenna ignites her Parliament Light, takes a huge puff and exhales, motioning to the waitress at the same time. "I could start with my friend from work, who, oh God, witnessed something horrible in Union Square the same night as your party. She's still traumatized, and I need to go see her, so I only have time for like a latte or something. Did you read the story in the *Times*?"

"You mean the story on my launch party, or the story about Lennox's murder?" Josh leans in, already ready to talk.

"You made it!" says the waitress, startling Jenna. "Can I get you something, ma'am?"

"Yes, I'll have a latte please"—she matches the waitress's sugar-sweet tone—"and could you please bring it in one of those little porcelain cups? Not the take-away cup."

"Sure thing." The waitress smiles.

Jenna raises her eyebrows at Josh, who responds with a shrug. The waitress grabs the two menus on the table and heads back inside the restaurant.

"It's awful, isn't it?" he asks.

"Yes, she is."

"Lennox, smartass." Josh leans back and stares into space. "It's hard to believe, really. I mean, I've only hung out with Lennox a couple of times since, you know, we broke up and stuff. But still."

"Um, 'broke up' is a bit of an understatement, don't you think? I think you mean after Micah found out about you two and ordered you to stop seeing him, stop talking to him."

"That."

"I can't believe it either. I loved that man." Jenna's emotion surfaces and her voice cracks. She pretends to cough as she rests her cigarette on the side of the empty place setting in front of her. "Sure, he was a complete mess at times, but he had such a good heart, didn't he?"

Recognizing her question as more of a rhetorical statement, Josh nods and allows her to continue.

45

"He was always there for me, even after you guys split up. Didn't seem to bother him at all really, my being friends with you. And I love Micah, despite how you may feel about him. He kinda fancies you, even though he hates you. And you do look quite similar, which I always found very weird and unnatural."

Josh nods again. He is used to Jenna's occasional way of speaking, a kind of sensible nonsense, as if she were on the side of a stage, speaking her own language in a run-on soliloquy to anyone who would listen. He realizes her need to process.

"I mean, we are such great friends. *Were* great friends." She coughs as her cigarette nub burns her fingers. "Shit."

"Do you remember when we first met?"

"Do I remember? You were hooked, my friend. Hook line and sink-, sink-, sink something." She extinguishes the butt on the black metal table.

"Sinker. Yes, yes, I was. He had this way about him. I couldn't get enough of him."

"That's the truth. You were at our office almost every day, which I loved. I got used to you using your relationship with me to spend time with Lennox. As a matter of fact, it was kinda fun being the one caught in the middle. God. Forbidden shit is always the best. I mean, do you know how many emails I had to delete from Lennox's account? The nasty ones between you and Lennox? Hundreds. And I musta missed a couple because isn't that how Micah found out?"

"I assume so, yeah."

A breeze rushes through, sending napkins flying through the air and silverware dropping to the cobblestones. Josh welcomes the wind. It soothes him. He closes his eyes.

"Josh, he's not here anymore. Lennox is dead." Jenna picks up her spoon, napkin and cigarette butt. "Do you realize that he has been *murdered*? Murdered, Josh. The paper says he was stabbed thirty-three times."

"Thirty-three?" His voice is calm, his eyes shut.

"Yes!"

The breeze grows stronger. Jenna begins to lighten up.

They each lean back in silence, as if reliving every moment they'd had with Lennox ... Josh with his sordid "one that got away" affair, his ensuing fight with Micah, his anguish over losing Lennox without getting to say goodbye; Jenna with her juggling Lennox's personal life and professional responsibilities, her covering up the affair, her hiding company secrets and lies according to Lennox's wishes. They are lost in very different memories.

"Do you think Micah could've done this?" Josh opens his eyes.

Jenna hesitates for a split second. "Absolutely not. God, they loved each other. If you didn't break them up, I don't think anything would." She lights another cigarette, takes a drag. "Plus, they just got married a year ago, *and* they had this, God, what was it, *three*-week trip overseas planned after tax season next year?"

"Well, we've both seen Micah angry. I think he totally coulda done it." The ensuing confrontation after the affair is permanently etched in Josh's mind, imprisoning it like a straightjacket.

"Impossible. Micah was with me at your event until he got home. The paper said the time of death was around that same time, and Lennox had been missing the entire night. Doesn't make sense."

"What do you mean it doesn't make sense? Maybe he kept him locked up or tied up, and then killed him when he got home."

"That's ridiculous. Why would he go to all that trouble?"

Josh pauses. "Things that make you go, 'hmmmmm.'"

They laugh.

CHAPTER 12

Micah chuckles at the question.

"How am I doing?" He repeats Shawn's inquiry back to him over the hotel landline. "I gotta take it moment by moment. But in this moment, I'm okay, I guess."

He turns off the television and walks toward the window. He holds the phone away from his face so he can lean into the view outside. Local news vans are parked all along the street outside his temporary residence at the W Hotel.

"I can't get used to seeing my face all over the news," he says, turning from the hotel television to the gray storm clouds developing above the media crews outside. "So there's that."

"I know, it's terrible, my friend, I can't even imagine." Shawn pauses to make sure his statement of validation lingers. He is doing his best to place himself there in the hotel room with Micah, to empathize, to soften Micah's fears, but he is already on the case.

Shawn is looking at the street just outside the crime scene of Micah and Lennox's condo at the corner of Henry and Rutgers. He is jotting down notes to hand off to his private investigator.

1. Why all the broken glass? Necessary?

2. Any witnesses from the church across the street?
3. Does the god-awful television monitor outside the church have anything to do with any sort of security camera? Or is it just tacky advertising?
4. Anyone in the building hear anything, or see any strange people lingering about?
5. CCTV across the street?

Something isn't right here, he thinks.

Shawn breathes in the air that sweeps across his face. He looks up at the afternoon sun and closes his eyes just as a row of clouds blocks the light, and rain begins to pelt his cheeks with a stinging drizzle. He pinches his phone between his shoulder and his ear, removes his suit jacket and maneuvers it over his head. He grabs his bag, limbos underneath the crime scene tape, and enters the Garfield Building. Just inside the small lobby, he sees a stairwell and, brushing the shards of glass to the floor below with his yellow legal pad, sits down on the bottom step next to the elevator. Watching the sheets of rain pelt the broken glass on the sidewalk outside, he continues his conversation.

"Hey, listen, Micah, I'm afraid I have more bad news," Shawn says. His voice is a little loud to compensate for the weather. "There's a chance they may arrest you later today on preliminary murder charges. Now, even though that may sound terrible, I fully believe this is just a formality for now, to keep you from leaving the country, blah blah blah. I'm meeting with my firm later today to see if we can get this ridiculous false confession thrown out. They don't have anything else I'm aware of that will keep you inside for long."

"Shawn, you gotta help me. Everything keeps swirling around and around in my head. I can't stop it. If I go to prison, I think I might lose it. I wanna go home, if I even can."

"I'm here right now. At your home."

"You are? Why?"

"Just wanted a reminder of the building, snoop around, do some preliminary work. I know you wanna come home, buddy, but it's gonna be a while." Shawn removes a piece of glass from his shoe. "But soon enough, Micah. Shit, you haven't even had a chance to mourn yet."

"Oh, I'm not so sure about that. I didn't sleep. I kept rolling over, thinking he'd be there, then I'd just, you know, cry. Like those awful cries that you can't control. I can't."

"I hear you." Shawn tries to reassure him. "Hey, I'm gonna come visit you in a few to discuss some details."

"Okay. Be prepared, though, police have been outside the hotel all night. I think they've been watching me."

"That's pretty standard, Micah. You're a person of interest, actually the only one they're focusing on, which is a mistake they're gonna pay for. They just want to make sure you don't go anywhere."

"How could I? Have you seen the news crews out there too?"

"It's a mess, yes. But there's a lot of hope, too, Micah. Much to discuss. I'm on my way to you now."

"Okay. If anyone can help me, it's you, my friend."

A flash of lightning illuminates the now-darkened sky. Shawn moves his bag closer to him, as if trying to shield himself from the approaching storm. "Well, I'm here, buddy."

"Can you do me a favor and call Jenna real quick and fill her in, if you haven't already? You can tell her anything you need to. She's pretty much my only other connection out there."

((Boom!))

Shawn jumps at the thunderous sound, which rattles the remaining glass of the lobby facade. "Sure, buddy, see you soon. Be there in a few."

"Hey, Shawn?"

"Yeah, buddy?"

"Thanks."

"No problem. It's what we do, right?"

((Click.))

((Beepbeep.))
"Call Jenna."
(("Calling Jenna Ancelet."))
"Shawn! Thank God! How's he doing?"
"As well as can be expected, I guess. He wanted me to call you and fill you in."
"I've already read the *Times*, and it seems to be the only thing on the news right now, isn't it?"
"Yes, it is. Jenna, listen. Lots of questions were raised in that article, and I have some myself. We both know Micah didn't do this, but he may be arrested later today."
"Oh my God, why?"
"Well, since he asked me to fill you in, I can tell you that there's a confession of sorts, but it's nothing you need to worry about. But it seems Lennox may have been alive when Micah found him, and Micah panicked and tried to save him, but may have ended up making the situation worse."
"That doesn't make any sense. I mean, he was trying to save him, right? And if he was alive when he found him, then he couldn't have killed him."
"Listen, Jenna, I know how close you are to Micah, and especially Lennox, so I'll be able to fill you in on some stuff, but not all of it, right? I'm Micah's lawyer, and can only divulge so much. But know this. I smell something odd. Off. Something sinister, even. I'm going to find out who did this and why. I think it might go deeper than any of us think."
"Really?"
"Yes. It's still early, so don't give up hope."
"Oh, I won't."
((Boom.)) The lightning and thunder are synching.
"And Jenna, I'm just assuming he'd want this, but can you keep an eye out on the property for Micah? Since you live close by, once the dust settles and the crime scene has been cleared, maybe you could even help Micah with some preparations, you know, for

Lennox? I'm just assuming he'll want to have some sort of service soon."

"Oh my God, of course! I've felt so helpless, it's the least I can do."

"Thanks."

"Hey, Shawn. I can't help but think … well, you know how you said the word 'sinister,' which reminded me of a word I used to describe, well …"

"Jenna, spit it out."

"I think I might know what this is all about."

CHAPTER 13

Rain engulfs the sidewalk outside and begins to pool in the interim area of the doorless lobby. Shawn knows he needs to get to Micah soon, but he cannot pass up the opportunity to find out anything and everything that might point to someone other than his client. His friend. His mind spins, exploring all the facts that could point in other directions, but the ones that point to Micah are those he fears the most. Instead of hanging up the phone and running in the rain to the W Hotel where Micah is staying within walking distance, he takes out his iPad, brings up his car service online, and orders a pickup. That way, he can actively listen to Jenna and go to Micah at the same time.

"Jenna, tell me everything."

Jenna braces herself. She'd sworn to Lennox that she would never reveal what she was about to share. On the one hand, she could point Shawn in a clear direction that could lead to exoneration for Micah, and on the other she could tarnish the reputation of a dead man, not to mention land herself in jail. She makes a decision.

"You know I used to work with Lennox, right?"

"A little, but give me the CliffsNotes refresher course," Shawn answers, taking out his legal pad to begin writing.

"Let's see. Okay, I worked with Lennox as his secretary at Élan Publishing for two years, until I was publicly let go due to, quote, budget restraints, when in reality I quit."

"Why did you quit?"

"I'm getting to that!"

"CliffsNotes, Jenna."

"Oh, dear God. Okay, okay, I'll try, but bear with me so you have the context." Jenna begins to talk very rapidly. "Shortly after I quit, I started working as the administrative assistant for the CEO of Élan's biggest competitor, which as you know, is Cooper Harlow. Now, this switchover caused quite an uproar 'cause it was right at the start of the Pub War."

"Right. Never liked that moniker. Couldn't the *Post* have called it something a little more evocative? 'Ooooohhhh, Élan and Cooper Harlow are battling it out over print and online viewership, it's a 'Pub War.' Please."

"You weren't in it, Shawn. These companies are behemoths. You may just know Cooper Harlow for their iconic fashion magazines, but did you know they quietly absorbed four powerful media companies and became one of the first tenants of One World Trade Center? Meanwhile, Élan shows up with new, young, smart, stylish, left-of-center publications, taking advantage of their proprietary integrated online platform that seriously began to threaten Cooper Harlow's market share. Then, as a final blow to the coffin, Élan goes public and begins its own media acquisitions. And there you have the beginning of the Pub War."

"Please, Jenna, come in for a landing."

"Anyway, employees and clients were poached by Élan from Cooper Harlow, and vice versa. Nondisclosure agreements were broken, meetings and interviews were held offsite under the most secure circumstances. Friendships and partnerships were either weirdly entangled or irreparably harmed. Especially mine and

56

Lennox's, for a while, anyway."

"Finally," Shawn says.

"Things at Élan were becoming secretive and scary. About two months before I left the company, I was privy to a cover-up of some sort, I'm not sure what."

"A cover-up?"

"Shawn, this could really get me in trouble." Her voice quivers.

"Well, Jenna, if you know something that might help Micah, I'd love to hear it. I can't promise what I will or won't do with the information. My client is Micah. But I understand if you need some time …"

"No, no, I know, I know." Jenna takes a deep breath. "Okay, so, being Lennox's assistant, I had complete access to all of his files, and he knew that. He also knew that I didn't just blindly respond to things, nor simply file papers without knowing exactly what went where. So he took me to dinner one night and explained that he'd been asked to doctor some books, and that if anyone knew other than myself, we'd both be in trouble."

"In trouble? How?" Shawn asks as he places his blazer over his head again and steps through the glass into the waiting limo. He climbs into the back seat, covers the mouthpiece of his iPhone, and, overcompensating for the pounding precipitation outside, yells to the limo driver, "Seventeenth and Park, W Hotel, please!"

"Well, that's what I asked. All he said was, the less I knew the better, and to trust him. So I did."

"What were these papers about, specifically?"

"Near as I could tell, they were purchasing agreements, vendor contracts, intents to purchase office equipment and the like. Mostly I simply input numbers on line items based on documentation and percentages I was given via private email. You know, those chatroom thingies we all use to talk with each other internally."

"So there's a record of these conversations?" Shawn raises his voice mid-question. The driver has his windshield wipers on high, but they are barely keeping up.

"Um, no. That's how I knew it was serious. Lennox told me that's the easiest thing to get rid of, these private messages."

"Get rid of? Haha, that's funny, there's a digital paper trail everywhere. I'll find it."

"I don't think you will. See, that's the part I wanted to tell you about. Élan doesn't mess around. They've been under investigation before for not playing by the rules. No one knows how, but they've always managed to sneak right past anything and anyone to get what they want." She pauses, as if putting two and two together for the first time. "Don't you think it's kind of strange that two people from Élan were murdered on the same night?"

((Flash. Boom!))

"Jesus," says the limo driver, as calmly as he can. "That was a close one."

Shawn had been suspicious of a separate incident involving one of Élan's consultants being gunned down on the street near Union Square the same night as Lennox was found stabbed and left to die. Aside from both of them working for Élan, the two were deemed unrelated in the press.

"Wait, the papers said the two have nothing to do with each other. One was a random man caught in the crossfire of something he wasn't a part of, and the other was Lennox, which the papers called a domestic homicide, which we all know isn't true." Shawn pauses and squints while raising one eyebrow. *This is why I felt something was off.*

"But what if they're related?" she asks. "Listen, it's complicated and weird, and I know things, and I'm still trying to make sense of it."

"Okay, Jenna, now you're talking. What do you know?"

"Well, before the other night, all I heard was rumblings. People who'd been fired and never heard from again. Like *never* again. I'm not talking about killing people, but there've been conversations around the office both at Élan and Cooper Harlow about Élan bugging phone conversations, following and documenting people's private lives, employees being shipped overseas to work in remote foreign offices, stuff like that. But now not just one, but two people were killed that worked for Élan? In the same night?"

"Ahhh, that's what you mean by 'sinister' stuff."

"Exactly! Which is why I knew I needed to say something. If Lennox was in under his head, and God forbid he flew anywhere outside the lines, the company would nip it in the butt."

Ignoring Jenna's hodgepodge of metaphors and idioms (something she does quite often when she's trying to make herself sound more American than French), Shawn looks out and sees he has arrived at the W Hotel. Police are placing Micah, who is wearing handcuffs, in the back seat of a squad car.

"Shit, shit! I wanna talk more about this, Jenna, but I'm at Micah's hotel." Shawn leaves the car and runs into the downpour.

"Okay, but that's really all I know. But I'll just bet, if you get access to Lennox's bookkeeping files, you might make more sense of it."

CHAPTER 14

Shawn is too late. He rushes back to the limo and tells the driver to follow the police car. They head across town, then down Avenue A, maneuvering through the outskirts of Micah's neighborhood. They pull into NYC's Seventh Precinct at the corner of Pitt and Broome.

Shawn looks at the Williamsburg Bridge in the background, and for a second, he thinks of telling the driver to just keep going straight, to take him home to his wife in Brooklyn. But Jenna's revelation has hit him hard. He's committed.

"Just bill it to my account, add 20 percent." He gets out of the car with his navy-blue jacket serving as his umbrella. He moves toward the building with increasing intensity.

Such an odd squatty building for New York City, Shawn thinks, *only four stories high, such a waste of space*. He'd been here the night before to see Micah, but was too shaken by what had happened to Lennox to pay much attention.

He runs up the handicapped entrance, a curved, brick-walled path that leads up to the dark-red brick building. A looming canopy with huge metal letters that reads "New York City Police Department Seventh Precinct" covers the top of the entrance. He bolts through both sets of heavy, metal-and-glass double doors and enters the brick waiting area.

"So much fucking brick," he whispers to himself.

"Can I help you?" the young pimply-faced policewoman asks from behind the desk. She is low to the ground, like a character from *The Princess Bride* in some sort of brick pit, which makes Shawn laugh out loud.

"Shawn, Shawn Connelly. Here to see Micah Breuer." He brushes the rain off his shirt with his drenched coat. "They just brought him in."

"And you're his lawyer, I'm assuming?" she asks, looking at the sign-in sheet.

"Yes."

"Since he was just brought in, you're gonna have to wait. Probably a while."

Grabbing the ledger, Shawn nods and writes his name just under Micah's, and then searches for a place to sit. He sees a set of four green, mid-century fiberglass chairs connected by a silver stainless-steel base.

How could I have missed these last night? He wonders why he hadn't noticed such a prime example of his favorite type of design. *Looks like this was ripped directly out of a 1960s airport lobby.*

He pulls out his phone and goes to work. All of the chairs are scratched, beaten up, worn down from other people's boredom, with carved initials, filthy suggestions, and phone numbers etched along each curve. The thick humidity outside intensifies the putrid stench of sweat and blood that continues to cloak these halls, despite the top layer of disinfectant.

"Call Wallace Holcomb." Shawn speaks into his phone. He mentally justifies talking with Lennox's father in two ways: one, Wallace Holcomb is by far the more rational and civilized of Lennox's parents, and two, Wallace isn't a lawyer. *Okay, that's redundant.*

"Aw, hell no," says the woman deep within the masonry, pointing to the sign above Shawn's head.

He turns around.

NO CELL PHONE DISTURBANCES IN THE LOBBY.

"You've got to be shitting me," Shawn says out loud, forgetting to end the telephone call he's just made.

"I shit you not. You think I wanna sit here all day underneath this fluorescent nonsense, going through this mountain of fuck, *and* try to ignore people's phone conversations?" the young woman behind the counter answers, making Shawn wonder if she's rehearsed this retort before. "You can go outside and talk all you want."

"Jesus. Ma'am, can you at least let me speak to the detective in charge?"

She looks up at him blankly.

He realizes his rudeness. "Please."

She pauses. "I can tell him you're here."

"Thank you." He grabs his computer bag, then mumbles, "This is why I live in Brooklyn."

Annoyed by the interruption, yet happy to breathe fresher air, he opens the first set of double doors and raises the phone back to his ear.

"Shawn? Is that you?" says a female voice on the other end.

"Mrs. Holcomb?" Shawn covers the mouthpiece and whispers *Shit shit shit.*

"Yes, Shawn, it's Elaine. Wally kept calling your name and was about to hang up, but I said, 'Hell no, lemme talk to him.' What the fuck is going on, Shawn?"

Quite the normal reaction from Lennox's mom, Shawn thinks. Shawn not only knows Elaine and Wallace Holcomb personally from when Lennox and Shawn were best friends at Harvard, but he also knows of Elaine's reputation since.

A no-nonsense lawyer who speaks her mind no matter the cost, Elaine Holcomb was a New York County Assistant District Attorney for well over a decade before she ran for mayor last year and narrowly lost to the Democratic incumbent. Shawn, along with the rest of Manhattan's legal world, hold her in high regard as the Queen

Bitch of Manhattan's judicial system, and even call her that to her face. Shawn knows firsthand that she's proud of the nickname. He also knows that she'll stop at nothing until there's justice for her son.

"I'm sorry, Elaine. I'm here at the police station and couldn't talk inside. I just called to see how you two are doing. I've been thinking about you both." The gesture seems empty, but he decides to run with it.

"What are you doing at the police station? You need some help? They don't think you had anything to do with it, do they?"

"No, no, I'm here to see Micah. He's been arrested."

"About goddamn time. You know I never trusted that boy."

Shawn thinks her resentful statement is unwarranted. Before this emotional reaction, all Shawn had seen was Micah and Elaine's unmentioned respect for one another—Micah for Elaine's forthrightness and cunning intellect, and Elaine for Micah's resolve and unwavering commitment to her son after the affair. *Apparently, she's changed her mind and become fixated on Micah as the killer. Great, that's all I need*, Shawn thinks.

"What do you mean?" he asks.

Rather than let her know he is defending her son's husband, he's chosen a different route. Shawn knows how Elaine works. He's heard stories from attorneys at his firm who have gone up against her in many a court proceeding. She is meticulous and is not afraid to skirt the boundaries of the law, and she knows the system too well to let it get the best of her. Shawn knows Elaine is already two steps ahead of him. No doubt she is already talking to the new prosecuting attorney and may have information he needs to know. This could be his last chance to get any information she may attempt to hide in the future.

"What do you mean 'What do I mean'? You're a lawyer, aren't you?"

"Yes, ma'am."

"I'm sorry, dear." She takes a deep breath. "I know you loved my son, I should be more considerate."

"It's okay, Mrs. Holcomb. But I'm curious, I thought you cared for Micah."

"I tried to, yes. Before he killed my son."

"But isn't that a little far-fetched? I mean, we both know Micah. He loved Lennox. Like, really loved him something special." Shawn knows this is pushing a little hard and could give him away, especially to someone as smart as Elaine Holcomb. But he also means every word.

"You know, I wanted to believe that for the longest time," she answers. "But let's go through the facts, shall we? One, we have the Lennox and Josh affair, which my son fully admitted to. However, Lennox told me about the subsequent confrontation with Micah, and if you ask me, some psychiatric files need to be pulled on this man. Two, this was a brutal murd—"

She stops. Shawn wonders if he has lost the connection, but then hears a soft clearing of the throat on the other end of the line. *Could this be the stoic Queen Bitch actually feeling something? Could this be...*

"A brutal, unforgiveable murder," she continues as if she never stopped. "And we all know what that means. Crime of passion. I don't think he ever forgave my son, or maybe Lennox was involved with someone else, or maybe Micah *thought* he was. Whatever. Micah had motive. Three, apparently Lennox wasn't the only one Micah threatened because the prosecution has the testimony of that poor Josh fellow on video saying he felt so threatened that he didn't leave his apartment for an entire six weeks. Four, Micah beat my son to death even after knowing that he was still alive. Lenny was *still alive*. And finally, here's the kicker: turns out my son has a life insurance policy worth one point five million. *One point five*. And you'll never guess who the sole beneficiary is."

Silence.

"Now tell me again how much he loved my son."

Shawn doesn't speak. He's trying very hard to write all of this down without her hearing his pencil scratching on his legal pad.

"Mrs. Holcomb."

"Elaine."

"Elaine. All of that happened over two years ago, including the life insurance. I helped them with that myself. And I hear there might be other leads, other suspects. I truly think Micah was trying to help Lennox."

"Believe what you want, Shawn. I'm sure you could cook up quite the defense ..."

Her voice trails. She knows.

"Elaine, there's something I need to tell you."

"You're defending that sonofabitch."

"Yes."

((Click.))

CHAPTER 15

"Mr. Shawn Connelly, I'm Detective Bronson Penance. You wanted to see me?"

Shawn is leaning back on what he has now deemed *his* green chair in the foyer of Precinct Seven. Almost two hours have passed since Lennox's mother hung up on him. He's just finished writing two highly detailed lists, one of the evidence and potential theories the prosecution may use to convict his client, and one of potential leads to mount an ironclad defense, leads that perhaps the detective doesn't know about.

"Yes, detective, I remember you," Shawn answers. "I want to see my client, but I have a few questions first."

"No need, counsel. I'm sure you know that the victim's mother, Elaine Holcomb, used to be a highly respected New York County ADA, so it shouldn't surprise you that this case is on the fast track." He hands a folder to Shawn. "Arraignment is Wednesday. Here's what I can give you right now. On Wednesday, of course, you'll receive a copy of the updated police report, as well as statements from witnesses who saw Micah exiting and entering, as well as from the ex—Josh Harrison, I believe, is his name."

"Wednesday? It's Monday and I haven't even gotten to talk to my client yet."

"It's tough, isn't it? We haven't even explored all our leads yet."

"My God, that woman," Shawn says.

"Tell me about it. Micah killed her son, no doubt about it. Not sure if he started it, but he definitely finished it. It doesn't look good. Micah's waiting for you. Interrogation room 4, past the brick wall and up the stairs, end of the hall."

"Thanks, Detective. Hey, can you do me a favor?"

"I just did."

"I want you to check Lennox's work computer."

"On it already."

"No, not his laptop, which I'm sure you have, but his work computer. I think it might point to something criminal."

"Attacking a dead man already, are we?"

"It's not that," Shawn says. "The company he works for. I think there's something there."

"Ahh, the double murder theory. Already considered it, but they're completely different crimes." Even as the words exit his mouth, something in the detective's gut tells him that something isn't right. He decides to go out on a limb and offer something else to Shawn. "There's something else. You know of any drug dealers who use a ghost emblem on their packaging?"

"I'm sorry?"

"Look, I've been around the block enough to know that your client did it, but I wouldn't be doing my job if I didn't explore every lead, including this computer thing you're talking about." He nods in the direction of the folder Shawn is holding. "But take a look at this and see if it looks familiar."

Shawn opens the folder to see crude drawing of a skinny house with a curved wavy base and a thick horizontal black line straight across the middle.

"I don't know what that is," Shawn says. He sees a thick arrow pointing up with left-right protrusions that look like stubby blocks.

"A ghost, maybe?" Detective Penance says.

"I mean, okay, maybe, but what is it? Like what does it have to do with anything?"

"This emblem was found on several heroin bags that may have belonged to the deceased. One of the bags was half empty. We believe Lennox may have been involved in drugs, perhaps even dealing."

"Shit." Shawn is filled with disgust that his friend could have been using again, mixed with hope that he might have yet another lead.

"Yep. Now I know it's a little unorthodox to share this kind of information at this point, but this one has got us curious. I'm already on it, but I'm sure your private investigator could find him quicker. Maybe?" Detective Penance knows Shawn works with Lyte & Morgan and has access to high-priced, better-connected P.I.s that could make the difference in this case.

"They're already pulling video footage from every camera in the vicinity, but I'll put them on this as well. Thank you, Detective."

"Contrary to popular belief, we do our job here. Concentrating on one perp has bitten us in the ass before."

"Alleged perp."

"I stand corrected. Now go see your client, Mr. Connelly. Just past—"

"The brick wall," they say in unison.

CHAPTER 16

The white entrance reads 228 in aluminum-carved, sans-serif numbers. Freckled hands unlock the front door with a key. They are careful to use the key only, leaving no fingerprints on the handle.

"Super here. Hello? I'm here to upgrade the wall sockets," he says in a gruff and powerful voice. No answer.

He is dressed in navy overalls. His spiky hair is covered by a baseball cap. As he walks past the kitchen, can lights from above illuminate the back of his uniform, which displays "LES Janitorial" on a large embroidered patch. He continues down the hall, slipping his fingers into heavily worn carpenter gloves.

"We have an appointment, I don't mean to scare you."

Again, no answer. He seems to be in the clear.

He pulls a shiny laptop out of the chest pocket of his overalls and continues past the first bedroom and into the second at the end of the hall. He walks into the dark, perfectly ordered room. He puckers his lips with approval.

The blinds are drawn. He places the laptop on the bed and opens the closet.

On the right side of the top closet shelf sits a stack of notebooks and papers. He lifts the stack and places it next to the laptop on the bed. Then he grabs the laptop from the bed and places it where the stack used to be. Almost as if he has rehearsed this exchange, he then turns and grabs the stack of notebooks and papers from the bed and places it on top of the laptop, making sure all the corners line up.

He reaches to the ceiling of the closet and removes the envelope that has been taped there, and places it inside the same pocket of his overalls.

Using his gloved hands, he smoothes the bed, removing the indentations left by the laptop and stack of papers.

"Thank you. I'm done," he says out loud, with a smirk.

He leaves.

CHAPTER 17

Shawn enters interrogation room 4 and sees his client staring right at him, sitting straight up, smiling. The room is flooded with fluorescent lighting, which bounces off the stark white walls in all directions, causing Shawn to squint until his eyes adjust. He looks up at the camera in the corner over Micah's right shoulder and waves with a single jazz hand.

"How you holding up?" Shawn asks, noting that Micah's demeanor does not match the situation.

"I'm practicing." Micah forces a grin.

"What the hell are you practicing?" Shawn places his notebook and laptop on the table between them. He touches it. *This is quite possibly the ugliest piece of furniture I have ever seen*, he thinks, noticing the newer light-maple slats that have been interwoven with the dark oak table base. The whole piece is covered in a light coat of army-green stain that looks like someone has simply shellacked piss over the top, hoping it would bring the look together.

"Hmm, let's see," Micah says. "A gay guy who's been all over the news for killing his partner, about to be shipped off to the Manhattan Detention Office or God forbid, Riker's Island ... I'd say I'm practicing my 'Don't fuck with me' stance, what the hell do you think I'm practicing?"

"Oh, Jesus, Micah. You'll be fine, I mean, look at you," Shawn sits down, squirms, tries to make the most of a small bistro chair. "You're short, sure, but there's not an ounce of fat on you. Who would want to mess with that?"

Micah ignores the comment. Statements about his physique have always made him uncomfortable. "I really don't know how we got here, Shawn. I mean, one minute everything was fine, and the next I'm trying to save my husband then end up being hauled away for killing him."

"You didn't kill him."

"I know that!" Micah barks, startling Shawn. He lowers his voice. "At least I think I do."

Shawn places his bag on the table with a loud thud and an even louder glance.

"I'm sorry I raised my voice. Thank you, thank you, Shawn, for helping me."

"No worries, buddy. Lennox was a dear friend, one of the best people I have ever met, and I know how much he loved you."

"Thank you."

"Okay, let's start from the beginning," Shawn says. He pulls his laptop and legal pad from his bag. "Is there anything else you remember from that night?"

Micah leans his full torso against the table in front of him, elbows supporting him, and runs his fingers through his hair. "Well, before I got home, the only weird thing was I couldn't get ahold of Lennox. I called a couple of times, I think … or texted, I can't remember how many times."

"Think, Micah. Remember. Details can be important."

"Well, I texted twice, I think. And I definitely called him once and left a message."

"What did you say?"

"Something like 'Where are you? You said you'd be here.' I sounded kinda angry, I'm sure, like frustrated meets worry, ya know?"

"Yes, okay, good, that's good to know, and completely understandable. Okay, continue."

"Like I told the police, James West was asking about Lennox at the party, which seemed strange to me, cuz he never asks me to get Lennox to come find him."

"What do you mean?"

"Well, our conversations are always very surface-y and trivial. It seemed a little heavy for the moment, especially since he was in event mode, meaning he needed to talk to everyone, be the life of the party. So why the need for business, especially through a third party?"

"I'm still not clear."

"I dunno. Just trying to make sense of what happened, who else could have done this."

"I see. Okay, so James West was acting a little weird, that's good. We're already exploring some sort of company angle."

"Really?"

"Yes. Jenna told me about an alleged bookkeeping scheme."

"That Lenny was involved in?"

"Potentially. We're looking into it."

Shawn does not want to tarnish Lennox at this crucial point in someone's grieving process. Nor does he want to tell Micah of a possible link between the two murders that happened that night. He changes the subject.

"Tell me about who saw you at the party, when they saw you, what time you arrived, what time you left, all that you remember."

"God, I have relived this over and over." Micah sits up. "But I understand. I said good-bye to Lennox around 7pm, maybe 7:15? I remember it being around 7pm, and I was at our condo waiting for him to finish getting ready, but he said to go on ahead because he had to meet someone real quick."

"Wait, meet someone? This is new. Do you have any idea who?"

"Actually, no, I don't. Since the thing with Josh, I've been working on just trusting him, ya know? So even though I was curious, I didn't ask. I just figured it was a work thing."

"You didn't have a fight or anything?"

"No, we'd been doing really well, like *really* well." He thinks of the night before the awful event, how Lennox had been so loving, as if he knew it was the last night he'd have the chance. Micah begins to feel teary but snaps himself out of it, blinking and shaking his head at the same time.

"That's good," Shawn says. "We're pulling the videos from anywhere near your place, so if we can find he last person who saw him alive, then maybe we have something."

"That's good, that's good. The video to our place hasn't worked for a while, but I'm sure the whole block has cameras. Nine-eleven initiative and everything."

"Yep. Okay, go on."

"I catch a cab outside my place, going uptown, probably around 7:20, 7:25."

"Did anyone see you?"

"Nah, I don't think so. But I'm sure I'm on the cameras."

"Good, good. You got to the event around what time?"

"Traffic wasn't bad, so I'd say around 7:45?"

"Again we'll pull the videos, maybe look through some social media photos to make it definite. Go on." Shawn is busy typing everything into his laptop.

"We were supposed to meet Jenna there at 7:30, so I was looking for her at our meeting point just next to the red carpet, but I didn't see her. I did see Josh, though, looking fucking dapper as ever."

"Ha ha, well, he was the man of the night, according to the *Post* AND the *Times*."

"Fuck off," Micah says with a half-smile. "I ran into him, like literally, partly by accident, partly on purpose. Okay, mostly on purpose."

"Oh my God, you are a child."

"Then I saw you trying to talk to Meryl Streep. Did you have any luck with that?" Micah looks at Shawn.

"As a matter of fact, she looked at me." Shawn smiles.

"Well, there you go, lucky bastard."

"I didn't see you there, so I can't really vouch for that, but I'm assuming you ran into Jenna at some point?"

"Well, first I talked with James West, the CEO of Élan, who asked to talk to Lennox, I told you about that. Kinda strange. Then I ran into Jenna."

"And what time was that?"

"Oh, wait, I texted Lennox before that at some point, I'm not really sure. They took my phone, otherwise I'd tell you exactly."

"Okay, don't worry about that. I'll have the files from the police on Wednesday, that'll tell me exactly when."

"Okay. Jenna and I talked a little bit, maybe laughed just a little at you and Haylee trying to talk to Meryl. Then around 9:00pm, everyone started gathering for the programmed part of the evening, you know, presentations and sizzle reels and shit. But I called Lennox right before that, he didn't answer, so I started getting worried. I left, took a cab and got home maybe around 10?"

"It took an hour for you to get home?"

"No, no, it didn't take that long."

"So what happened between 9 and 10?"

"Oh, shit. You're right. I must have the timeline wrong." He pauses and works through the times in his head. "I remember checking my time on the way to the event, around 7:45, and remember thinking I was already 15 minutes late. Then on the way home, I checked my phone and it was 9:55 somewhere along the way."

"This helps a little. I guess we can fill in the blanks when we get a better idea of time stamps from videos and cell phone records."

"This is the timeline I told the police though. Roughly, I think."

"Don't worry, you were a mess, and timelines are totally fuzzy after a trauma. Trust me, please don't worry about that."

"Okay."

"Then you got home. Now here's where I need as many specifics as possible."

"Well, I remember as the cab was pulling in, I looked up at our place and saw that the lights were off. But the shades were still up. If Lennox had left, he woulda pulled the shades down. He always does that. So I figured he might have fallen asleep or something." Micah loses himself in thought. "Honestly, I pictured Lennox having someone up there, that's where my brain went. That's where it always goes, ever since …"

Shawn fills in the subsequent silence with his own knowledge of the Lennox-and-Josh-cheating-saga. Shawn snaps his fingers. "Micah, I need you to concentrate. What happened when you got out of the cab?"

"Right. Okay, I searched for my keycard, swiped it, and went through both sets of glass doors. I went up the elevator, hoping it wouldn't make much of a sound, cuz if there was someone up there, I wanted to catch them in the act." He pauses and looks at Shawn. "I know, I have serious issues."

"You're being honest. And this will go a long way, if only for me and the way we play this. You didn't tell the cops or the detective any of this, did you?"

"No, no, I was way more vague. In fact, I didn't even remember any of that when I talked to them."

"Okay, good. Go on."

"The elevator doors open, and everything is dark. I keep the lights off and sneak around the corner to the bedroom. I'm about to peer into the room when I hear a gurgling sound from the living room. By instinct I know it's Lennox, and I rush over to him, thinking he's choking on something. He is lying there, barely moving, and I freak out."

"Freak out? How so?"

"Well, all I could think about was getting whatever it was out of his throat, and just started pounding him and pounding him. Over and over."

"Jesus."

"I know!" Micah looks at Shawn, whose cheeks are slightly raised, eyes at half-mast, nostrils pinched. Micah agrees with the disgust and begins to feel his eyes well up. "I did kill him, didn't I?"

"Micah, no. No! Of course not! He'd been stabbed thirty-three times, for God's sake. He was already near death. I'm not sure there was much you could do to save him, and you did what you thought was right."

"But it wasn't. Right, I mean. I didn't do the right thing. I deserve this."

Shawn feels the need to lighten the dark turn the conversation is taking. "Friend, stop. You did not kill Lennox. You tried to save him. And from now on, this is what you say, again and again. 'I did not kill Lennox.' Any mention of you killing Lennox, or even thinking that you killed Lennox is off the table. And especially this ugly-ass table. Am I clear?"

"Okay, okay." Micah laughs through some sniffling and wipes his nose on his sleeve.

"Now. Is there anything else you remember?"

"He was naked."

"Naked? Why? Wait, you said he was getting ready for the event. Did he just get out of the shower?"

"Maybe. Before the shower, he said he was gonna take his time, eat a snack, 'mosey on over there,' I think are the words he used. I kinda just yelled from the elevator door on my way out, I needed to meet Jenna at the event, so I didn't pay attention."

"You don't think this was sexually related, do you?"

"I don't think so, but honestly I have no idea."

"Well, once we get the autopsy results we'll know for sure. Anything else?"

"No, not rea—wait, there were some weird flashing red lights in the corner of our living room, you know, where the living room meets the kitchen?"

"Cop lights?"

"No, I hadn't called the cops at that point."

They both pause in silence.

"Weird," Shawn says, typing 'red lights', then formatting it in a red color with an underline. *Red lights in the corner, what the heck?* He begins tapping on his laptop. "Micah, is there anyone else who could have done this?"

"His fucking ex-boyfriend maybe? It would explain why Lenny was naked." Micah watches for Shawn's reaction, which is nothing more than a closing of the eyes. "Come on, Shawn. Heck, I don't know. It wasn't Josh. He is way too much of a wuss. Plus, I saw him at the event."

"I'll definitely put my men on it. No stone unturned."

Shawn types again and then turns to Micah, watching to see Micah's reaction to what he was about to ask. "Hey, you don't think he was doing drugs again, do you?"

"Who? Lennox? Hell, no. He was working that program better than even me. And he had two sponsees who called him every day. He'd go out and meet with them all the time. In fact, maybe *that's* who he was supposed to see that night!" He throws his hands up and back. "Oh my God, I'm a horrible person."

"There could be a sponsee who saw him that night too?" Shawn begins typing frantically. "Do you know their names?"

"Just their first names. Talbot and Frank. Frank's last initial is 'J' I think, not sure about Talbot."

"Good, good, this is good. There could be a shit ton of people we could at least throw at them as having access to Lennox that night, and work on potential motives."

"Christ, Shawn, that's awful."

"Not as awful as your spending the rest of your life behind bars."

Micah nods and looks down. Shawn continues typing.

"Why would you ask about the drugs?" Micah says. "Cuz if he was, well …"

Shawn looks up. "Well, what, Micah? No stone unturned."

"Well, there's this letter Lenny wrote, said if anything ever happened to him, to read the letter and it would lead you right to him. 'Him' meaning whoever did him harm, I guess."

"Micah, what the hell? You're just *now* bringing this up? Something did happen to Lennox, Micah. He was brutally murdered, in case you forgot. And you basically confessed to it."

Micah releases his tense grip on his chair and looks up with tears in his eyes. "Shawn, if Lenny was even thinking about drugs again, then this guy woulda known about it. Hell, he could even be the cause."

"What guy?"

"The guy in the letter! He's definitely the one that woulda killed Lennox, if he had reason to. Lenny was petrified of him."

"By 'what guy' I mean do you know this guy's name? Where he lives? What the letter says?"

"I never read it. The envelope was sealed, and I buried it in Lenny's files."

"Buried it how? Where?"

"The only thing I know is that this guy had something to do with Lennox's past. The drug stuff. All Lennox told me was to file the letter under some silly title that didn't mean anything."

"Micah. For God's sake, what title is this goddamn letter or fucking folder under, so I can go find it?"

"Oh my God, geez." Micah, feeling annoyed, grabs Shawn's pen and searches for a nearby sheet of paper. Feeling Shawn's impatience, he begins to write on one of the light maple slats on the wooden table between them.

"Okay, so it's a folder, and it's under this … okay, well, it's not really a title, it's more of a picture. Lennox told me exactly how to draw it."

Micah scribbles the outline of a skinny house, colors it in, then draws a thick line through it.

CHAPTER 18

"At approximately 10:50pm on August 17, I was called to the home of Micah Breuer and Lennox Holcomb, to ascertain the events that had unfolded at 142 Henry Street earlier that evening." Detective Bronson Penance addresses the slew of media that have gathered to hear an update on one of two murder cases that had happened in the city on the same night. A bouquet of microphones is directly in front of him, with the Seventh Precinct brick façade in the background. A crowd of both local and national media has overtaken the entire parking lot outside the station.

Dressed in a light tan summer blazer, Detective Penance straightens his black-and-white-striped tie and looks directly into a camera in front of him.

"Upon entering, we found Lennox Holcomb, age thirty-six, brutally stabbed and dead on the living room floor of his home at the Garfield Building in lower Manhattan. The suspect, Micah Breuer, was taken downtown for questioning, and confessed to the murder of his husband of two years, Lennox Holcomb, the victim. Micah Breuer is currently being held in custody, and murder charges are pending."

No stranger to media press conferences, Detective Bronson Penance is adept in interacting with the media, and prefers being the one on camera. He has experienced too many untrained police commissioners and other personnel divulging information too early, resulting in botched cases before they had even started.

Having been prodded by influential players like Elaine and Wallace Holcomb, Penance feels pressured into this particular media event. Yet he also wants to fulfill his responsibility of getting ahead of public opinion, to secure a quick conviction should the case go to trial.

"What evidence do you have that Micah Breuer is the one and only suspect?" asks a reporter from the *Times*.

"Blood evidence and a confession." He flinches, but the statement is factually correct.

"Two murders in the same night. Both victims worked at Élan International. Are the two connected?" asks a reporter from CNN.

"At this time, we're pursuing the two murders as being separate cases, with no known link other than the fact you just stated."

"My sources say there were drugs involved in the Micah Breuer/Lennox Holcomb case. Do you have any comment on that?" The *Times* reporter presses closer.

"That information is part of an ongoing investigation, and we cannot divulge any details at this time."

Shawn, watching from the back of a taxi, pounds on the monitor. "You sack of shit. She got to you. Elaine Holcomb got to you. Fuck me."

CHAPTER 19

"You know you have to think like Elaine Holcomb," the district attorney says to Astrid Lerner, the assistant district attorney handling the case of The People vs. Micah Breuer. He has accosted her in the narrow hallway just outside her office, before she has even had the chance to put her things down in her office, much less enjoy the coffee she holds in her hand.

"Think like her, be like her," he says. "Now this sonofabitch is going to plead 'not guilty,' cuz he's already hired the top defense firm in the city. He's also well-connected and rich as shit, plus his mother-in-law is who?"

"Elaine Holcomb," Astrid responds with little affect.

"Right. Now the arraignment is tomorrow, but the trial? My God, it might start in less than two months if this woman has her way."

"Good morning to you, too, sir. I am on it, sir." She fumbles with her coffee, her folders and her keys, trying to get her boss to realize she has just arrived and has her hands full already.

"I have no doubt, but you need to be ready," he says. "Second degree murder, manslaughter, we need it all, back-up plan upon back-up plan. And we need this on the fast track. There's too much publicity, in addition to the goddamn fact that I don't need this woman in my hair. I thought I got rid of her once and for all."

"Sounds like someone had a phone call early this morning."

"I'm sorry," he says, walking backwards a step.

Astrid pauses, realizing how badly her boss must need to get this off his chest.

"Sir, she was one of the best you ever had," she says, placing her hand on the doorknob to her office. *Shut up shut up shut up*, she thinks. *Why does he always seem to do this at the very start of my day?*

"And now she and I both want you to be even better." He walks away mid-sentence.

Astrid tries to use her key to unlock her door but realizes it's already ajar. She pushes it about two-thirds of the way open, until it's blocked by a brown box of papers on the floor. She forces her way through the small opening.

Three paralegals are sitting at a round circular table next to her desk, with stacks of folders on their laps. She is concerned about how they got in, but grateful they are so eager. *The boss has spoken. We've got a job to do.*

A driven young woman from a wealthy Pennsylvanian family, Astrid Lerner is 38 years old with medium-length ash blonde hair. She stands at five-foot-ten, and usually towers over her colleagues, both men and women. She owes her height to each of her parents, whom she both admired for their work ethic and hated for their relentless focus on achievement. Her father wanted her to be a doctor, which is why she became an attorney. She's always had mixed feelings about the law. She hates the practice of it but loves the doors it opens. Confident, well-rounded and empathetic, she fancies herself a judge-in-training but can also see an eventual run for mayor, following in the quasi-footsteps of the infamous Elaine Holcomb.

Her light-grey office walls are covered with awards and commendations, with graduation diplomas and framed photos of her parents. One rather large window looks out into the main work area of the felony unit, but no windows with direct natural light, a fact that has always bothered her about the tiny office. Astrid turns on her desk lamp, then reaches behind her and turns off the harsh artificial lights in the drop ceiling above her. She looks at the paralegals to hint that they should have made this particular lighting choice themselves.

"Good morning, have we found the video yet?" she asks, enjoying the darker, cozier atmosphere she has created.

ADA Astrid Lerner feels the electricity, and now the pressure, of her first major publicized case and is anxious to be a success. After all, the person whose shoes she is filling is ankle-deep in her own son's murder and is actively looking to the new ADA to prosecute on the fast track.

No pressure filling the shoes of the legendary Elaine Holcomb.

"Not yet. We've done everything but knock on doors within the radius," her young assistant says, fumbling through an unorganized mound of papers.

"Well, then let's start doing that. Wait. Radius of the camera, is that what you mean?"

"Yes."

"Tell me more."

The young paralegal smiles as he searches the messy stack in his lap and finds a folder marked CAMERA. "Well, the camera is a Chutter ProHD, and it looks like the video we are looking for had to be recorded within, say, five hundred or a thousand feet of the apartment, sorry, condo." He pauses and puts his finger on a line in the file. "Hmmm, okay, it's battery-operated and has a motion sensor, meaning it only records what's moving in front of it. Night vision up to twenty-five feet, so even if it was dark, it would record whatever it was pointed at. So all that to say, it says here in some sort of conclusion one of us drew up, 'After a sweep of the computers in question, no laptop or desktop in evidence has any recordings from this camera. But it was most likely recorded somewhere in or outside the house.' So if you ask me, if it was the latter, it had to be extremely close, maybe even on the same Wi-Fi."

"Okay, so the sweep of the condo didn't produce anything. Any luck with the neighbors?"

"Micah and Lennox own the entire seventh floor. And in the complex, there are five condos that are full-floor units, two floors that have half-floor units, and one downstairs basement condo, which is the biggest and probably the coolest one out of all of them, didn't you think?" He looks at another paralegal, who gives him a robust validation in the form of a giant head nod.

Astrid claps her hands.

He jumps, looks back at his notes. "We have spoken to the other ten occupants, and none of them have any idea what we are talking about."

"Oh, then they must not know anything. Oh my God, get me search warrants for all the neighbors."

"Yes, ma'am," replies one of them. Astrid doesn't know which.

"And I want a full report from all the laptops and computers and cell phones, of course including the victim's and the defendant's," Astrid says. "Internet search history, email search of key words, all of it. Now what about the murder weapon?"

The paralegal fumbles again, this time taking longer.

"Look at me, look at me, look up here." Astrid mimes two fingers poking herself in her eyes. "I understand this is a lot of pressure I'm putting on you guys to help me prosecute in this amount of time, but just concentrate. You know the information, you don't have to find it. I simply want to go through what we have. I need the high points."

Astrid sits back, proud of herself for not reaming the shit out of him.

He diverts his attention away from his folders and closes his eyes for a full two seconds. "Right. Okay, the murder weapon is still in question. Analysis of the utensils left in the sink reasonably confirms that none of them was the actual murder weapon, although the puncture wounds prove almost conclusively that the thirty-three stab wounds were from one of the steak knives found in the sink."

"What does that mean?" she asks, already knowing the answer.

"Okay. First, the knife in the sink could actually be the murder weapon, but it could have been wiped clean. However, there was food on it, which means it's not. Shit."

"Calm down. You're on to something, just take your time."

"But we don't have time, you said."

"You're right. Here's the deal. First, we know it wasn't the actual murder weapon because of the analysis, but what we do know is that it could be part of a set owned by the defendant. Second, the murder weapon is still out there, and could be hidden somewhere close. Do we have someone on it?"

"Actually, we do. The same team who's looking for where that video could've recorded to."

"Okay, what about the African case that housed the wireless camera?"

"Near as we can place it, it was hand-made, and it came from Africa."

Astrid bites her lip. She looks at the girl sitting next to him.

"You, what about the drug use? The initial results from blood and saliva rule out heroin consumption in the previous 48 hours. Can anyone confirm or deny that Lennox and/or Micah have used drugs recently?"

"We've talked to friends and combed social media," the second paralegal answers. "We've even visited two twelve-step support groups we know they have attended and asked around. Everyone we talked to seems to think they were both sober."

"And what about the icon on the drugs found at the scene, any idea who the heroin came from?"

"A vague recollection from a few months ago," says the third paralegal. "Someone at what's called 'the Red Door A.A. meeting' in the Village said he remembers buying heroin with that emblem. He said he was too fucked up to remember exactly who it came from, although he did remember buying it from someone at a party in Chinatown, around Grand and Chrystie."

"Good, good, start there. Speaking of drugs, I want hair follicle analysis as soon as the results are in. They'll tell us if either of them had been using in the past three months or so. These drugs they found may be old, meaning we don't know how recently he was using, if he got sober again or what. Talk to his friends, his friends' drug dealers, whoever you can. If he was using, it might be argued that it could be an additional motive for Micah to kill him, maybe a reason for a fight, maybe a lingering resentment."

"On it," two of them say in unison.

"Okay, we have a savage murder, people, possibly sexually motivated, with a possible drug angle, possible resentment for infidelity from two years ago, possible murder weapon, a confession of sorts, a one-point-five-million-dollar insurance policy, and the possibility that the whole night was caught on tape. Sounds pretty good, but we have to get specifics beyond circumstantial. I want that tape."

"Actually, it's probably digital," says the first paralegal.

Again, Astrid chews her lip, this time almost bringing blood.

He notices. "But I know what you mean. I'll make that a priority."

"What about tape surveillance from nearby sources?" She continues to talk directly to him. "Where was Micah before? When? What did he do?"

"Well, the video from his condo complex is not working, but there are two outside within a block of his house, one facing the front of the building, the other down the street, pointing north towards Essex," he says authoritatively, this time referring to notes from a folder he has quickly located. "According to the one just outside his building, Micah Breuer was spotted leaving the condo at 7:17pm, and the camera just outside the new Élan building caught him arriving at the party at 7:57pm on the night in question. I know what you're thinking, how can it take that long to drive uptown? We checked on that. Traffic wasn't bad that evening, according to GPS records and several video sources at vantage points along the way. But we have the vehicle clocked at a gas station at 7:40pm just east of the Village, which could explain why it took so long."

"Great work, so now we have the beginnings of a timeline. Do we have any other people coming in or out of the building during that time?"

"Yes, a few, but they're accounted for." He grabs 8x10 photo stills from the folder and lays them on the table in front of them. "These two are neighbors who live upstairs. One's an actor and the other is a model. We talked with them and they were both together all night, said they barely know Lennox and Micah other than the occasional party they all attended. They didn't hear anything that night, but not sure they would, considering no one shares a wall with the full-floor units."

"What about this person in the thingies, what are those called?" She points to a different photo.

"Coveralls. That's the janitor of the building, we think. We haven't been able to find him yet."

CHAPTER 20

"Make sure we find it."

CEO James West is used to giving orders and watching his minions scramble to fulfill them. He has risen to power at Élan Publishing in a relatively short amount of time, based largely on his ability to delegate.

"Yes, sir," two dark-suited men say, exiting the office in unison, as if marching to war. James closes his office door behind them.

"Now, you people," James says, turning to the three persons seated at the large conference table, all backlit by the sunset off the Hudson River.

James West's office, designed by renowned interior designer Benjamin Vanderweiss, is decorated with an eclectic mix of furniture, including a steel-and-glass conference table surrounded by fourteen vintage walnut Herman Miller chairs. Six poster-sized black-and-white safari photos from his African travels are displayed on the walls throughout the room, and a bulky and weathered thousand-year-old Italian desk is the designated focal point, semi-obscured by the mound of cardboard boxes leaning against it.

"Fill me in, please." James walks across the room in front of them, scooting a half-filled box across the jet-black floor with his foot. The box is stopped only by the far wall to his right, and the jostling of its components makes his audience wriggle in their chairs.

"The two have nothing to do with each other," says one of the nameless faces in silhouette.

"I should hope not."

"What I mean is that we can't figure it out. We've taken care of one issue, but the other seems to be shedding some unwanted light."

"Ya think?" James West says, walking toward the window behind them. He stares at the new Élan International headquarters to his left, his pride and joy, the third tallest building in Manhattan, nearing completion in Hell's Kitchen and about to open its doors. The structure itself is being heralded by the international press as "one of the most remarkable and technologically advanced architectural works of the last two centuries." The design is the brainchild of the respected architect Enrick Goldman, known mostly for his dramatic and timeless residential works that fit in perfectly with the landscapes surrounding them. He was tapped by Élan and its corporate investors to bring the same aesthetic to a commercial skyscraper, and according to most critics, he had not disappointed. With a hefty base that houses an entire mall, convention center, indoor golf course and twelve floors of parking, the new Élan headquarters then tapers inward in three sections that match the exact heights of the skyscrapers that surround it. The first section is a 3,200-room luxury hotel, the second section is a sprawling forty floors of Élan headquarters, and the top section boasts thirty floors of high-end condos, with glass penthouses offering sweeping, majestic views of New York City and beyond.

James West watches as a gigantic crane hoists an enormous Élan logo to its final resting place on the new building's façade. "Look, we're moving in less than three months. Our building and our ugly-ass logo are all over the news, we have stockholders asking questions, two employees dead in the same fucking night, and multiple detectives talking to our people *and* obtaining search warrants for our goddamn computers and servers." He pounds on the window to emphasize the latter point. "Now, do I have to be worried about anything *else*?"

"Not at all, sir. We have erased any—"

"'Not at all' is fine. I don't need to know what that means."

CHAPTER 21

"I'm sorry, I'm not sure I understood you," Shawn says to the taxi driver, covering the mouthpiece of his cell. They are parked just outside the courthouse on Centre Street, just south of Canal.

"That is because you are on the phone," replies the Pakistani cabbie, enunciating in a more purposeful accent than before. "I said $14.50."

"I gotta go," Shawn says into his phone. He swipes his credit card, opens the door, and begins to exit just as Chinatown's subtle smell of fish and soot fills his nostrils.

He leans in to the taxi. "You're why Uber is taking over the world." He slams the door.

"I cannot understand you," mouths the taxi driver, not really caring if Shawn sees his face. He peels away.

Shawn is directly in front of the Manhattan Criminal Court building, staring up at the large bronze and marble spires that bookend each of the two entrances. Quotes about the importance of justice are carved in concave relief all along the walls of the two courtyards. To his left, a gigantic copper mast protrudes from the building's façade. The pole, weathered and oxidized over time, still manages to wave a proud but tattered American flag.

He walks up the steps through the first security screening and past the information booth. Just above the booth hangs a beautiful 1930s black globe timepiece with the clock reading 8:45. Shawn nods in approval as he makes his way to the waiting area. He checks his phone just to make sure the timepiece is still working. *Yep. Beautiful.*

Shawn sits on a long wooden bench surrounded by beige marble walls. His briefcase makes a thud on the green granite floors, echoing down the long hallway.

Micah should be here soon, he thinks. *The Tombs is right next door. The Tombs. What a dreadful name.*

◆

Having been transferred from the police station to the Manhattan Detention Complex, aka "The Tombs," Micah is dressed in MDC-issued tan scrubs. The prison escort accompanies him across the twelfth-floor walkway that connects the Tombs to the courthouse. Micah is scared and shaking, looking for Shawn, who'd said he'd meet him. He wasn't sure where.

The elevator doors open to the lobby of the courthouse. Micah sees the public for the first time in days. As he exits to his left, he becomes aware of his clothing, his appearance. For the first time throughout this ordeal, he feels like a common criminal.

He turns the corner with the escort and sees Shawn. His pace quickens as he walks toward him.

"I thought you were meeting me earlier," Micah says, trying not to shiver.

"I'm so sorry," Shawn answers. "There's no public access to the twelfth floor here."

"For protection from people like me, right?" Micah look down at his scrubs, his handcuffs.

"Hey look, it's gonna be fine," Shawn says, trying to maintain a positive tone. "This is all just temporary. Let's do this."

He motions for Micah to follow him, prison escort in tow. They reach the thick double-door entry of the arraignment room that reads "Criminal Court, City of New York." Bronze Roman reliefs adorn each door panel, representing justice in the most antiquated of ways. Shawn forces them open.

They walk down the center aisle between two rows of pews filled with onlookers, fellow criminals, lawyers and law enforcement officials. Shawn and Micah take their places in the front row.

As he awaits his docket number, Micah begins to shake.

"It's so fucking cold in here," he whispers.

"Yeah, these people stand in here all day, so they crank the AC," Shawn whispers back, as he pulls today's paperwork from his briefcase.

Micah scans the room. He listens to the judge explain the various proceedings as he looks each remanded suspect in their eyes. *He seems nice enough*, Micah thinks. Policemen stand both to the judge's extreme right and distant left. Large, white vintage cone fixtures with dark brown nipples hang from the ceiling, and long vertical windows light the top half of each wall to his right and left.

Micah looks out one of the windows, concentrating on a peak-a-boo glimpse of the distant Manhattan skyline. Some of the buildings are similar to his and Lennox's view from the rooftop of their condo in Two Bridges, and he is lost again in memories.

The day they first met.
The last time he saw Lennox alive.
The pounding on Lennox's chest.
((Pound pound pound.))

"Case #LS 454556-1471, the People versus Micah James Breuer, on for arraignment," the courtroom deputy clerk exclaims.

Micah jumps back to the present; he and Shawn stand up. Shawn unhooks the rope that separates the waiting area from the court, invites Micah through, then places the rope back in the locked position. They approach the long, slender podium that separates them from the judge. Micah, having paid attention to the last four arraignments, stands to Shawn's left. Shawn places his file on the tall slanted part of the podium, struggling to keep its contents from hitting the ground. He opens the file fully just to be safe.

The clerk continues. "Counsel, please state your name for the record."

"Shawn Connelly, your Honor, representing the defendant."

"And the defendant, please state, of your own accord, your name for the record."

"My name is Micah Breuer, your Honor."

"Mr. Breuer, your attorney has waived the reading of the charges against you." The judge speaks to Micah with a soft yet stern undertone, like a concerned father addressing a teenage daughter. Micah smiles and nods.

"However, due to the magnitude and sheer number of charges," the judge continues, "I'm going to indicate that you are being charged with second-degree murder, first- and second-degree manslaughter, and criminally negligent manslaughter. Now, these are merely allegations at this point, and they do not imply at all whatsoever that you are guilty of any of these charges. It will be up to a jury of your peers to decide guilt. Right now, everyone in this courtroom assumes that you're innocent."

A cough emanates across the room. Micah and Shawn turn to see the back of what looks to be Elaine Holcomb, a stout woman with short grey hair, making a swift but noisy exit. The door closes behind her.

"Now, you did get copies of the information that's been filed?" asks the judge.

"Judge, we acknowledge receipt of a copy of the criminal complaint," Shawn says.

"Great."

"A copy of the supporting affidavit, which is two pages," Shawn continues. "Also a copy of the medical examiner's death confirmation summary."

"Yep. How does your client plead?"

"If it pleases the court, we enter a plea of not guilty."

"Well, that went the way I expected. Very well."

"May I be heard in terms of bail and scheduling, your Honor?"

"I will hear. Is there an ADA present?"

"Standing ADA Minerva Johnson here, sir, representing The People," says the blonde-haired woman to their right.

Shawn notices the purposeful absence of Astrid Lerner. *Turning lackadaisicalness into grandstanding. Awesome.*

"Mr. Connelly, you may proceed," says the judge, marking the record.

"Mr. Breuer has never been charged with any capital offense," Shawn says. "He is a respected member of the community, especially in AA, where he has been clean and sober for over eight years. In addition, the litany of charges brought forth by the prosecution is both damaging and unwarranted. Evidence obtained has no bearing—"

"Save it for the trial, Mr. Connelly."

"Yes, your Honor. My point is that Mr. Breuer should not be considered a flight risk, as he has fulfilled all obligations, cooperated with police, and has no prior convictions. Also, due to the severity of the ridiculous charges, we would ask the court for at least ninety days to prepare for trial."

"Thank you, Mr. Connelly. Due to the severity of the charges, ridiculous or not, bail is denied. And your defendant has a right to a speedy trial, so date is set at October 15. Six weeks should give you ample time. I know your firm well."

((Pound pound.))

Shawn grabs his file and takes Micah back through the rope and out the double doors. They find the nearest bench.

Micah turns to Shawn with defeated eyes.

"I know," Shawn says. "But we knew this could happen."

Shawn tucks his files away in his briefcase while Micah simply sits, staring straight ahead.

"Micah, you gotta bear with me. This is not going to get easier. Now, later I'm going to give you some information on applying for a corrections administration permit to attend the funeral."

Micah says nothing.

"Did you hear me?" asks Shawn. "Elaine is holding an open memorial service for Lenny."

Micah closes his eyes.

"Look. I don't want to alarm you." Shawn begins to explain, knowing he has little time before Micah is taken back to the Tombs. "But in case you didn't notice, the standing ADA in there didn't say a word, which is extremely odd, especially when discussing bail. And even then, bail was denied. I thought we had a shot, but I can see Elaine's influence is a little deeper than we thought."

Micah remains steadfast in his silence.

"Whether you want to talk about it or not, Elaine is holding an open memorial service," Shawn continues, "and she's probably going to try and block your request with the detention complex. However, since we are applying for leave on compassionate grounds, I'm hopeful they will find that compassion and let you attend."

Micah is escorted away, staring straight ahead as he's led down the hallway.

CHAPTER 22

Shawn looks out the window of his Midtown high-rise office, pondering his next move. Having removed the coat and tie he had worn at arraignment, he now leans back in his large black leather chair with a pen in his mouth, arms and hands behind his head. His sleeves are rolled up just past the elbow, revealing an antique Rolex with the time reading 8:28pm. A photo of his wife rests on a shelf in the library behind him, a half-empty beer bottle in front of him, and his unopened gym bag next to his feet. A file box full of documents is strewn across his desk.

His private investigator sits across from him, flipping through a large mound of paper, held together by a struggling black clasp.

"In addition to the files the prosecution and police provided, which I pored over at length to develop points of exploration," the P.I. says, "I spent over a day and a half going through all the files printed off of Lennox's work computer, and there is absolutely nothing here that suggests foul play or any sort of cover-up," he says.

Shawn says nothing.

"As far as we know, the weird ghost-looking emblem is part of a small heroin operation on the Lower East Side. Promising leads from friends of theirs who have used this guy, but apparently this dealer is a pro at covering his tracks. Funny that someone who brands his heroin wants to keep a low profile, huh?"

Still nothing.

"The ex-boyfriend Josh Harrison has a solid alibi, but he's still on my radar. The transcript from his police interrogation is pretty alarming, don't you think?" Again, he receives no response. His questions seem rhetorical at this point. "I mean, your client seems to have quite the temper, based on this confrontation about the affair. Not to worry though, there's plenty of dirt on this Josh guy. Many skeletons in his closet, mostly from when he was in one. I've got a man following him to see if he spends any time with shady characters."

Shawn is listening to every word. This silent contemplation is how he works when he feels overwhelmed. He is methodical, meticulous, and dangerous in his planning, according to those who have pitted themselves against him.

Shawn's detective is used to this, even amused by it.

"And here's a photo of the video camera that may have recorded the entire episode. You'll notice it's very small and not very advanced, which means it may not leave a trace we can pursue. However, we have contacted the manufacturer to determine all direct purchases in the last six months, and of course information on who distributes them at large. I have that info right here. It's a lot."

He dumps the folder on Shawn's desk with a loud thud that makes Shawn jump.

"Shawn, the bottom line is that there are many leads in different directions, so I feel confident we have a good shot at directing our defense in at least one of them, if not two or three."

"It was this Ghost guy. I can feel it," Shawn says. He picks up his land line.

"But the Ghost letter you told me was in Lennox's files isn't there. Not with the police either. We have no way to find the guy at the moment, and we have nothing substantial connecting this man to the murder."

Shawn puts his hand over the phone's mouthpiece and whispers, "Except the warning of a dead guy."

Shawn uncovers the mouthpiece and says to his assistant, "Sandra, set up a press conference on the Breuer case. Yes, as soon as possible. Yes. Great, thank you."

He returns the phone to its cradle and turns to the detective.

"Let's see if this Ghost appears out of thin air."

CHAPTER 23

Shawn's cab parks in the cobblestone parking lot of the Manhattan Detention Complex, known to most New Yorkers as the Tombs, a foreboding nickname given to one of the previous buildings that stood in its place back in the 1800s. Being an architectural history buff, Shawn is always disappointed as he approaches the building, a tall rectangular reddish-brown monstrosity.

Looks more like self-storage, hoarding away people's big-ass furniture that won't fit into their tiny apartments, he thinks, *rather than the Roman masterpiece that actually used to look like a tomb.*

Careful not to make eye contact or talk with the cab driver this time around, he swipes his credit card and gets out. The wind is both warm and cool on his face in an autumnal stasis. He walks up one of two sets of corner stairs leading up to the brownish-gray stone courtyard and enters through a grid-like glass-and-metal entrance, noting the decades of grime accumulated on the glass panes.

He signs in, hands over his bag to an awaiting officer, places his keys and cell phone in one of the small gray metal lockers to his left, and walks through the airport-like security structure. Everyone he approaches is silent, carrying out their jobs like Stepford wives in some sort of mechanical rote.

A tall, gruff female correctional officer escorts him past Micah's cell block in 5 South, a newly renovated subsection of the Tombs. The fresh décor has a subway theme, and Micah's cell number 13 is located just above the F line, designated by an orange circle with a large white F in the middle.

Fitting, Shawn thinks, remembering the F train is the subway that runs from his condo in Cobble Hill to Micah and Lennox's place on the Lower East Side.

Shawn clomps across the intermittent vinyl and cement floors, the sound of his footsteps bouncing off the canary yellow corridors. He enters the meeting room without any fanfare, any sense of danger or gloom. Again, he is relieved Micah is not at Riker's Island. *It wouldn't have made sense*, he reasons.

Micah is doing push-ups in the center of the space. He is wearing a fresh set of tan scrubs, this time with a white T-shirt underneath. His muscles are too large for his tee, and they flex and expand, as if trying to break free from their confinement. As he enters, Shawn can see Micah through the window, despite the giant round metal speaker in the middle of the glass.

"Micah? How're you holding up?" Shawn asks as the correctional officer closes the door.

In one powerful, fluid motion, Micah pushes himself up to standing. "Well, I guess I'm okay." He brushes the dirt from his hands. "I just keep to myself, kinda used to that. Everyone is leaving me alone for the most part."

"See? I told you. But let me know if I can get the missus to talk with you. She's the best listener I know. That's why I married her." Shawn sits on the metal chair in front of a long thin desk and places his open briefcase next to him.

"Shawn, you know I love Haylee, but I've already got a therapist. How's it going with you? Did you find the letter in that folder?"

Micah sits down in the chair and looks up at him.

"I'm glad you asked. We have several leads. You may not like hearing this, but it seems many people had far more motive to kill Lennox than you."

"You're right. I don't like hearing that."

"That being said, we didn't find the letter, but I bet if we find this guy Lenny was so frightened of, we have the man who killed him."

"Jesus, you really think?"

"Yes. Problem is, this guy is good at covering his tracks, which is probably why Lennox wrote that letter. If I was a betting man, which as you know sometimes I am, I'm guessing it has some pretty incriminating stuff in it, maybe even a way to find him, I don't know. We're still on the hunt for it. I'm gonna comb the evidence room, and maybe talk with the prosecuting attorney and see if she remembers anything."

"Sounds good, thank you."

"To recap from your arraignment, they're going after you with murder 2, manslaughter 1 and 2, and least, criminally negligent manslaughter, which technically is the only one I'm afraid might stick. I'm fairly confident we can show state-of-mind at the time and rid you of *all* charges. But honestly?"

"Yeah?"

"I still think Elaine is pulling the strings. And I think they're pushing everything they have at this case, so bear with me. I'm holding a press conference in a few hours and need your permission to do so. It's a little risky, but ethically I can hold one to offset the damage done by Detective Penance. We need to see if we can push this Ghost out of hiding."

"The guy in the letter?"

"Yes, that's what we're calling him based on that sketch you drew and the pictures of the heroin bags."

"Heroin bags?"

The correctional officer enters and whispers in Shawn's ear. Shawn's eyebrows lower. He looks back at Micah.

"It's my private investigator. Called me here. Must be important. I'll be right back."

Shawn exits the meeting room, and the officer hands him a wireless landline.

"Hey, in a meeting with the client. What have you got?" Shawn scratches his forehead. "Can you repeat that?"

He places the phone between his shoulder and his cheek, so he can better mime a pen writing on a piece of paper in the air, hoping the officer will help him. She does not react.

"Okay, thanks, I'll call you back when I hit the road," Shawn says. "Find that hard drive."

((Click.))

Shawn thanks the officer and goes back into the meeting room.

"Okay, Micah, you won't believe this. So, remember I told you that Jenna said to check Lennox's work hard drive for some information about a cover-up?"

"Yeah, but I thought you said that didn't turn up anything."

"It didn't, according to *them*. I wanted my detective to check it himself because I didn't trust the printouts and summaries the prosecution gave us. Trust me, I've been burned before by very, very similar instances of prosecutorial misconduct. And sure enough, I'm glad I did."

"How so?"

"Get this. My team went to evidence to check out the actual hard drive, and it was gone. Like disappeared from the fucking police evidence room."

"No shit? They must know who did that. Aren't there cameras and security guards everywhere?"

"That's the thing! No record of anyone. And the evidence room's camera footage is gone for three days surrounding the day it disappeared. Both the original footage, *and* the backup on the outside server. They don't think the camera was even working."

"No shit," Micah repeats.

"Yep. Gone. Missing from goddamn evidence. Not sure of who or why or how, but the fact that someone had the gall to take it means we're onto something. Which is good news."

"Wait. You're talking like we're still going, like this isn't that big of a deal. The evidence was stolen, Shawn. Can't the case be thrown out completely? I mean, it's evidence about my case. That *they* lost!"

"Hold on a second. Hear me out. Yes, it's the people's duty to preserve evidence, but only certain evidence is covered by that protection. I've seen this before. Prosecution has a piece of evidence analyzed, logged, and submitted. Nothing is found relevant to the defense. Evidence disappears for one reason or another, can't find it, chain of possession broken, lost it, whatever. Defense wants to have the evidence re-analyzed, but can't find it. Defense moves for a dismissal of the case. Judge rules that the evidence was already analyzed and proven neither material nor exculpatory to the defense. Wastes everyone's time, so it doesn't matter."

"That's insane. It was *stolen*."

"But we can't *prove* that it was stolen. Micah, this is still good news. It'll work in our favor."

"I'll believe it when I see it." Micah drum-rolls his palms on the table and shakes his head. "Shawn, can we back up a little? You mentioned heroin."

"Yes. Sorry, the heroin bags." Shawn pulls photos from his case files and holds them up to the glass one by one. "Evidence gathered in your condo shows several heroin bags with stickers matching the ghost emblem you drew from the folder. One bag was open and half-empty, which the prosecution intends to argue as another motive for you to kill your husband."

"That's— that's impossible. Lennox was not using again, trust me, Shawn. He couldn't have been. Not only would I have known about it, but he would have never bought from that guy again. I've never seen him like he was when he was telling me about that letter. All shaky and paranoid. Scared me to death."

"You're right. Toxicology from fluids and hair samples has confirmed that Lennox hadn't used in at least three months. But that doesn't mean he didn't relapse before that, something he may have hidden from you. That's why it's so important to find this guy. I mean, think about it. If Lennox, God forbid, was using again and got reconnected with this guy, who knows what could have happened? This is our best shot at pointing them in another direction, and potentially arresting the right guy."

"Shawn, please don't do this. You don't want this guy on your bad side, trust me. Plus, if you're on the news talking about my case, my profile in this place is gonna go way up. It's a lose-lose, I swear it is."

"I hear you, Micah, I really do." Shawn collects the heroin photos and shoves them in his briefcase. "Micah, let me be honest. We may have many suspects, but we're not in as good shape as we initially thought. My detective seems to think otherwise, but me? Not so sure. So far, the company angle has stalled, the hard drives are missing from fucking evidence, the roads to Ghost aren't leading anywhere, and the camera found at the crime scene is worthless if we can't find the recordings."

"You found, wait, what? A camera? Jesus, Shawn, it feels like I don't know anything."

Shawn pulls out another stack of photos and holds one up to the glass, letting it linger. "The evidence list and photos of the scene show a camera in your living room that could have recorded the entire murder."

"You're kidding me. Wait!" Micah leans back, his forehead wrinkling. "Do you think the camera could've been the source of the red lights? Remember? The red blinking lights I saw in the corner of our living room?"

"Holy shit." Shawn recalls the camera specifications from the discovery documents. "From the documents we have on the camera,

I remember it was battery operated. Blinking red lights to let you know there's no more power, maybe?"

"My God, I've been wondering about that ever since that awful night! There was a camera in our living room? Like right here was a freaking video camera?" He points to the picture, his finger touching the corner of their living room, opposite where he found Lennox lying in a pool of blood.

Shawn peels the photo off the glass. "Yes."

"I can't. That's too strange."

"Micah, do you have any idea why someone would want to film you and Lennox? If it was in your bedroom, I'd be asking another question."

"This isn't funny." He looks again at the photo now resting on Shawn's lap. "I'm trying to figure out why someone would want to film our lives. Wait, is it a monitor or a camera? Was someone just watching us, or filming us?"

"That's a great question. But it looks like a motion-recording video camera, works over Wi-Fi, meaning it recorded to a computer we have yet to find."

Micah hesitates to let his brain catch up to this present moment.

"I guess the good news is, if this camera recorded this godawful night, you'll see for yourself that I didn't do this."

"I have no doubt. We'll keep searching. We'll keep hoping that hard drive shows up, and maybe it will have something the prosecution missed. But Micah, that's a lot of hopes and maybes. Every other lead is going cold. We have just one more month until the trial starts. You gotta help me out, my friend. This Ghost guy. You need to let me go find him, by any means necessary. I have to do this press conference."

"Do it."

CHAPTER 24

Shawn's wife Haylee is in their palatial brownstone, searching for her keys in order to make it back to work for her 2:30 appointment at her office in Greenpoint.

The five-point-five-million-dollar, four-bedroom, three-bath brownstone was Shawn's major splurge after being promoted to senior partner. He wanted a place out of the city, a home for him and Haylee to raise a family in the best possible neighborhood he could find. When Warren Street came on the market, he'd offered $120,000 over list price to secure it.

Tucked away on a majestic tree-lined street in the heart of Cobble Hill, Brooklyn, the four-story townhouse is tastefully appointed with vintage furniture by Arne Hovmand Olsen, Shawn's favorite mid-century designer. A long teak coffee table rests in the middle of the first floor living room, surrounded by a custom couch in a 1950s black, tan, and white-speckled tweed.

Just off the living room, Haylee is in the walnut-paneled kitchen, moving around the piles of mail, kitchen utensils, and vegetable remnants on the Carrara marble countertops. Taking a long lunch break from her sometimes brutally demanding psychotherapy practice has become a refuge of sorts. Fixing herself a fresh salad, usually paired with whatever protein was left over from dinner the night before, and watching whatever noon-hour programming is the most interesting has become her daily routine.

She finds her keys on the coffee table next to the remote, which she picks up and points at the television. Before she has a chance to turn the TV off, she sees her husband on the screen, approaching a host of microphones. She can't make out where he is, but she is intrigued. She unmutes just in time to hear the very start of his press conference.

"Thank you all for coming today. Just a few short weeks ago, on August 17, I began representing Micah Breuer, an innocent man accused of allegedly murdering his husband, Lennox Holcomb, who worked in financial data analysis for Élan International here in New York City. It was a particularly brutal event on an extraordinary evening that saw two different Élan publishing employees murdered. And I'm sure New Yorkers want to know that everything possible is being pursued to keep this city safe."

Haylee places her keys on the table and sits back down.

"Based on facts omitted or unknown by police during their initial press conference"—Shawn waves a brown folder for emphasis—"we have reason to believe that overwhelming evidence obtained in the condo of Micah Breuer and the late Lennox Holcomb points in several directions, none of which is linked to my client Micah Breuer." Shawn waves the folder again, then sets the left heel of his hand on the podium, while still holding the folder halfway toward the camera.

Haylee thinks this is odd. Since she knows her husband quite well, she also knows he wouldn't do something so awkward without a reason. It's as if … *Wait, what's that?*

Shawn continues. "Although the prosecuting attorney claims there is a confession, the presumption of innocence has been detrimentally and haphazardly …"

Haylee hears none of the rest. She pauses the television and squints at the folder. She notices a small sticky note with the ghost illustration on it. She walks closer to the television. Her eyes widen then squint in one singular motion.

She takes her phone out of her purse and begins to text.

```
"Honey, the stickie note. I think I've
seen that logo thingie before."
```

CHAPTER 25

Astrid pauses the television. Shawn's torso is frozen on the screen, with the folder in his hand.

Elaine and Wallace Holcomb are watching the press conference from Astrid's office and have been waiting for an update on their son's case. They are seated in front of Astrid, catty-cornered to the TV on top of the side console.

"See what we're up against?" Elaine points to the television. "He plays dirty. He knows goddamn well that folder is showing everyone that stupid heroin emblem. What is he doing? Does he hope that somebody recognizes it and points us to some hoodlum that supposedly got my Lenny to take drugs again? Divert, divert, divert. Pure and simple evil."

"Sweetie." Wallace Holcomb tries to comfort his wife, laying his hand on top of hers.

"Don't." Elaine pulls her hand away.

"Elaine, I'm with you," Astrid says. "It's a red herring. But rest assured, we've got more than enough to put Micah away for good."

"Then fill me in. I'm done with this sideshow."

"Okay," Astrid begins, wordsmithing as she goes. Elaine Holcomb is powerful and respected in this office, with devoted followers of the way she used to run the place, including her own boss. But Astrid also knows that even though this case involves the murder of Elaine's son, she is under no obligation to divulge everything, nor should she. "Micah's hard drive was clean. Too clean, if you ask my opinion. He's either engineered it that way, or he's like no other gay guy I've ever known."

"Funny, but not helpful. What else?"

Astrid hates being cut off, or cut down as the case might be, especially when there's more to share on the topic. She wants to pick her battles, and this is not one of them. "We have character witnesses aplenty. First, we have Josh Harrison, Lennox's former boyfriend. Now, even though Josh's testimony will show Lennox was unfaithful, I believe overall it will be a win for us to show motive: jealousy, resentment, et cetera. Josh will also testify that Micah has a snapping point."

"Yep."

"Micah has a melting point that registers on a psychopathic scale, which we will demonstrate with expert testimony."

"Not sure how that will fly, but I like the thinking."

"Thank you. Then we have the two sponsees, Frank Jabali and Talbot Lexington. Now, in a follow-up interview, Micah had said that perhaps Lennox was going to meet them that night, but Frank and Talbot's testimony will reveal that they did not see Lennox that evening. Micah lied, tried to divert. Furthermore, they will confirm Micah's jealousy. Apparently, he was outwardly jealous of the time Lennox spent with them."

"See, what did I tell you?" Elaine says in the direction of her husband, placing her hand on his. He places his hand on top of hers.

"We also have Jenna Ancelet as a character witness. She has misgivings about Micah as well. She can also back up her best friend Josh's account of the breakup, when Micah went off the rails. One caveat. She will also be a witness for the defense. She is loyal to them as a couple, even after she left the employ of Lennox to work for the competition. They were super close. We're talking vacations, house parties, everything. We're unsure of how this will play out, but I'm developing a strategy."

"Don't like that."

"The video camera," Astrid continues without missing a beat. "No one has been able to locate where the recordings went, or even if there were recordings at all. I'm going to file a motion that the camera be inadmissible as irrelevant to the case."

"That doesn't make sense. If it recorded the murder, you need to find it."

"We're still working on it, but if it makes it into the trial, it could swing against us. I think the defense would suggest the recordings were part of some Élan company conspiracy in which Lennox could have been involved. It could sway the jury."

"I heard about that. No evidence. Go on."

"The only other thing besides presence of the camera, but lack of video evidence, is the absence of a murder weapon. As you know, we're sure that the knife used to stab Lennox thirty-three times was a knife matching a set found in the apartment. Now, we have a photo of Micah leaving the condo that evening, and he is carrying his bag, his briefcase. Not sure why he'd need that at a formal event, so we checked and double-checked. The DNA from the case showed nothing abnormal. No blood, no hair samples, just Micah's fingerprints. Plus, witnesses corroborate that he always carried that bag. He considered it his purse. We still think he may have carried the knife with him and disposed of it somewhere along the way to the event. However, the actual knife was not and is not anywhere in the vicinity."

"Obviously, he's hidden it somewhere, and CIU is too stupid to know where to look."

"I'll pass that information on to them. Now, for the good news. Four-prong attack: motive, opportunity, DNA, and confession."

"Oh, I like the sound of this."

"I thought you would. Motive. One, Micah was resentful of Lennox's affair, as evidenced by witness testimony. Two, a life insurance policy was taken out to the tune of one point five million dollars with Micah as the beneficiary. We will call attention to that number as being exorbitant. Next is opportunity. Micah's recollection is all over the place, with pretty big omissions, up to almost an hour here and there. Our timeline will show that Micah was the last to see Lennox alive, had ample opportunity to almost kill Lennox, dispose of the murder weapon and anything else linking him to the crime, go to the party, come back to find he hadn't completed the job, kill Lennox and subsequently try to fool the police into thinking he was trying to save him. We even have a moment we will pull out at trial about the lights being on in the apartment when Micah got home, when he swears he couldn't see a thing."

"Like Perry Mason," Wallace Holcomb says.

Elaine replies with a swift and pointed *Shh!*, which is barely audible except to her husband.

At this point, Astrid realizes she is divulging way more than she should, but she is enjoying the ego boost from the reactions on Elaine and Wallace's faces.

"DNA." Astrid continues. "Lennox's DNA is all over Micah's body. It was all tested, and it all points back to Lennox and Micah. No other relevant DNA was found at the scene, not a speck."

"Not true, they had a housekeeper."

"Yes, I said relevant. The housekeeper's DNA was there, and she was taken into consideration. But she was ruled out as a suspect. She was in Cuba with her family at the time. Verified."

"Oh, okay."

"Lastly, there's the confession. Micah has confessed that his so-called 'life-saving' techniques ended up killing your son. So even if we get a gullible jury, which Shawn Connelly is known for, and they can't see the connections with all the evidence we present, we have

Micah on criminally negligent homicide, plain and simple. Done. That's a given. Boom. One to four years."

"That's not enough, but I get it. Backup plan. No plea bargain, right?"

"None will be accepted."

"And if all this goes wrong, we'll still sue in civil court." Elaine is somewhat satisfied, yet feels the need to have a backup plan for the backup plan.

"It won't go wrong."

CHAPTER 26

"Right. Here's everything."

Shawn drops a huge box on the closest desk he can find.

"Get to work," he says, motioning to the gaggle of paralegals waiting to devour the new discovery files.

The Lyte & Morgan law firm offices are considered by most in the legal world to be "old school," like the firm itself. Herbert Lyte, the founding partner, is approaching 65 years old, and although he is no longer part of the day-to-day operations of the firm, he still has a solid vision for it. This overarching brand strategy is one of timeless trust, and that philosophy trickles down to who he hires, who he selects as clients, even how the office is decorated.

Even though Shawn's tastes have evolved to a more streamlined look, he can appreciate the old-school mentality. Being a Harvard graduate, and having grown up with a father who appreciated the classic and timeless, he feels equally at home here as he does in Brooklyn.

The paralegals' corral is a massive, ornate, hand-carved wooden cylindrical half-wall for which there is one entrance. All the desks are arranged to interact with each other, to foster camaraderie and collaboration. Shawn is enjoying the energy, is fueled by it even.

"Comb through everything you can find, and if you can't find what you need, find it," Shawn orders. He chuckles to himself at his repetitive word choices as he walks back to his office.

"I guess that speech makes you one of the finding fathers," jokes his private investigator, who has been eavesdropping from Shawn's office. He looks more disheveled than the last time they met.

"Maybe I can find you a shower." Shawn closes the door to his office.

Dimly lit except for the extraordinary view of the Midtown skyline, the office is encased in floor-to-ceiling walnut built-ins on the remaining three walls. The bookcases are filled with sports memorabilia, countless reference materials, and of course framed photos of any celebrity Shawn could talk into taking a selfie with him.

"I know you have everything under control here," the P.I. says. "And I've hit everything you've asked me to cover, and then some. All there in my report."

"Yes, Allen, I've read it, and thank you. Again."

Allen Pinchot sits back and relaxes. He has been Shawn's rock-solid sideman for over five years now, uncovering things that few private investigators would even think of. He is a tall and slender man with a bit of a belly, forty-two years old with thinning dark hair that still manages to sport a wave.

He has been the unsung hero in Shawn's meteoric rise in the New York City legal landscape. Now he finds himself struggling, trying to save the day yet again.

"I know it's not much, but there are some new things of note, like the WiFi at Micah and Lennox's condo," Allen begins. "I took my laptop over there to see what networks show up, you know, see if we can find a lead to what server or hard drive may have those camera recordings. There are 72 networks that pop up, and all have passwords. All of them. I started trying to crack a few but ran out of time. If you wanna send someone out there to do the rest, that might save you some money. If not, I'd like to continue."

"Money is not the issue. However, the timeline is. Look at this," Shawn says, pointing to Allen's report. "This is the first time I've seen Micah's follow-up timeline next to the one he initially gave to the police. This one is the latest version of what Micah told police, which is sworn. The other one, this one right here, is the timeline he told the police right after the murder. He still has major gaps. Right before the event, right after."

"Yeah, I wanted to make it clear that we have some work to do. The one he told the police right after the murder was a little more in our favor."

"In our favor? Interesting. Sounds like you might not be sure of his innocence?" Shawn is half-joking, half-serious.

"Oh, I'm absolutely sure Micah is not the one who killed his husband. I think this Élan company surveilled them both for God knows how long, then found out Lennox knew too much about a financial cover up and hired someone with ties to Lennox, probably the Ghost guy, to go kill him that night. Then the poor bastard Micah got caught up in all of this in some random night of shitty luck."

"Wrong time, wrong place."

"Yep."

"Any word on the missing hard drive from the police evidence room?"

"Still nothing."

"And any follow-up to what Jenna said about the sinister corporate culture at Élan? People disappearing, shipped off overseas?"

"There are a few people who've taken jobs in other countries, sure, but nothing out of the ordinary. Social media feeds of these former employees show everyone happy and thriving. I gotta say though, people who work at Élan are creepy. Tight-lipped. Very 'Theranos,' if you get my drift. Anyway, give everything a once-over. I gotta head home to the wife. She's been baking some sort of paella all day."

Shawn looks up from his papers and smiles.

"I know, I know. Wish me luck."

"Good luck, Allen," Shawn says. "Thanks again. Be safe out there."

CHAPTER 27

On the lower east side, between the footings of the Manhattan and Brooklyn Bridges, lies a vast expanse of cemented waterfront. Full of bustling life during the day, the boardwalk is the loud foreground to Brooklyn's DUMBO skyline and its silent reflection on the East River. In the pitch of night, the shadows of the bridges, overpasses and surrounding mid-rises shield much of the area from streetlights, enabling patches of darkness to begin their nightly commerce.

Squeaks and thuds give way to a constant hum as a wheelchair glides from cobblestone to concrete. Spotted hands push the wheels from light into shadow, situating the chair at a perfect 90-degree angle to the glorious nightscape glistening in the water.

He waits.

Up the hill, a young man arises from the F train staircase at Madison and Rutgers. He clutches the right pocket of his tattered skinny-jeans and shakes his head, as if trying to rid himself of a persistent gnat.

"You got this, pussy," he whispers to himself out loud, the sound almost echoing as the wind spits his words back at him. He scrunches his arms to bring his black overcoat closer to his body to shield himself from the cold, both real and imagined.

He turns right and walks down toward the river, remembering the emailed instructions.

Wheelchair near the waterfront. Left. Say nothing.

He walks forward, leaning into his uncertainty. His head begins to rise, and his confidence begins to build. To his left, he sees the figure in the wheelchair and approaches. He looks around, reaches into his pocket and pulls out his cash.

"Not sure what this will get me."

"Shhh," says the figure, taking the boy's money and pulling out a bag of heroin from his dusky tweed jacket.

The young man glances at the bag, sees a familiar emblem, and speaks again.

"Whoa, you're the Ghost guy?" he asks, looking at the heroin. "Aw man, some cops were asking about that logo at my NA meeting the other night," he says, reaching for his fix. "I've been dying to try this stuff."

Without hesitation, Ghost takes the package and places it back in his coat. He reaches into the pocket on the other side of his jacket and pulls out a handkerchief. He unveils a bigger bag of heroin, roughly twice the size as the other.

"For my biggest fan." Ghost offers the entire contents of his freckled hands in a passive, upward gesture.

"No way, really? Thank you," says the young man. No ghost sticker, but he doesn't want to complain. With cupped hands, he envelopes the handkerchief and its contents as if it were precious frankincense, pushes it deep into his pants pocket, and skip-sprints back to the subway.

Ghost closes his eyes and sighs. He turns the wheelchair and begins the journey back to his son. Even with an uphill slope, he muscles his way through the two-mile digression until he turns from Avenue D onto 10th Street, to the end of the roundabout, the center of which is obscured from the streetlight by the foliage surrounding it. He hops out of the wheelchair, kicks it, then throws it to the very back of its usual resting place, next to his rickety old bicycle among a series of useless garbage cans devoured by hungry bushes.

"Shit," he says, running to the back of his building, which all but disappears among a forest of similar, larger ones.

"Shit shit fuck."

He opens the heavy metal door at the back entrance of the housing unit and bolts up the four flights of stairs that lead up to his small solemn apartment in Alphabet City. He unlocks the deadbolt and enters. Using only the light from the streetlamp outside trickling in through the tiny window in his living room to guide him, he tiptoes down the narrow hallway to the bedroom door. He opens it. A vertical shaft of light makes its way across the room until it bathes his child in an ambient glow, like a sliver of hope reminding him of the why of it all. The boy awakens and pushes himself up. He says nothing, lies back down, and turns away from the light.

Ghost walks to the bed, pulls back the covers, lies down and wraps himself around his son, one arm tucked underneath the boy's pillow, the other around his waist. He pulls him close.

"It's almost over, *mon cœur*. Daddy almost has enough to take us home."

He rubs the back of his son's head. The child lets out an audible sigh.

"Shhh. Sleep."

CHAPTER 28

"How did you sleep?" Haylee asks, bringing a cup of coffee into the bedroom. Darkness still fills the room, as the sun has just begun to illuminate the Brooklyn sky. Shawn, face down, pulls the Egyptian cotton sheets with his hands and stretches across the king-size bed.

"What time is it?" Shawn grunts. "Better yet, did you remember where you saw that ghost emblem?"

"Geez, baby, you are obsessed." Haylee moves toward her husband with the coffee, which is her signal for him to sit up and start the day. "No, I haven't remembered where I saw it, and yes it's time to get your lazy ass outta bed."

"It's quite the logo. Can't make sense of it, but it's key to acquitting Micah." He sits up, takes the coffee and sips it like it's nectar. "I just know it. Oh, that's good, thank you, honey."

"That's why I can recall seeing it, but I can't remember where." Haylee scooches herself halfway into bed, almost causing Shawn to spill his coffee.

She stares out the window that looks onto the tree-lined street. Shawn notices.

"Honey, it's okay, we'll find this guy some other way." Shawn places his hand over hers.

"No, no, it's not that. I was just dreading seeing this client of mine today. It's always so heavy."

"That's because my baby feels *everything*." He pulls his hand away from hers, and in a loving jab he grabs a pillow as if he's about to hit her with it.

"I hope you spill that coffee," she says as she climbs off the bed and heads toward the bathroom.

"Baby." Shawn puts his pillow down and stands up. "What's up with this client of yours that has you so poopy?"

"Oh God, honey. It's awful. He's been spiritually abused in the worst way."

"Spiritually abused? Did you make that up?" Shawn places his coffee on the nightstand.

"No, it's very real, and it's pretty common. The church can do a number on you, trust me. I have three clients who moved to the city because, I don't know, they wanted to escape?" She plugs in her flat iron to warm it up.

Shawn moves toward the doorway, his body backlit by the morning sun.

"Escape what, specifically?" He knows she won't answer.

"Nice try," she says, opening the floor-to-ceiling glass door of their seamless shower and pressing the electronic control knob to start the water. She speaks louder so Shawn can hear her over the ceiling showerhead pelting rain drops onto the basalt floor. "The confidentiality of my patient-client relationship prohibits me from …"

Her voice fades into the noise of the shower, as Shawn mouths a *blah, blah blah* at his own reflection in the mirrored medicine cabinet. He places his hands on either side of the sink and pushes his upper body toward the mirror. He nods in approval at his scruff and decides to keep it for the day. He opens the medicine cabinet, pulls out his dental floss, and begins twirling it around his finger.

"But what I can tell you," Haylee continues, her voice louder to make her point, "is that these abused religious people move to the city to escape the church, but they can't seem to escape their core beliefs. Like they're in there. Way in there. Deep. So it's a constant internal battle. I mean, we didn't grow up that way, you and me, so we don't have a frame of reference, nor do I want one. But I hear story after story like this all the time. It's rampant. The weirdest thing, don't you think?"

Shawn closes the cabinet, his reflection coming back into view. He looks at himself and squints as if a light had just turned on above him.

◆

((*Honk honk.*))

Across the East River, the loud noise causes the young man to stumble into the traffic going the other way. With no memory of how he got there, he now finds himself in the middle of 42nd Street and 8th Avenue, in early morning rush-hour traffic.

((Honk honk honk.))

The cars swerve and brake to miss the man, who is desperate to find a resting place for his flailing limbs. His skin is a pale blue, and his tattered skinny-jeans are the only thing that remain on his cold and shivering body. His bare chest is splattered in crusty puke from the neck down to the waist, and his shoeless feet find it hard to figure out what his brain is telling them.

"You got this, pussy," he says out loud. "You got this, pussy."

He zigzags toward the sidewalk next to the Port Authority Bus Terminal, only to be struck by an oncoming cab, catapulting him onto its hood and discarding him onto the pavement below. He lands face up, contorted but moving. A brown soapy mixture foams in his mouth, as if he'd been spit from the sea. He convulses. Yellow pus begins to ooze from his left nostril down the side of his cheek, followed by a cascade of blood that carries the entire mixture to the ground.

◆

Jenna squeezes the last of her concealer onto her fingertips and spreads it under her eyes. She is at the offices of Cooper Harlow at 7am, as she often is, along with most of her coworkers. She is finishing the last of her makeup when she hears the ding of her text go off. She washes her hands, puckers her lips, and winks at herself in the mirror on the way out.

Morning light floods the offices of One World Trade Center. Jenna's office is on the 52nd floor of the magnificent steel structure. As she walks to her desk, Hermès Birkin bag in hand, she relishes the breathtaking views of lower Manhattan and beyond.

Back in 2012, Cooper Harlow made national news as being one of the first tenants to sign the lease at One World Trade, which prompted other media companies to relocate downtown. The headline-grabbing move was also the major impetus that prodded Élan CEO James West to try and one-up his competitor by building the even more technologically advanced, more secure building to house Élan. Cooper Harlow has felt the hit, sparking countermeasures to offset their premature real estate move.

Even though she has had to live through the media giant having to sub-lease many of the floors because of their rival Élan's dominance, Jenna closes her eyes for a second and smiles, grateful she has the opportunity to work here.

She grabs a quick cup at the small coffee station just next to her maple-clad, well-appointed Knowles desk station, which houses her and another assistant.

"Good morning," she says to Petra, the other "her." Petra is on the phone and does not acknowledge her.

Jenna tucks her white D&G blouse under her buttocks so it does not wrinkle, reaches into her purse, and pulls out her iPhone as she sits down. The phone's face recognition doesn't work fast enough for her, so she enters her password. 1-2-3-4-5-6.

She squints to see who sent the message. It's James West, the CEO of her former company Élan.

Would you please come see me?

"What on earth?" she says out loud. Seeing a text from James West, her former boss's boss, sends shivers down her spine. And she cannot recall a time when he was so formal. They used to work down the hall from each other, and when he wanted to speak with her, the usual subject was television shows and other pop culture nonsense. Most of the time he would just yell her name, with a loud "Get in here!"

"Petra, I've gotta run out, can you handle this nonsense while I'm gone?" She criss-crosses an open hand in the general area of her desk.

"Sure," Petra is now off the phone. "You don't do anything here anyway."

The two assistants are both European, with similar senses of humor, so the sarcasm is not lost on either.

"Oh Petra, you always know *just* what to say!" Jenna does her best Karen Walker impersonation.

Jenna grabs her Jimmy Choos and slides them on without buckling the straps as she moves toward the elevator. She begins to call Josh on her way out, all the while dreading the long process of exiting the building through all the extra security protocols that had been put in place because of the murders and investigations.

She trips on the threshold of the elevator, losing one of her shoes as well as her phone.

"Josh, Josh!" she yells at the phone on the floor while she slips her shoe back on. She bends down and buckles the leather straps. She is fully aware of the three people in the elevator with her. "Josh, don't hang up!"

She composes herself with little to no grace, and grabs the phone, only to find there's no service.

"There's no service," says a short bald man in the elevator.

"No shit," Jenna says.

She turns to the front of the elevator to await her exit at lobby level. Ray Montagne's "Trouble" begins playing over the speakers.

"You've got to be shitting me," Jenna says.

"Somebody has a favorite word," says the bald guy.

Jenna, never diverting her gaze from her straightforward elevator stance, mumbles, "I'll show you my favorite word, you sonofa—"

((Ding.))

Jenna exits and hits redial.

"Jenna, are you okay?" Josh says.

"Yes, darling, I'm about to go through security, lemme call you back."

"You coulda just wait—"

((Click.))

Jenna throws her Birkin onto the conveyer belt, removes her David Yurman earrings and bangle, and throws them in the dog food bowl, as she calls it, along with her phone. She's done this before. As her accoutrements go through screening, she walks through the metal detector.

((Beep.))

"It's your shoes, ma'am," the security guard says. "Those particular Jimmy Choos have metal spikes."

"Dear God, is every man on this island gay?" She reaches down and begins to undo her heels, the leather straps making a whipping sound from the sheer force of her frustration. She throws them onto the conveyor belt. The guard smiles as he hands her back her phone and jewelry.

Jenna hits redial while she begins to re-accessorize. Josh answers.

"Jenna, I'm busy. I don't have time for this."

"I'm so sorry. Thanks for your patience. You gotta help me." She halfway throws on her shoes and hobbles toward the door.

She exits the building and turns left toward the west side highway. She bustles through the gathering tourists waiting in line to visit the top of the trade center. As the light above the intersection turns red, she motions for a taxi, which swerves to the right to pick her up. She ducks into the cab and catches her breath.

"Up, up, up, 45th and 12th, quickly please," Jenna says to the taxi driver. "And don't take the highway all the way, there'll be too much traffic during rush hour."

"Yes, ma'am," replies the driver.

Jenna turns her attention back to Josh.

"I'm listening," Josh says in an impatient tone.

"James West just asked to see me, so I'm headed there right now."

"Wait, what? Why?"

"Hell if I know. But I think it may have something to do with Lennox."

"Lenny? What do you mean? Is that why you're calling me?"

"No! I mean yes. I mean kinda. You know how Micah is about to go on trial for killing Lennox?"

"Yeah."

"Well, I told Shawn that I knew certain things about a corporate cover-up, and now I'm scared the corporation knows something."

"What are they covering up now?"

"Josh, did you hear me? I think they know something. I think they *know* something."

"Oh."

Jenna notices the taxi is not moving.

"Excuse me, what is going on?" Jenna asks the cab driver. "I thought I said don't take the highway all the way up."

"We're on 8th Ave." The driver is on the phone with his dispatch. "Sorry, ma'am. Apparently, some kid just got run over in the street a few blocks from here."

◆

"I like this getting ready together in the morning thing." Shawn tightens his tie. "We never get to do this."

"Eh." Her unenthusiastic responses are a running joke between them. She finishes straightening her hair, lays the flat iron on the floating teak vanity and sees her husband in the mirror heading in her direction.

Shawn grabs his wife by the waist and pulls her toward him.

"I love my wife," he says, then pushes her away from him as he backward-dances out of the bathroom.

"You better," she says, as she grabs her lipstick.

He doesn't reply.

"I have a giant life insurance policy," she says louder.

Nothing.

Haylee finishes putting on her lipstick and places it on the countertop. She peers through the door to the bedroom. Shawn is sitting on the bed watching the large television hanging on the wall.

"Come on baby, that was funny … Micah? Lennox? The life insurance policy? Too soon?" She walks toward him.

"Shhh, shh, shh." He grabs the remote and turns up the volume. The ticker at the bottom of the big screen reads HEROIN OVERDOSE?

"Eye-witnesses close to the scene described the man as 'half-naked, pale, and foaming at the mouth,' and have questioned if the young man struck by this Manhattan taxi cab just minutes ago may have been in the middle of an overdose," a voice-over reads as footage shows a shaky Facebook live video zooming in on the man's face. The ticker quickly changes to RAW FOOTAGE.

"Jesus," Haylee says.

"Sources have confirmed that the young man is twenty-four-year-old New York native Frank Jabali, a computer programmer who lives on the Lower East Side. He was rushed to a nearby hospital and is reportedly still alive. We will continue to update you on this tragic and …"

"Holy shit." He turns off the television and grabs his briefcase. He pulls out a folder, then another. He opens the second. He scans each one of the pages until he comes across a witness interview transcript for Frank Jabali.

That's him! he thinks. Frank Jabali, or Frank J. as Micah called him, one of Lennox's sponsees who might have been the last to see Lennox alive.

He tucks the paper in his lips, while he shoves the folders back in his briefcase. He takes the paper out of his mouth and kisses his wife.

"Gotta go." He shuts the door in an anxious exit.

Haylee stands there.

"Oh, okay," she says.

CHAPTER 29

"Oh, oh, it's right up here," she says to the driver.

Jenna's cab approaches Élan's current office, a modest building compared to the new headquarters, at the corner of 45th Street and 12th Avenue, right on the edge of Hell's Kitchen. She texts her former boss, James West.

Almost there.

She pays for the cab with her phone. *$67.50?* she thinks, then remembers she's been in the taxi for almost an hour.

She enters the giant lobby, which is fully enveloped in early golden daylight. The entire fortress is glass, from the front and side windows to the plexiglass furniture. The transparent landscape serves to highlight a large linear structure of dark, bent-plywood slats which curve like an ocean wave from the 30-foot ceiling down to the reception desk.

Remembering how much she used to admire the cold beauty of her former workplace, Jenna walks toward the front desk, noticing the reverberation of her metal heels on the marble floor. She readjusts her walk to compensate, but realizes she's simply added a prissy note to her loud pace.

Slut-clacking, that's a new one.

God, this place, she thinks, knowing how much money was poured into this building not eight years ago only to be usurped by the new one being built across town. She continues to walk, a little nervous about being here, a little grateful that she does not have to be here every day.

A simple row of thin brass pendants illuminates two beautiful young women directly below. Jenna recognizes one of them but cannot remember her name.

"Jenna! So good to see you," the familiar one says.

Good to see you, too, nameless person I used to see every day, Jenna thinks.

"Good to see you too," she says.

"Mr. West is expecting you. Here's your security badge. Through security and up ... well, you remember."

"I do," Jenna says with a half-smirk. She looks at the security area. She takes a deep breath and closes her eyes.

◆

((Ding.))

She exits the elevator on the thirty-first floor, flashes her badge at the executive receptionist, a dapper young fellow who winks and waves her through. She walks past her former desk, hoping not to be recognized. Distant memories flash by as she makes her way to the corner office. She can almost hear Lennox screaming at her after he found out she was leaving, coworkers whispering the words *traitor* and *bitch* in those final two weeks.

She approaches James West's assistant, whom she recognizes. They used to work together, him as West's assistant, and her as Lennox's assistant. They were in constant communication. An older man with a crewcut and week-old scruff, Kimberly Nicholson, or Kimbo to most who know him, is considered loyal to his boss,

144

almost to a fault. Being an assistant herself, privy to her boss's business and personal lives, Jenna knows he knows what's going on.

He is typing on his computer. *Probably messaging West*, she thinks.

"Mr. West is expecting you." Kimbo gives a friendly wink.

"Jenna? Is that you?" James West says from behind the half-open door. "Get in here!"

There we go, Jenna thinks as she enters, breathing a sigh of relief at his familiar tone.

"Close the door, would you?" he says.

And there we went, she thinks. Jenna is now uneasy.

"Packing up already?" She glances at the boxes on the floor.

"Yeah." He acknowledges the mess. "Jenna, we don't have much time. The police detective in charge of Lennox's murder case is on his way, so I'm just gonna get right to the point." Mr. West motions for her to sit down. She remains standing. "I know you must still be quite shaken about Lennox. But for the record, we had nothing to do with his horrific death. You understand that, don't you?"

She fumbles with a response. *Is he fishing for information that she might share with the police? Is he winking at the fact that they both know there's something else going on, and that she should also act just as dumb as he is?*

"I do, Mr. West." She decides to play his ambiguous game. "I don't know what you're talking about, but rest assured I know you had nothing to do with Lennox's murder."

"Sir, Detective Bronson Penance is here to see you," his assistant says over his phone's speaker.

"One moment," Mr. West responds to Kimbo, then looks at Jenna. "Sorry, I thought we would have had more time. I'm going to be blunt here. I know that you helped Lennox with certain, let's say, transactional dealings. And I think you might know where these transactions have been collected, so to speak. Now, as you can tell by the commotion here, our company is in a bit of transition, and I need your help. I'm going to ask you a question, and trust me, you'll want to answer it truthfully."

Jenna tries not to swallow. "I'm listening."

"Do you know where Lennox hid this account, and most importantly how to access it fully?"

Jenna knows where the account is, and is fairly certain she knows how to access it. *The files and account numbers and passwords are all safely tucked away from this ridiculous company.*

"Sir, I can with one hundred percent certainty tell you that I have no idea what you're talking about. My job was to input numbers and to not ask questions. So I did input the numbers, and I didn't ask questions. Period. End of the road."

James West laughs. He's always loved the way Jenna speaks. "Thank you, I just wanted to make sure, in person, you know, so I could see your face."

"Oh, absolutely." She musters as much confidence as she can while trying to understand the importance of his seeing her face. "Sorry I was so late."

"And please refer to the nondisclosure agreement you signed when you left us, just to make sure we're on the same page. I wouldn't want you to lose anything else you hold dear."

She feels another gulp begin to form in the back of her throat. She knows Mr. West can read fear, and she wants to reassure him that she knows nothing.

"Absolutely," she says. "Is that all?"

"Yes." He motions through the window to Kimbo.

Jenna turns to leave, while Detective Penance enters.

"Oh, after you." Detective Penance motions for her to pass.

"Thank you." Jenna leaves with her head down, as if she'd just been punched in the gut. She waves a defeated goodbye to Kimbo as she passes him.

"Detective, so nice to meet you in person," Mr. West says, with a half smile.

"We have a warrant for your servers, so my guys have begun that little process." Detective Penance jumps right in, hoping to elicit a response he can use. "Quite the past few weeks for your company, don't you think?"

"Stocks go up, stocks go down. We've seen worse."

"Ahh, yes. And the murder of one of your consultants in Union Square. Oh, and yet another employee right in his home."

"This city can be quite random, can't it?"

"Too much random might be considered by some to be a pattern." Detective Penance picks up an ebony-and-ivory elephant trinket off Mr. West's console table. He has remained standing, continuing to pace the room.

Mr. West says nothing.

"What can you tell me about Lennox Holcomb?" Detective Penance asks. "What exactly did he do for you here?"

"As vice president of finance, he was in charge of all aspects of accounting, payroll, financial reporting, overseeing transactions related to general ledger—" Mr. West stops himself after he realizes he is simply orating the job description. "You know, stuff like that."

"As I mentioned, we are seizing your servers, sir." Detective Penance looks at James West. "Seems a tiny little hard drive is missing from our evidence room, so we have decided to see what's in the motherboard, so to speak."

"Great, have a look. We'll get anything you need, Detective. Lennox was a good man and didn't deserve what he got."

Bronson Penance is a seasoned detective and takes note of West's phrasing. He walks toward the window. "Quite the monstrosity, isn't it?" Detective Penance is looking north across the skyline at the mostly completed new building, the one to house Élan's growing empire. "Building a high rise, consistently outperforming Cooper Harlow, hiring and hiring and hiring … with all that money, I bet you can find someone who knows the system, who can break into an evidence room with no one noticing and disappear something like it was never there."

Mr. West sits back in his chair and places his arms behind his neck.

"Well, we noticed, Mr. West," says Detective Penance. "We may not have proof yet, but we noticed."

"Detective, I appreciate you coming by. If there's anything else you need, do let us know."

Detective Penance walks toward the door and picks up an African box from the console. "Souvenirs are always great reminders, don't you think?"

He sets the box down next to a wooden elephant and leaves.

CHAPTER 30

"Thank you for the reminders. I'm actually in a cab pulling up now, talk to you soon."

Shawn ends his call with his lead paralegal, who has not only found out which hospital Frank Jabali was taken to, but has also gone through all the highlights of the witness statements of both of Lennox's sponsees, Frank Jabali and Talbot Lexington. The paralegal even texted photos of both of them. Shawn wants to be prepared just in case he is able to talk to either in person, with no ethical repercussions.

After paying his fare and walking down the block that houses St. Catherine's West, he finally finds the emergency room's modest side entrance off of 60th Street between Amsterdam and 9th. Ominous blue-and-white–striped ambulances line the curb just outside. He enters through the metal and glass doors and is hit with a smelly mix of urine and mildew. He walks past the waiting area of blue pleather chairs and approaches the desk to the right. A security guard, dressed in what looks like a police-issued black-and-white uniform, is peering at Shawn with inquiring eyes.

Shawn looks at the receptionist lady, then at the police officer, unsure of whom to direct his inquiry. He decides to split the difference.

"Yes, I believe Frank Jabali was just admitted here?" Shawn asks, looking first to the lady, then to the officer.

"And you are?" asks the lady.

"His lawyer, a lawyer," he says.

"His lawyer, a lawyer, there's a big difference," the hospital admissions girl says.

"Careful how you answer that, not that either makes a difference," says a woman's voice from the direction of the blue pleather chairs.

He turns and recognizes the face.

"Astrid Lerner," he says.

Shawn is comfortable with the fact that they both had the same idea. After all, this particular witness was to offer testimony for both the defense and the prosecution.

"Shawn Connelly. Your reputation precedes you."

She lifts her arm off the black plastic armrest and outstretches her hand. He walks toward her, takes her hand to shake it. He tries to let go, but she holds on.

"Come sit down," she says, pulling his arm and sliding herself to the next seat in the row of welded-together aquamarine chairs.

He sits down. They let go of each other's hands and look straight ahead.

"Shawn Connelly." She breaks the long pause. "Harvard. Second in your class. Had your pick of New York City's top defense firms. Settled on Lyte & Morgan. Established. Good ol' boys. Wouldn't have been my first pick, but I get it. Paid your dues. Became one of the most sought after up-and-coming criminal defense attorneys in the city."

"Astrid Lerner. Elaine Holcomb's bitch."

Astrid's eyes flinch but she is undistracted. "Shawn Connelly. Most recently second chair to the highly publicized trial of our good mayor's son, who had allegedly killed his housekeeper late at night in a drug-induced frenzy. Legend has it that *you* were the one who sussed out the housekeeper's background of mixing pills before bedtime. And get this. You argued that the murder was not about your client's drug use at all, no no no no ... but a self-defense reaction to a housekeeper's midnight delusions brought on by her own drug abuse."

Shawn remains quiet, relishing this walk down memory lane.

"Now, normally," Astrid continues, "*normally* this type of Hail Mary reasonable doubt introduction would be considered nonsense by any regular jury. But not yours. You knew you had collected some stupid, gullible sons of bitches in the twelve. You somehow not only turned the verdict into a full acquittal by the end, but also turned yourself into a hero at your firm. Hell, this entire city."

"What are you doing here, Astrid?"

"I'm here to talk to Frank's family, so maybe I can see him, make sure he's okay. He's one of our star character witnesses. I'm sure you've read his statement."

"I read it. He loved Lennox. We all did."

"And his encounters with Micah, did you read that part?"

"I did."

"And?"

"Are we talking about this? If we are, then murder 2? And manslaughter 1 and 2? *And* criminally negligent homicide? Are you for real?" Shawn's voice rises for the first time since they began talking.

"Your client did this. I don't care how clever you've been in the past, but clever doesn't acquit psycho."

"Pay attention, Ms. Lerner. Even your own detective knows Micah didn't do this. *Someone else* did. The same person who almost killed this young man you're waiting to see. A hundred bucks his toxicology report will come back positive for some sort of poison that someone *other than my client* used to spike this poor boy's heroin, and you may need to, God forbid, add someone else to your suspect list. If you continue to pursue Micah and only Micah with as much vigor as Elaine Holcomb wants you to, you'll not only end up ruining your reputation, but you'll allow the real killer to remain at large. Stop this, Astrid, while you still can. You continue, and you'll lose."

"You're the blind one, Mr. Connelly. Your client may not be as close a friend to you as his husband was, but your prejudice has nonetheless pulled the wool right over your eyes. Time to wipe the tears and focus on what is clearly in front of you. Your client did this, start to finish. The drugs have nothing to do with it. Try, just try, looking at it from every angle like we are."

"Filling Elaine's shoes by jumping right in bed with her. Wow." He gets up and walks toward the exit. "Talking is pointless. See you in court."

"We never talked."

Shawn walks out onto 60th Street and begins to look for a taxi. A gush of cold air sweeps over him, and he redirects his face to ease the brunt. He sees a young man walking around the southwest corner of Amsterdam. He is dressed in dark jeans tucked into black boots, a long T-shirt sneaking past the bottom of his vintage navy peacoat. Over the young man's scarf, Shawn can make out most of the face enough to recognize Talbot Lexington, Lennox's other sponsee.

"Talbot!" Shawn yells and makes his way toward him.

Talbot stops in his tracks, contemplates bolting on the spot.

"I'm a friend of Lennox's." Shawn slows down and stops about 25 feet from Talbot.

"Lenny is dead, motherfucker."

"I know I know, I just wanted to talk to you about your friend Frank and what happened to him this morning. I think it might have something to do with Lennox."

"Lenny was killed. Frank just overdosed, man. How the fuck you even know me? Leave me alone."

"I'm not sure Frank overdosed, Talbot, that's the thing. Do you know what happened to Frank last night, who he saw? Who he bought the drugs from?"

Like a defiant child, Talbot puts both hands in his coat, then jerks his coat down, forcing himself to attention. He looks at Shawn and doesn't move. He is expressionless, resolved.

This isn't defiance, Shawn thinks. *He knows something.*

"Hey, there's a Starbucks at the end of the block up here," Shawn says. "How 'bout I buy you a coffee?"

CHAPTER 31

Shawn stares at his cold latte, then looks at Talbot's empty coffee cup. Twenty minutes have passed with barely any words between them except, "Good coffee?" and "Yep."

They are sitting at a window bar on metal stools with worn wooden tops. A pop singer Shawn doesn't recognize is playing over the loudspeaker, while two construction workers with thick Bronx accents stand nearby, talking about how much they hate Starbucks while sipping from their green-and-white cups. A woman with black dreadlocks and combat boots is just outside the doorway, screaming "Left! Right! Left! Right!" into her worn and raggedy mittens. Shawn is annoyed by the incessant city clamor and would much rather be home with his wife in Brooklyn.

He stretches his feet onto the windowsill and leans back. Across the street, he admires a wrought iron fence with fleur-de-lis endcaps housing the garden area of a generic condo building from the 1980s. Barren trees line the street, their trunks surrounded by caged plants doing their best to stay relevant in the changing season. Shawn tilts his head to see past the obtrusive window graphics displaying the holiday spice latte du jour and sees a St. Catherine's parking sign. Shawn wonders if Astrid is still there, perhaps talking with Frank or his parents. Now that he seems to be striking out with Talbot, Shawn thinks about going back to the ER. Then he thinks about Astrid. *No thanks.*

Instead, he deems himself content to stir cold coffee while watching the after-work frenzy of New Yorkers heading home in the freezing drizzle that had just begun.

"Talbot, I could tell that you wanted to share something with me earlier," Shawn breaks the monotony. "When I mentioned the drugs, the heroin, your face completely changed. I want to help find who killed our friend Lennox. And I need to know what you know about your friend Frank."

"It was a mistake." Talbot stares straight ahead.

"I don't think so. It's not just chance that had us bump into each other, Talbot."

"No, I'm talking about last night. Frank texted me that he was gonna do heroin again. He'd been clean for almost four months."

"Heroin can grab ahold of people, and it's hard to let go," Shawn says. "Lennox had several relapses before he got his shit together. I remember one night in college, he was so fucked up I thought he was just gonna lay there and die. I spent the entire night holding his hand, cleaning up his puke."

"I know, he told me."

"He did?" Shawn asks. "Oh, right, of course. Sponsor, sponsee. Doesn't get much closer than that."

"How do you know so much about me, anyway? You a cop?"

"No, no, hell no. I'm an old friend of Lennox's from a long, long time ago. We basically grew up together." Shawn hesitates to reveal anything else but takes a chance. "I'm also a lawyer representing Lennox's husband Micah."

"Micah, huh? Fucking jealous woman." Talbot laughs.

"Did your friend Frank tell you what happened that night?" Shawn doesn't comment on Talbot's insensitive remark. He is grateful that Talbot did not clam up and that his rapport-building techniques are paying off.

"Yeah. Well, no." He sorts out his thoughts. "Well, see, he told me he was thinking about it, and that he had set up some sort of meeting with a new drug dealer. Sounded kinda scary and a little stupid. I told him not to go. Wanna see the texts?"

"Sure." Shawn shrugs, hoping he looks nonchalant.

Talbot removes his phone from his pocket and begins to flip through it.

"Here. It starts right here."

Shawn reads, barely breathing between scrolls.

11:07pm, Frank:
   Doing it. Made a new friend LOL
11:08pm, Talbot:
   New friend? WTF?
11:37pm, Frank:
   Dude says to meet him at 3am down by the
   river. Says he'll be in a fucking
   wheelchair.
11:40pm, Talbot:
   No. Don't do it. Not worth it.
3:03am, Frank:
   Got it. And get this. It was Ghost guy!
   Creepy AF dude, all freckly and shit.
   Iconic.
3:07am, Frank:
   Swear to God, he had that heroin with
   the ghost thing on it. I've got some
   good shit.

Shawn scrolls down one more frame.

3:08am, Frank:

```
Had to snap a pic of the Ghost before he
vanished haha! I've got the shit baby.
Come join me!
(photo attached)
```

Shawn looks at the attached snapshot, taken on the run. He can barely make out where it is, but he can see someone in a wheelchair sitting in front of what looks like the East River.

Unmistakable reasonable doubt, Shawn thinks, *if this is the same guy Lenny was involved with.*

"You didn't tell me there was a picture." Shawn tries to contain his excitement.

"Well, look at it, you can barely tell what's going on. Frank was probably high already."

"I'm gonna need screen grabs of all these texts, Talbot. And the picture too. Send them to me now, please."

"Sure," says Talbot, scrolling and taking screen shots of the entire exchange. "Where do you want me to send them?"

"Text me."

Shawn grabs Talbot's phone and presses in his number. He hits enter.

((Swishhh.))

CHAPTER 32

The jail cell door rolls across its glider, striking its familiar crash as it locks into place. The sound startles Micah, who is reading the Bible, one of the only books he finds available in the Tombs' library.

"You have a visitor," says the well-built guard of mixed race, dressed in prison blue, with a dark brown crew-cut and wire-framed glasses. He has been eye candy of sorts for Micah, who often wonders what the man's life is like outside of his workplace.

The guard grabs Micah by the arm and begins to escort him down the subway-themed corridor to the visiting room. Micah doesn't mind.

Fellow inmates heckle as he passes each cell.

"Oooohh, a visitor," says one. "Maybe it's your dead husband."

Micah gives the man the middle finger and continues walking.

"I've seen porn that starts like this," says another.

Micah lets out a single laugh. He turns his head to see if his escort has had a similar reaction, and is rewarded with nothing. *Or was that a grin?* He couldn't tell.

They walk through the white metal door to the visiting room. The walls are cement blocks, so the sound reverberates with every footstep he takes. As he clomps another couple of steps, Micah watches his neighbor from the A & C train cellblock arguing with what looks to be his wife or girlfriend. In the corner, he notices a prison guard cleaning up a child's puke on the speckled vinyl flooring. Then he sees beautiful Jenna sitting amidst the ugliness that surrounds her.

He smiles.

Jenna smiles back, stands up from her white table and makes a small waving gesture along with an air kiss. She is dressed in a cream-colored Gucci sweater with Snow White embroidered on the front, black slacks and navy blue off-brand pumps. She stands out amongst the slew of other visitors in sweatshirts and jeans.

"Thanks for coming," he says, sitting in the plastic chair across from her. "You're my first non-lawyer visitor."

"Are all the guards that, um ..." Jenna's eyes follow the guard.

"Um, no. Just the one."

"You didn't think we'd abandoned you, did you?" she says, trying to figure out what to do with her hands. She puts them under her ass and leans forward.

Micah shrugs in a defeated affirmative. He is comfortable in the silence. Jenna is not.

"The funeral was nice." Jenna wanted to at least acknowledge that it happened. "I really wish you coulda been there."

Micah looks down.

Jenna senses his loneliness. "I know this might sound trite, but I really want to know. How are you going?"

"How am I going," Micah says, rolling with the Jennaspeak. "Fucking miserable. Keeping myself busy. Reading. Staying up to date on my case through Shawn."

"Shawn. What would we do without him?" Jenna is trying her best to make her pronouns as inclusive as possible, making sure that Micah knows he is not alone.

"Ain't that the truth?" Micah bows his head.

"Speaking of the case, I spoke with James West."

Micah's head jerks up. "You did?"

"Yes, and it was quite the experience. That's partially why I came, Micah. I'm scared. Like shaking in my skin scared."

Micah reaches his hands across the table. Jenna pulls her hands from her seat to hold Micah's, sees the guard moving toward them, then moves them back with a head tilt to Micah.

Micah places his hands back in his lap. "Why? What happened?"

"He threatened me, kinda. And I'm not sure why."

"Threatened you how? Did you tell Shawn this?"

"Not yet. While we were talking, Mr. West just wanted to make sure that if I knew anything, it would remain confidential. He even mentioned my nondisclosure agreement, and said something like 'We wouldn't want you to lose anything else dear to you.'" She stops, looks downward to her left. "Do you think that was about Lennox?"

"Good question. My question would be, did he threaten you because of Lennox, or because of the Union Square killing? Cuz that company was involved in both, if you ask me." Micah leans forward. "Two people from the same company, on the same night, killed by different nameless people who are still at large? If any of that's true, he's simply trying to throw his weight around, to make sure he can contain information as much as possible. You're good, Jenna, you're good."

Jenna sits back in her chair. He sees that she hasn't really felt his words of encouragement.

"Jenna, it's all gonna be okay. Trust me."

She begins to cry, her shoulders shrugging as if she's laughing. She is smiling. "You always do this to me. I come to you to make sure you're okay, and you always end up being the one to comfort me."

"It's what we do, right?" Micah says, borrowing one of Shawn's catchphrases. He stalls a bit to let Jenna work through whatever she is feeling, then hits her with, "Wanna do me a favor?"

"Anything."

"Find the letter."

"The letter."

"The one that Lennox filed away, the one that implicates the drug guy. In the folder with the ghost logo."

"Micah, I don't want to get further into this," Jenna says, deflecting. "This is all out of my horizons."

Micah realizes she is mixing metaphors again but can't figure out what they are. He lets it go.

"Jenna, I remember he wrote the letter about the same time you were his assistant, because it was right after his affair with Josh. Now, listen to me ... Shawn says the letter isn't in any of the files they confiscated from our condo, and it's not in the discovery from the prosecution, so the only other place it could have been was in his files at work, or your files you took with you when you left."

"I don't know." Jenna looks uncomfortable, which is annoying Micah. "I remember Lenny asking me to delete it several months after I transcribed it for him, and I barely remember what was in it. Plus, I don't want to do this anymore."

"Do what anymore?"

"This. All of this." She flattens her palm and rotates her hand around in a circle. "I want to help, I really do. But I'm scared to get any further into this."

"Please just check, would you?" Micah finds himself over-enunciating. "I never read the goddamn thing, but because of everything Lennox told me about this guy, I think it might be key to who the company may have hired to kill him. Seriously. Help me here. Jury selection is beginning this week, for Christ's sakes. Shawn has a plan for securing the right jury, but I'm not so sure about it."

She sits there, lost in thought.

"Please, Jenna. Do it for Lenny," Micah prods. "He didn't deserve this."

"I'll do my best," Jenna says, forgetting the request as soon as she leaves.

CHAPTER 33

I deserve this, Astrid thinks, congratulating herself as she takes off her high heels and pours herself a glass of cabernet. Although she hasn't had the opportunity to spend much time at home over the past few weeks, she has set aside this evening to relax by working on her opening statement.

Two months ago, Assistant District Attorney Astrid Lerner bought the home of her dreams, a modest one-bedroom end unit in the historic Christadora House across from Tomkins Square Park in the East Village. The condo is shotgun style, on the fourteenth floor, with sweeping north, east, and south views. Manhattan is majestically highlighted through thick black iron-framed windows against stark white walls.

She fancies herself a bargain hunter, which was evident in the way she negotiated the deal on the condo itself. Even after her offer of $30,000 below asking was accepted, the appraisal came in way below offer. She stood her ground and decided not to walk away, forcing her real estate agency to handle further negotiations so they wouldn't lose the sale. She ended up getting the $1.2 million condo for just under a million.

She tops off her glass and revels in her victories, not only her condo purchase, but also the fact that she has just negotiated the jury of her dreams ... An all-male, all-Republican set of twelve. *Almost. Just two questionable peers separate me from convicting him*, she relishes. One is a lesbian activist, the other is the female CFO of a high-tech company. In this moment, she is confident with her odds, despite her suspicions of her opponent Shawn Connelly.

Three days of jury selection and only one peremptory challenge? She asks herself. *It's so unlike him to buckle like that.* She takes another sip.

((Buzz.))

Astrid places the wineglass down, disturbed by the buzz kill, yet fully expecting the arrival of Detective Penance.

"Come on up," she says into the intercom, and presses him in.

She takes her glass of wine into her bedroom, places it on her nightstand, and grabs a notebook from her briefcase. She reads the opening paragraph:

LADIES AND GENTELMEN OF THE JURY.

"Good beginning, Ass," she says out loud. "Ass" a nickname she calls herself, especially when she notices something stupid like her own typo.

((Knock knock.))

She puts the notebook under her arm, grabs the glass of wine, and walks to the door.

"Detective."

"Ms. Lerner." Detective Bronson Penance does his best imaginary hat removal.

"Why, do come in."

"Don't mind if I do."

"God, we are dorks."

"You speak the truth, m'dear."

Detective Penance sits down in the chair where Astrid was enjoying her wine, takes out some papers and photos and spreads them across the coffee table. Unshaven, with his shirt half untucked, he appears tired but restless. He feigns excitement, if only to boost his adrenaline for the conversation that's about to happen.

"Let's get to work, shall we?" He knows that Astrid has a lot of work to do the night before a trial.

"Before we start, did you hear about my jury?" She is still standing.

"You mean how you basically ran right over the legendary guru, Shawn Connelly, and negotiated the perfect jury? You found ten full-on conservative religious men. In New York City, for crying out loud."

"Yeah, it's strange. I would have thought he would have objected more, it was like we were looking for the same people, except those final two. Although I do like the lesbian as a person. And I think the CEO and I could be friends."

"Maybe that's his strategy. All he needs is one or two. A hung jury maybe?"

"Yeah, maybe, although he knows we'd turn right back around and pursue it again," she answers, then gets distracted. "Oh, oh, get this … Do you know that one of the jurors actually made the statement … Wait, let me find it."

She bends down, reaches into her bag and pulls out a notebook, never putting her drink down.

"Here it is." She begins to read. "Okay, so he says, 'Faggot priests who abuse young children should be hung by their balls and have their fingernails ripped off one by one.' Then he did the sign of the cross." She mimes the movement using her wine glass. "Can you believe that?"

"In the courtroom?" He tries to hold in his laughter. "In front of Judge Wilson?"

"I thought he was gonna have a heart attack," she says, sipping her wine.

"Please don't tell me that guy is on the jury."

"He's foreman. Shawn was actually the one who asked the question about Catholic priests."

"Something fishy there," he says. "Who did he use the peremptory on?"

"Some juror who went on and on about her cats during *voir dire*."

"That's what they call the questioning of the prospective jury, right?" He's trying to remember the terminology.

"Yes," she replies. "Now, this lady ... this cat lady ... she had on these tight black gloves with white tips. Looked like claws. Toward the end of her questioning, she said something that sounded vaguely like gay-bashing, and Shawn immediately moved to strike her. Which I really didn't mind, cuz she was annoying as hell."

"Sounds like he knew what he was looking for, and maybe he got it too."

"Yeah." She brings her wineglass up to her mouth to take another sip. She stops, letting the glass rest on her lips.

"Let's get to work, shall we?" he repeats, breaking Astrid out of her thoughts.

"Let's do this." She sits in the chair opposite the view she was enjoying before Detective Penance arrived.

"Okay, so we have the phone calls and texts from Micah, which we have in the timeline," he starts. "We also have the phone call from Talbot to Lennox that night telling him that he couldn't make their meeting, whatever that means, and another voice message from James West, who basically said he was at the party, he had just seen Micah, and everyone was wondering where he was. Are you gonna use the Talbot and James West phone calls?"

"Yes, I think we have to if we talk about Micah's. By introducing the one call, we open ourselves up to the rest of the them during cross."

"Well, you gotta do what you gotta do. I know you can handle it."

"Yep. What's next?"

"Despite Lennox being found naked, the autopsy results showed no signs of sexual battery, plus the shower DNA results showed mostly dark hairs from Lennox. We think he had just taken a shower and was grabbing a snack, which matches what Micah told us in his voluntary deposition. Stomach contents included barely digested cereal and milk, which goes along with the half-eaten corn flakes we found on the desk."

"What about the chair? What's your feeling about that?"

"The bloody desk chair that was moved across the floor during the attack? No one doubts that the chair is where the initial murder took place. My guess is the victim was rolled and dumped on the floor. The perpetrator either finished stabbing him there, or just discarded him and left him for dead."

"My God. I dare someone to convince me this wasn't a crime of passion. Poor guy, not a care in the world, having some cereal at his desk. If I get caught up in the emotion of that, I'm done for. Moving on."

"So the Wi-Fi camera that may have taped the murder, where is it, here it is." He moves the photo of the camera found inside the African trinket box to the forefront of all the other photos. "Now, we still haven't found any recording, but I leave to you to introduce the camera to the jury."

"I filed a motion to dismiss it," Astrid says. "Since nobody knows what the hell it even did. But *if* the camera is entered into evidence, I've been thinking about a counter. Something about sadism ... wanting to video his own crime. We don't know that he didn't set this up himself."

"Actually, we might know who did. I went to see James West this week and found a number of souvenirs from his African travels in his office, including a box that looks remarkably similar to this one." He points to the picture of the box from the crime scene, then unearths a magazine photo of James West next to the console in his office, with an African box clearly on display. He circles the box with a red grease pencil. "Now, might be coincidence, might not, but again, something to consider."

"Considered. I read your report."

"Now, along the same lines, we confiscated the main servers and combed any interactions with James West and Lennox Holcomb. We found nothing. Well, we found chats, but any conversations between the two of them from about six months ago until now are gone. Wiped. Not even a trace. Which I thought was kinda strange, especially considering that all other emails, interoffice messaging, everything on virtually every single employee was still there."

"Wait, so are you saying we should be looking at this company, this CEO, instead of who we arrested and charged?"

"Not exactly. See, my colleague is working the other case, the Union Square murder case, and with all the knowledge I have of the two cases, I have a theory that Élan Publishing was keeping tabs on key conspirators in some sort of financial cover-up, and they may have been keeping tabs on Lennox by placing a camera in their living room, which might have recorded the murder that night. Accidentally."

"May have, might have. Speculation. You can't say that on the stand."

"I could work it in somehow. If the camera's admitted into evidence."

"Good luck with that. What's next?"

"Jenna." Detective Penance pulls out a photo of Jenna Ancelet. "Now, I saw this chick ... excuse me, lady ... when I was leaving James West's office. I remembered her from the night we took in Micah. She was the one Micah saw as we were leaving the murder scene, and he yelled at her to call his lawyer. That's not even the juicy part."

"I should say not, you interviewed her as well. I have the transcript."

"Right, right. She was cleared. Alibi, everything. Done. But get this. I saw her at Élan talking with Mr. West right before I got there. She doesn't work there anymore, I remembered, so why would she be there? I combed the servers and found out that all of her emails and instant messaging to Lennox were gone from the same exact timeframe, too."

"Wait, I thought you said everyone else's emails were still on the servers?"

"I said *virtually* everyone else's. Jenna's is gone, too. Zip. Nada."

"Jesus Christ, this company. Does that lead you to believe we're on the wrong path here, Bron? Seriously?"

"Look, I want to be a team player." Detective Bronson leans back, rubs his eyes. "I know you have a lot of pressure on you. I know there's something off here, but I just can't wrap my mind around it. On the one hand, too much evidence points to this crooked company in two murders of two different employees in the same night, and they're really good at getting rid of evidence. On the other hand, evidence supports motive and opportunity for Micah to kill his husband, apart from any company angle … Not to mention a confession, albeit a weak one, and DNA evidence."

"Exactly. DNA evidence."

"But that's where I stop and think, should we ask for a postponement? Or at least consider a plea deal?"

"That's not your job."

"You asked."

Astrid sits up from her chair. She lets out a sigh that feels like it's been screaming to be released. "I did. I did ask. Not because I wanted to know, but maybe because I wanted to hear it out loud."

Detective Penance leans back in his chair, mirroring Astrid.

"These are lives we are talking about," he says. "Like I said, I know you're under a lot of pressure on this. But we gotta remember, a human being is dead. Drugs or not, conspirator or not, gay or not, not that I have a problem with that."

Anyone who says they don't have a problem with that clearly does, Astrid thinks.

"Plus, I am not letting go of these wiped emails and missing hard drives. I just need more time to find better resources," he continues. "And from what I've heard, Lennox was a decent man. He just got caught up in the wrong place with the wrong people. Did these people include Micah? I think that's the real question here. If we believe it, then let's go for it. If we don't, then we have an ethical responsibility to hold off until we know for sure. Both of us."

Detective Penance plops the photo of Jenna he had been waving around throughout his monologue onto the table, like a drop-the-mic exclamation to end his point. *And THAT is doing my job*, he thinks, somewhat relieved to get his concerns off his chest.

Astrid pushes herself up out of the chair and begins pacing around her condo. Normally she would look at cases from many different angles before landing on a truth, a passion behind her representation of the People. But regardless if she wanted to believe it, this woman, this predecessor, this Elaine Holcomb, has control of her decisions. Astrid wants to prove herself. She wants to advance her career.

But is it just that? she wonders.

Something else is nagging her. An overwhelming feeling that Micah somehow orchestrated his husband's death. Call it intuition, call it experience. She begins to talk out loud, outlining her own "on-the-one-hand" dissertation.

"True, there's evidence to suggest this company could've orchestrated the murder, and Micah was the innocent victim in all of this. But isn't it also true that there's more evidence to the contrary? We have a timeline with massive gaps, we have blood all over the alleged perp, we have a taped confession, we have Micah's beyond-squeaky-clean hard drive, witnesses that corroborate a psychopathic switch that turns Micah from a Christian-raised schoolboy into a raging luna—" She stops mid run-on. "Wait a second, that's it. That's our argument."

"Hard to believe, but I'm actually following you," he says.

"Then get out. I've got work to do."

He continues to sit, smiling at Astrid's sarcasm, while gathering his documents and pictures. "You should start by subpoenaing Micah's therapy notes. He's got tons of receipts from this Jewish lady in the Flatiron District."

"It's cute that you think I haven't already done that. Now go on. Git!" Astrid says with a shuffling gesture.

"Okay, okay." He stands up to leave. "I heard you, I heard you."

CHAPTER 34

"Oyez. Oyez. Oyez. All rise."

Shawn and Micah stand along with the rest of the court. Micah looks at Shawn, who winks as if to say, *We got this.*

"New York County Supreme Court is now in session," the court clerk continues. "The honorable Judge Christopher K. Wilson presiding. All persons having business before the Honorable Court are admonished to draw near and give their attention, for the court is now sitting. God save the great state of New York and this Honorable Court."

A quiet hush covers the room, followed by squeaks and shuffles as lawyers, jurors, and audience members sit down in their seats. The wooden spectator pews are filled with various local and national media and interested onlookers, each wanting a glimpse of the first "Pub War Murder Trial," as the *New York Post* has dubbed it. Contrary to the second Pub War case involving the other Élan employee murdered on the same night, this case has a suspect, a confession, an arrest, and its trial is now underway.

The courtroom, with twenty-foot ceilings and original eight-foot mahogany wainscoting, is a throwback to an older age of tradition, respect, and admiration for the justice system. A hodgepodge of renovated additions over the years includes the same speckled vinyl flooring as the Tombs next door, thin black microphones that look like they were ripped from the hands of Bob Barker himself, and large flatscreen television monitors next to the jury box on the left and in front of the defense on the right.

Shawn is sitting next to Micah, who is dressed in a dark-grey wool suit and a blue tie, both of which were gifted by Shawn the night before. Shawn is paying close attention to the jury, and at the same time watching Astrid get her notes together.

"Good morning, ladies and gentlemen," says Judge Wilson, high atop everyone else on his large, looming wooden bench that has been covered in layer after layer of stain and shellac over the years. "Quite the weather we're having, huh? Had to keep my boots on cuz m'feet are cold."

The packed courtroom shows respect by snickering. The judge recognizes the mild feedback.

Judge Christopher K. Wilson, originally from South Carolina, is one of the few judges in any New York municipality who has an unblemished reputation. With no questionable ethics, no violations of code or process, he is sixty-six years old and considered by most in the legal profession to be a bit eccentric, very old school and by the book. He attended Vanderbilt University Law School from 1974 to 1977 and began working in New York as a defense lawyer in the late seventies. After rising through the legal ranks, serving in various capacities as judge for several civil and criminal courts, the Mayor of New York City appointed him to serve out his remaining years as a New York County Supreme Court Justice.

"Now, before we get started, I'd like to make something clear. My courtroom is formal. I will not stand for gimmicks, for outbursts, for anything not pertaining to the case. We are on the people's dime and we don't have time for any nonsense."

Great, a Republican judge too, Shawn thinks. He takes a deep breath. *Am I in Manhattan?*

"Calling the case of the People of the Great State of New York versus Micah Breuer-er," the clerk says, fumbling over the last name.

"Are both sides ready?" asks the judge.

"Ready for the People, your Honor," ADA Astrid Lerner says.

"Ready for the defense, your Honor," Shawn says.

"Will the clerk please swear in the jury?" asks the judge.

"Will the jury please stand and raise your right hand?" asks the court clerk.

The jury rises. Astrid Lerner gleams with approval and looks to the audience where she knows the Holcombs are sitting. Elaine is stoic.

The clerk begins to scan the jury. "Do you solemnly swear or affirm that you will try the matter of the People of the Great State of New York versus Micah Breuer in a fair and impartial manner and render a verdict according to the law and the evidence, so help you God. Do you so truly affirm?"

"I do," they state in unison.

"You may be seated."

"Thank you," says the judge. "Ms. Lerner, you may begin."

Astrid, dressed in a navy-blue pinstriped power suit, is seated right in front of the jury box. Her hair is styled in an updated Marlo Thomas *That Girl* style, straightened and flipping up at the ends. She places her hand on the slick varnished wall that separates her from the jury risers and begins.

"Thank you, your Honor. And thank you, ladies and gentlemen of the jury. The defendant has been charged with the murder of Lennox Holcomb, his husband.

"Lennox, or Lenny, as his family and friends called him, was stabbed thirty-three times on the evening of August 17, 2018. And that man, Micah Breuer, sitting right there in the dark suit, confessed to killing him. That is a fact. Our evidence will show motive to commit murder, our timeline will prove opportunity to commit murder, and our DNA evidence of the murder is undisputed.

"Now, the defendant over here might look like an all-American Christian boy, and he is. Born and raised. He grew up with a loving family. Church-going. God-loving. But the defendant had another side. One that he hid from both his parents up until the day they died. Expert testimony and even the defendant's own words will show a pattern of lying and hiding his true self beyond those early years, well into adulthood, ultimately up until the time his husband was murdered.

"The defense attorney, Mr. Connelly over here, is going to try to sway you with conspiracy theories, corporate espionage, and even ghosts."

The jury chuckles.

"I know, but it's true." She begins to march across the front row of the jury box. "Oh, it'll be interesting. Sometimes it'll be hard to stomach, as the brutality of this crime is well-documented in the evidence we will present. But throughout this process, I would like for you to ask yourself: Is it easier to believe in ghosts, or that a conflicted young man living a double life could be a real-life murderer?"

Astrid looks at each member of the jury, one by one.

"Thank you for your time and service."

She spins on her heel and takes her seat.

"Mr. Connelly?" Judge Wilson prompts.

"Thank you, your Honor." Shawn begins his opening statement. "Ladies and gentlemen, Micah Breuer walked into his home on the evening in question and found his husband in a pool of blood on the floor. His husband was still breathing. Micah did what any of us would do: he tried to save him. He did CPR. Now, maybe CPR wasn't the best choice, but defense will show that his state of mind and lack of knowledge as to what exactly was happening with his husband caused him to act quickly."

He pauses, walks to his right, continues.

"Imagine for a second you're at dinner. One of your loved ones is choking on, let's say, some random meatball from your grandmother's under-baked, chewy, lumpy beef stew."

The jury laughs, louder than they had with Astrid.

"Objection," Astrid Lerner states. "Meatballs, your Honor?"

"I think it's a metaphor, Ms. Lerner, kinda like your ghost thing," the judge says. "Overruled."

She tries not to react. *That's completely different*, she thinks.

"You know the Heimlich, right?" Shawn continues, looking at the jury. "You go to do the Heimlich on your loved one. You're desperate. You push upward and push upward. But instead of releasing the meatball, you accidentally break your loved one's rib. That rib punctures the heart and your loved one passes away. Are you going to think you killed your loved one? Absolutely. But was that homicide? Absolutely not. Can any of Micah's acts that evening be considered homicide? No.

"When the prosecution has finished, the defense will bring to light the real truth: one they neglected to pursue any other line of questioning or suspect to the fullest extent they could have; and two, the evidence will show several other avenues, *several* avenues, that point to the real killer of Lennox Holcomb that fateful night.

"Reasonable doubt will definitely come into play here. Because there's a whole lot of doubt in the prosecution's reasoning. Thank you for your time and service."

"Objection," Astrid repeats.

"Sustained," says the judge. "The jury will ignore Mr. Connelly's personal conclusion regarding the prosecution's reasoning."

Astrid is pleased.

"The prosecution may present its first witness," says the judge.

"Thank you, your Honor. The prosecution would like to call Officer Mateo Palino to the stand, please."

The tall, burly Italian police officer walks in front of Astrid up the single step to the witness stand and sits down. He is dressed in full uniform.

"Please stand and place your hand on the Bible," orders the clerk. "Raise your right hand. Do you promise that the testimony you shall give in the case before this court shall be the truth, the whole truth, and nothing but the truth, so help you God?"

"I do."

"Officer, could you please state your full name for the record?" Astrid asks.

"Mateo Palino. That's M-A-T-E-O, last name P-A-L-I-N-O. I've worked with the police department of the Seventh Precinct for the past three-and-a-half years."

"Thank you. Can you tell me in your own words what happened the night of August 17?"

"At approximately 10:15 on the night of August 17, I received a 9-1-1 dispatch to the corner of Henry and Rutgers. Possible homicide, possible suspect still in the building. My partner and I arrived on the scene, pressed a button for apartment number seven, received no immediate answer, broke through the two glass entrances and entered the elevator. As we entered, we heard a voice on the speaker say, 'Come on up,' and then we heard a buzzer sound.

"When we arrived at the seventh floor, the doors wouldn't open, but then seemed to open automatically. The defendant then pointed to the victim and said, 'He's right over there.' I proceeded to ascertain the status of the victim, while my partner secured the—"

"Sorry, let me stop you for a second," Astrid says. "Can you tell me how the defendant appeared upon arrival at the scene?"

"Objection," Shawn says. "Calls for speculation."

"Your Honor, this witness is an officer of the law," Astrid chimes in. "His perception is based on experience, and he was the first one on the scene."

"Overruled."

"Continue please, Officer Palino," Astrid says.

"Well, the way he said 'Come on up.' It was kinda like he was having guests over for a party. *'Come on up!'* And then we entered. He was very calm. Simply pointed to this huge pile of blood with a naked body in the middle of it and said, 'He's over there.'"

"Can we play the 9-1-1 call, please?"

A loud *click* echoes through the room. The volume is high, but quickly resolves to a normal level.

"9-1-1, what is your emergency?"

"Please help me! My husband! Something's happened here! I tried to save him. He was alive. Oh God, please come, please! Maybe you can help him!"

"Sir, please slow down. Did you say something's happened to your husband?"

"Yes! I got home, and he was just lying there. Blood. Oh my God, I think he's dead! Please hurry!!!"

"Sir, what is your location?"

"142 Henry Street, #7, corner of Rutgers."

"Sir, we have an ambulance on the way, and police are very close."

"Oh God, how did this happen? I don't understand!"

"Now, I need you to calm down, okay? Is there anyone else in the house?"

"What?"

"Sir, could the person who did this still be there?"

"Oh my God, I have no idea."

"Do you have a neighbor or a nearby friend you can go to right now until help arrives?"

"I think I'm okay."

"Just to be safe, could you find a place to hide, maybe lock yourself in a bathroom, please, sir?"

"Yes, I have a friend who ..."

((*Audible doorbell.*))

"I think they're here."

((Click.))

"Does anything strike you as odd about that call, officer?"

"Yes."

Astrid looks at the jury with a knowing glance. She does not pursue this line of questioning at the moment and continues.

"Can you describe for the jury what the defendant was like for the rest of the evening?"

"Well, he was very fidgety and kept wanting to sit everywhere. I kept thinking, *this is a crime scene for God's sakes,* and kept asking him to remain standing. I asked him to tell me what happened, and he described hearing a gurgling noise in the dark. He says he knew it was Lennox, so his first thought was to approach and administer CPR.

"And the way he said he administered CPR seemed excessive," Mateo continues. "He said he kept pushing on the victim's chest over and over. *'Over and over,'* he said. I couldn't imagine beating on someone's chest who'd been stabbed thirty-three times."

"But officer, wasn't the room dark? I mean, can you blame the defendant for not knowing what had happened, and trying to administer CPR to save him?"

"That's the thing. The lights had been on the whole time, ever since the moment we stepped through the elevator, and there were no blood stains on the light switches."

"I don't follow."

"Well, if you do CPR on a man who's been stabbed thirty-three times, mostly in the chest, you're going to have blood all over you. I mean, allll over you. And he most definitely did, all over his face, his arms, his chest. So if the lights were off during the time he said he administered CPR, but they were on when we arrived, then why was there no blood on the light switch?"

Astrid again looks at the jury. Some faces are staring straight ahead. Some are looking down.

"No further questions for this witness," Astrid says.

Shawn recognizes Astrid's win. He did not draw the same conclusion from the photos of the light switch in the condo he had seen in the discovery photos. He mentally kicks himself and wonders how he will address the matter.

"Your witness, Mr. Connelly," Judge Wilson says.

"Thank you, your Honor," Shawn begins. "Officer Palino, do you live in a high rise?"

"Yes, in the East Village with my wife and two kids."

"And do you have a buzzer for visitors?"

"Yes, we do."

"Do you remember what you say to your visitors when you buzz them in?"

"Something like 'Hey, come up.'"

"Is it something *like* 'Hey, come up' or is it definitely 'Hey, come up'?"

"Sometimes it's 'Hey, come up,' sometimes it's 'Come on up.'"

"Sometimes, something like, huh? Is it possible that the reason why you don't know is because you do it so often, it becomes rote, like second nature?"

"It's possible."

"Thank you. You also mentioned a casual way about Mr. Breuer that was out of place, or *odd* I believe is the word you used. But isn't it also possible that people react differently to traumatic events?"

"Yes, but the defendant's demeanor went beyond—"

"'Yes' will suffice, thank you. And do you have any psychological credentials this court is unaware of?"

"No."

Shawn ponders a way to address the light switch but is wondering himself how there was no blood on it. He stalls by shuffling some papers on his desk, still figuring out his argument.

"Now, Officer Palino," he begins, then pauses. He is about to try another 'is it possible' themed argument, but decides not to risk it. "I have no further questions," he says, and stares straight ahead to the witness stand, as if he were about to say something else.

Officer Palino stands up, then halfway sits back down again, looks at Shawn, then shakes his head.

Shawn walks back to Micah. They lock eyes for a brief moment of unspoken confusion.

"Counselor Lerner, do you have anything further for this witness?" asks the judge.

"Nothing further at this time," Astrid responds.

"Very well. Next witness."

"The people would like to call Detective Bronson Penance, please." Astrid smiles and lifts up her laptop she has connected to the monitors. The first slide of her PowerPoint presentation reads *Timeline*.

Detective Penance approaches and is sworn in. A stark contrast to the disheveled way he presented himself at Astrid's apartment the night before, he is dressed to the nines in charcoal-grey pinstripes, with a red-and-black tie and a pocket handkerchief to match. He rattles off his credentials and lengthy history as detective for New York's Southern District, as well as his role in the investigation.

"Detective Penance, did you notice the absence of blood on the light switch?" Astrid begins, wanting to reiterate her Perry Mason moment, as Elaine Holcomb's husband had put it.

"Yes, yes I did."

"You were also the one to put together this timeline of that evening, is that correct?"

"Yes."

"Can you walk us through it, please?"

"Of course."

Astrid hands him the remote control. He approaches the large monitor in front of the jury.

"Based on eyewitnesses, footage from several public and private cameras along the route, social media photo timestamps, GPS tracking on the phones of both the defendant and the victim, and phone calls from the defendant to the victim, I put together the following timeline." He begins reading the slides and describing the events.

7:00pm–7:30pm: Initial stabbing
"Bloodwork and blood splatter results obtained from the scene indicate the murder happened between 7:00pm and 7:30pm. However, the victim was still alive after these stabbings."

7:17pm: Micah Breuer leaves/enters taxi.
"We know this from the footage and timestamp of the city camera at the corner of Henry and Rutgers, across from the condo, which is the crime scene in question."

((Photo of Micah leaving the building))
"The defendant, dressed in a black-and-white tuxedo, carrying a large Jack Spade canvas bag, gets into a taxi, which is corroborated by a receipt, direct from a company called LES Taxi and Limousine Service."

7:20pm: Micah texts Jenna
    Where are you?
"The defendant texts a friend asking, 'Where are you?'"

7:40pm: Gas station stop of 3 minutes
7:45pm: 14th St at 5th Ave
7:50pm: Micah texts Jenna
    Almost there
7:57pm: Micah arrives at event
"Notice the time lag here. Cameras at the event the defendant uses as his alibi clock him exiting the taxi at 7:57pm. It's important to note here that traffic was light that evening, so what should have been a twenty-minute drive from the Lower East Side where Micah and Lennox lived to Midtown, where the event took place, took almost fifty minutes.

((Photos and videos of various camera angles showing Micah's limo))
"Cameras did clock the taxi at a gas station at Houston and Lafayette at 7:40pm, which took a total of three minutes, as did a

camera at 14th and 5th at 7:45pm, and another at 7:50, three blocks from the final destination, which was the event."

"Thank you, Detective," Astrid says. "Do you have any information on the taxi and its whereabouts during the stretch of time unaccounted for between 7:17pm, when the defendant left his apartment and got in the cab, and 7:40pm, when the taxi carrying the defendant stopped for gas? That's over twenty minutes."

"We do not. We cannot place the defendant anywhere during that time period. We spoke with the cab driver, but there was a bit of a language barrier there."

"Continue," Astrid says.

8:20pm: Micah texts Lennox
> OH. MY. GOD. You said you'd be right
> here. Lemme know an ETA baby.

9:05pm: Micah calls Lennox

"Not much later, Micah calls Lennox. The voice mail transcript reads: *"Hey baby, where are you? I miss you. I can't tell you how many people are asking about you. Text me or call me, I have my phone. I hope everything's all right."* This will also be made available to the jury as a recording.

9:15pm: Micah leaves event

"Witnesses at the event report Micah leaving around 9:15pm."

9:34pm: Micah enters taxi

10:10pm: Micah exits taxi

"These times are corroborated both by cameras and taxi receipts. It wouldn't normally take this long for a taxi to drive from Midtown to the Lower East Side, but nothing too out of the ordinary."

10:15pm: Approximate death of victim, corroborated by both the victim and blood coagulation analysis

10:32pm: 9-1-1 call

"Note here that the 9-1-1 call came over fifteen minutes after the defendant comes home and discovers his husband in a pool of blood on the floor."

10:38pm: Police arrive on scene
10:50pm: Detective arrives on scene
11:15pm: Defendant escorted to police station
11:50pm: Defendant is processed
3:10am: Defendant confesses

"And there you have it," Detective Penance says, ending his timeline.

"Thank you, Detective. Correct me if I'm wrong here. The defendant calls his husband at 9:05 because he is very worried, yet doesn't make it home until over an hour later?"

"Objection," says Shawn. "Argumentative."

"Sustained," says the judge.

"Please fill us in on any other relevant findings, Detective," Astrid says.

"Well, Micah and Lennox had a one-point-five-million-dollar life insurance policy on one another."

"One-point-five? Isn't that a bit excessive?"

"Objection," Shawn speaks out. "Argumentative. Again."

"Sustained."

Astrid knew her snap judgment of the amount wasn't going to fly, but she wanted the $1.5 million on record, so she could use it in her closing argument.

"And when was this one-point-five-million-dollar life insurance policy taken out?"

"July of 2015."

"July of 2015." She reiterates the date while shifting her eyes back and forth from Detective Penance, then to the jury, then back to the detective. "Now I understand you've talked to several character witnesses, and have personally documented all testimony to be presented in this case?"

"I have. Transcripts and recordings."

"Thank you. We have nothing further for this witness at this time," Astrid says to the court.

"Your witness, Mr. Connelly," says the judge.

"Thank you, your Honor." Shawn stands up, grabs a folder, and walks toward the witness. He is holding the folder by his side as he approaches.

"Now, Detective Penance, you stated previously that it was you who discovered the absence of blood on the light switch, is that correct?"

"Yes, then I told Officer Palino, and we discussed it," Penance answers, anticipating where this particular line of questioning is heading.

"But Officer Palino just said, mere minutes ago, that it was *he* who noticed the light switch."

"Yes, but he did so *after* I asked him if the lights were on."

"Lots of this story is confusing to me, so forgive me for asking."

"Objection," Astrid says.

"Sustained," replies the judge. "Careful, Mr. Connelly."

"Detective Penance, these so-called gaps in the timeline, did they take into consideration the many events that were happening the evening of August 17?" Shawn asks.

"Yes, they did. When we say the evening was 'normal,' we mean information we have on traffic patterns of the evening, as well as registered events near the areas in question."

"Would it interest you to know that on the night of August 17, there were approximately two point five times the so-called 'normal' events in Midtown and surrounding neighborhoods?" Shawn asks. "We'd like to enter this document from the New York City Visitors Bureau as defense exhibit 40-B."

Detective Penance looks at the document and looks straight ahead. He says nothing.

"Isn't is possible, Detective, that Micah's taxi could've been held up in traffic … especially with more than twenty-five events of at least ten thousand people being held on the island that night?"

"It's possible but not probable, based on our information and the video footage."

"You have no route information for Micah's taxi, nor any footage of the taxi during those times, just before and after, and you did not procure a translator to talk with the cab driver, is that correct?"

"We do not, and yes, that is correct," Detective Penance states, realizing Shawn is trying to confuse him. "Except for the translator. We did procure a translator, but we believed the driver was confused about the night in question."

"You believe. Thank you. Now, Detective, you made no mention of my client's alleged confession, other than a line item on the timeline." Shawn feels confident in his proactive measures.

"Correct. I believe we are addressing that tomorrow."

"Mind if we address it now?"

"Objection," says Astrid.

"Your Honor, this particular confession goes hand-in-hand with the defendant's state of mind during this traumatic night," Shawn says, appealing to the judge. "I would like to address the trauma as it relates to the detective's earlier comments about the light switch, as well as the alleged confession."

The judge ponders his decision for a quick moment. "I'll allow it."

"Thank you, your Honor. Can we play the tape of Mr. Breuer's alleged confession please?"

The audio starts with a loud thud, which startles Micah. He crouches in his chair, realizing another memory from that night is about to be resurrected.

> "There's blood everywhere you touched, but there's no blood on the light switches. Can you explain that please? …

(pause) … Sir, why did you pound on your husband's mutilated body when you knew he was still alive?"

"Sir, I told you, I was freaking the fuck … (pause) …Geez, oh man, did I … (pause) … Did … Did I kill him? … (pause) … Oh dear God, I killed him myself."

Shawn looks intently at Detective Penance and asks, "You used to be married, didn't you, Detective Penance?"

"Yes, a lifetime ago."

"When your wife was still alive, could you imagine her lying in a pool of blood when you got home from, let's say, a Policeman's Ball?"

Janice in the hospital.

Janice at home in hospice.

Janice being lowered into her casket.

"Detective?" Shawn interrupts Detective Penance's thoughts of his wife.

"No, I couldn't, but …"

"And now, lights on or off, try to imagine the panic you must feel that your wife is in danger. Wouldn't you want to do whatever came to your mind to help her?"

"That's an unfair analogy."

"Exactly! Why? Because you, good sir, are trained in life-saving techniques. My client is not. He was in panic mode, both during his husband's dying breath, and during his interview when you, detective, were questioning why he would resort to the only life-saving technique that popped into his mind."

"Objection," Astrid says loudly. "Is there a question here, or is the detective on trial for killing his wife?"

"Mr. Connelly, do you have a question?" asks the judge.

"My question is …" Shawn continues in a milder tone. "My question is, would it be possible that someone, someone without life-saving techniques at their immediate recall during a traumatic event, perhaps *the* traumatic event of their entire lifetime up to that moment, could act in an abnormal manner?"

Detective Penance does not look up, nor does he answer.

"That's okay, we'll let the jury decide. Lastly, on your timeline, you mentioned the phone calls from Micah to Lennox that evening, even read the transcripts."

Shawn goes back to his desk and picks up the top paper from his folder.

"Can you read these other transcripts from that evening of August 17, 2017, from the two other people who called Lennox around the time he was murdered?"

"Sure," Detective Penance takes the paper from Shawn.

"7:30pm, Talbot Lexington:
> Hey dude, something came up, not going
> to be able to make it."

"7:30? That's shortly after Lennox was stabbed, is that correct?"

"Yes, but the cell phone records retrieved from Mr. Lexington pinged from up—"

"Yes will suffice."

"Objection," Astrid speaks out. "Argumentative. All of it. We see what Mr. Connelly is trying to do here. The cell phone ping is directly correlated to Mr. Connelly's reasoning behind this line of questioning. Talbot was nowhere near the scene of the crime, and the jury should hear from the detective on this matter. We ask the court to allow him to continue."

"Sustained," rules the judge. "Detective, you may continue."

"Thank you, your Honor," Detective Penance responds. "We had Mr. Lexington's cell phone records pulled, and the ping came from Midtown at the northern edge of Chelsea, so there's no way he could have also been on the Chinatown edge of the Lower East Side."

"Thank you, Detective. And could you please read the second transcript from James West, Lennox's boss?" asks Shawn.

"**8:30pm, James West:**
   Hey old boy, just saw your better half.
   Call me when you get this. It's
   important. "

"Mr. West says 'your better half,' which is Micah, his husband, whom he'd just seen at the event, correct?"

"That is a fair assumption."

"Do you have any idea what that was about? What's so important on the night he was killed?"

Even though he and Astrid had discussed this scenario, Detective Penance reflects on an appropriate answer.

"We pursued that with Mr. James West."

"Pursued?" asks Shawn. "What does that mean? How did you pursue it?"

"We interviewed James West roughly two weeks later, and he was cleared with a solid alibi."

"Where did you interview him?"

"At his office, Élan headquarters."

"So not at the police station?"

"No."

"And during this interview, did you ask him specifically what he meant by the message he sent to his employee the night he was murdered? What he deemed as 'important'?"

"No, we did not."

"Thank you. Nothing further," Shawn says, heading back to his chair next to Micah across the room.

"Ms. Lerner, your witness," says the judge.

"Thank you, your Honor," replies Astrid. "Detective Penance, your interviews, collection of evidence and alibi confirmations is enough to clear Mr. West of any wrongdoing in this case, is that correct?"

"Yes," he says.

"Furthermore, could you tell me why you cleared Mr. West as having an alibi, and why you did not clear Micah Breuer?" Astrid asks.

"Micah was the one we found over his dead husband's body, was the last one to see him alive, and was the one who confessed to the murder," Detective Penance replies.

"We have nothing further for this witness," Astrid says.

"Who's next?" asks the judge.

"The People would like to call Josh Harrison to the stand," Astrid says.

Josh, with his perfectly coiffed blonde wavy hair, in blue jeans and a tweed blazer over a crisp white button-down, brushes arms with Detective Penance, who is on his way out of the courtroom. Josh walks in front of Astrid's table, smiles at her and then the jury, and sits in the witness stand.

As he is sworn in, Shawn, still reeling from the one-two punch he'd just experienced, looks at his watch. He's surprised that Judge Wilson is still going strong so late in the day. Shawn was expecting Josh to be tomorrow, and wants to ask the judge if it's possible to postpone this witness, yet he's concerned how that might look to the jury. Instead, he turns to Micah and begins writing on a small pad between them.

Thought Josh was tomorrow. Mostly prepared. Don't worry.

Micah looks at him and closes his eyes in a long blink. He grabs the pen and writes.

We got this.

Shawn smiles and sits back in his chair.

"Mr. Harrison, did you have an altercation with the defendant in the summer of 2015?" Astrid Lerner starts.

"Yes, ma'am."

"Please tell us what happened."

"Yes, ma'am. For one thing, the guy is nuts." Josh tries to make as much eye contact with the jury as possible. "Like if there was a scale like this, he'd be like this."

Josh maneuvers his hands to represent some sort of invisible machine with a flittering needle that moves so much it blows up.

Shawn notices the improper character evidence and wants to object. He doesn't. *This should be fun.*

"Who is 'the guy' you are referring to, for the jury please?"

"That man right there." He points to his left, directly at Micah.

"Let the record reflect the witness is pointing to the defendant," says the judge.

"What makes you say he's nuts?" Astrid asks. She, too, notices the leeway, and takes advantage.

"He threatened to kill me."

"How so?"

"He said if I ever came near Lennox again, he was gonna kill us both. He meant it. With, like, these psycho eyes I've never seen before. Complete douchebag."

"Do you really think he wanted to kill you both?"

"Oh yes, ma'am." Josh nods so hard he hears his neck pop.

"Why do you say that?"

"Because then he told us *how* he was gonna do it. He said he was gonna stab us both in our sleep."

Light but audible gasps are heard from both the jury and the courtroom. Shawn and Micah act unshaken.

Noticing the violent reaction from his captive audience, Josh repeats himself using different words with a more dramatic emphasis.

"He threatened to take my life," Josh says. "I had this, this feeling, you know, that he was serious and would follow through with it, especially when he said, *'I'll kill you both in your sleep. Or maybe just one of you,'* he said. *'So the other will know what it feels like to lose everything you love,'* or something like that. Still sends shivers down my spine."

"And what was the date of this altercation again?" Astrid asks.

"July, I think, of 2015," Josh replies.

Astrid pulls out a piece of paper and hands it to the jury foreman.

"What I've just handed to you is a copy of the life insurance policy dated July of 2015," Astrid says, then turns back to Josh. "Mr. Harrison, when the defendant said, *'I'll stab you both in your sleep,'* what makes you think that he was serious and might follow through?"

"It seemed real. Different from the way he normally speaks, which has always seemed fake to me. How can I explain this?" He takes a moment. "Okay, Lennox told me Micah was an actor."

"Objection, hearsay," Shawn interjects. He's just messing with the prosecution.

"Your Honor, we have proof that the defendant was, in fact, an actor, if you'll allow the witness to proceed." Astrid is annoyed.

"Objection overruled," says Judge Wilson.

"You were saying, Mr. Harrison?"

"Lennox told me Micah was an actor. I saw that, many times, in our interactions. Micah would just seem like he was saying stuff. You know, like he was rehearsing lines or something."

"I don't follow," Astrid prompts.

"I don't either," Shawn whispers to Micah out of the side of his mouth.

"I remember this one day," Josh begins, "a few friends of mine were at the beach on Fire Island, pretty recently actually, and I was sitting fairly close to Micah. Didn't even realize it. Buncha hot guys watching other hot guys playing volleyball. Just didn't see him. Anyway, I guess he caught me checking Lenny out. So, Micah looks over at me and says pretty loudly, so all my friends could hear, 'I know you can't just turn it off, and I know it probably still hurts, but I appreciate the effort.' Now I know that doesn't sound weird, but it rang familiar to me, so I went home that night and looked at my DVR and there it was."

"There was what?"

"*Gossip Girl.*"

The courtroom erupts in laughter. The judge pounds his gavel to quiet the crowd.

"I know, I know," Josh continues, enjoying the attention. "Judge me all you like, but I like reruns of *Gossip Girl*. And this particular episode just happens to have been on the night before we were at the beach. So, I pushed play and sure enough, it didn't take me long to find it. Serena and Dan, they're these on-again-off-again ex-lovers on *Gossip Girl*. Anyway, Serena and Dan were at a bar. She is with someone new, and says to Dan, her ex-boyfriend, 'I know you can't just turn it off, and I know it probably still hurts, but I appreciate the effort.' Same words. The same exact ones!"

"Thank you, Mr. Harrison. The prosecution would like to play a series of recordings now to shed light on this testimony."

"I'll allow it," says the judge.

"What's happening?" Micah asks Shawn.

"I allowed these," Shawn says. "It's a show, grab your popcorn." Shawn leans back and smiles.

"Now this first recording is from an off-Broadway play in which the defendant played a supporting role," Astrid says, introducing the audio. She presses play on her iPad.

   (("*I'm not sure what happened. (pause). Blood. There's so much blood! (pause) I think she's dead!*"))

"And, as a reminder, this is the 9-1-1 call from the night of his husband's murder."

   (("*Yes! I got home, and he was just lying there. (pause). Blood. (pause) Oh my God, I think he's dead!*"))

Astrid turns off the recording. She holds up an 8x10 glossy of the defendant, with the words MICAH BREUER emblazoned in Helvetica Bold. She turns around and shows it to the courtroom, then the jury, and hands it to the jury foreman.

"We have nothing further for this witness," she says to the judge.

Shawn stays seated, pauses. Then, he begins clapping.

The judge bangs his gavel. "Mr. Connelly, there will be no clapping in my courtroom."

"No, sir." Shawn swats the air as if there's a fly around him. He stands up, continuing to clap the imaginary bug away from him, and walks toward Josh. "Quite the performance, Mr. Harrison. You're a fellow actor, are you not?"

Josh laughs. "You, too, Mr. Connelly, with the swatting. And the answer is 'No sir,' not for like a decade now."

Mimicking Astrid, Shawn unearths an 8x10 of Josh and presents it to the courtroom, then the jury, then hands it to the jury foreman. "Mr. Harrison, would it surprise you to know that Micah has not acted professionally in over eight years?"

"No, sir, not really."

"Is it true that you have a lot of actor friends, Mr. Harrison?"

"Some," Josh replies.

"By telling us about this alleged threat, what did you hope to gain?" Shawn asks, seeming to jump to another line of inquiry.

Perplexed at the question, Josh looks at Shawn and tilts his head. "I'm sorry?"

"What did you hope to gain by telling us that? Simple question."

Josh looks at the prosecution. Astrid gives him the equivalent of a shrug, using only her face.

"Uh, to show your client's state of mind to commit murder," he says, discouraged by his own grammar.

"Move to strike the answer as unresponsive," Shawn says to the judge with a soft, sing-song lilt to his voice, along with a dissenting nod. He never takes his eyes off of Josh.

"Granted. The witness will refrain from characterizing."

"I wanted to show I took a threat of murder very seriously," Josh says slowly, "and became fearful for my life because of it."

"Ah, yes, fearful for your life." Shawn walks back to the defense table and grabs another folder. He pulls out a photo and hands it to Josh. "Can you describe what you're looking at, Mr. Harrison?"

"Looks like a picture of Lennox, Micah, and me at the beach."

"Are any of you laughing?"

"I don't know. Smiling, sure. Laughing, maybe."

Astrid begins to fumble through her folders, looking for the photo he is showing.

"And in your opinion, is there a fourth person taking the picture?"

"No, sir, it looks like we're taking a selfie."

"And who might that be taking the selfie? In other words, whose arm is holding the camera?"

"I am."

"And who are you right next to?"

"Micah."

"So, you, Micah, his husband Lennox are arm-in-arm, smiling or laughing, taking a selfie at the beach?"

"Yes, sir."

"Lastly, there is a date right above it, can you read what it says, please?"

"Objection," Astrid gives up trying to find the photo. "This photo was not in discovery."

"Your Honor," Shawn interrupts before the ruling can be administered. "Is counsel seriously trying to say she did not have access to the Facebook feed of her own witness?"

"Overruled. You may answer," says the judge.

"July 4, 2018."

"July 4, 2018," echoes Shawn. "That's only six weeks before the murder took place. Can you tell me, Mr. Harrison, do you think someone who's fearful for his life would be laughing and taking a selfie with a friend whom he seriously thinks is going to murder him?"

"But Micah isn't my friend."

"Not your friend?"

"Correct."

"Are you familiar with what a ninth step is, Mr. Harrison?"

"Yes, sir."

Shawn begins to read an excerpt from a blue book. "According to the literature of most twelve-step programs, step 8 reads 'Made a list of all persons we had harmed and became willing to make amends to them all,' and step 9 reads, 'Made direct amends to such people, except when to do so would injure them or others.' So the ninth step is when you make amends to people you think you have harmed. Something someone does in recovery, is it not?"

"I'm not in recovery, but yes, sir, I think that's what it is."

"Have you ever had anyone make amends to you, sir?"

"Yes, sir."

"And would one of those people be Micah Breuer?"

"Yes."

"Do you remember that exchange?"

"Yes."

"Can you tell me about it, please?"

Josh squirms in his chair. He knows where this line of questioning is going and had forgotten about the conversation he'd had with Micah six months ago.

"Well, at first, he told me that the way he'd handled mine and Lenny's affair was wrong." Josh's recall is now in Technicolor. "Then he asked if there was anything he could do to make it up to me."

"Was he emotional at all?"

"Yes, he was crying."

"Did you feel like he was acting? Remember you're under oath."

He takes a moment. "It felt real at the time."

"And after Micah asked if there was anything he could do to make it up to you, what did you say to him?"

Josh looks in Micah's direction.

"I said, *'You can be my friend.'*"

"Isn't it true that since the time of the amends, you've become friends with Micah, even shared intimate stories of a similar upbringing, acting mishaps, trips to Fire Island, and so on?"

"Yes, but I still didn't trust him."

"We have nothing further for this ex-boyfriend of the deceased," Shawn says, returning to his chair.

"And why didn't you trust him?" Astrid stands and asks Josh.

"Because he threatened to kill us!"

"How?"

"By stabbing us."

"Because he threatened to kill you and Lennox by stabbing you," Astrid reiterates to the jury, emphasizing the words *kill* and *stabbing*. "Thank you, Mr. Harrison."

Josh leaves the witness box and begins to walk down the center aisle to exit the courtroom.

CHAPTER 35

Lilith McGuire stares at the photo of Josh, a picture from his Facebook feed that she's printed out. The paper is still warm from the laser printer.

"I can't believe we missed this picture of the three of them," she says.

"Well, that's what happens when you're trying to glean information from two high-profile murder cases going on at the same time," Detective Penance answers. "Not to mention the pressure of combing through piles of data from a clearly corrupt company at the heart of *both* of these murders, and a former ADA bearing down on us with her fat little thumbs."

Lilith McGuire and Detective Bronson Penance are in the main conference room at the Seventh Precinct police station. They are surrounded by boxes of paperwork, mounds of statements, photos, documentation, and brick, lots of thick, red brick on all four walls.

"The camera," Lily begins, as she shuffles through a collection of photos. "Remind me, I know the motion to enter the camera into evidence was denied just before trial, but I don't understand why."

"Because we can't prove that it recorded anything."

"But Officer Palino said it was still warm, so it must've been doing something. If we find those recordings from the camera, we will know who did this."

"You mean we'll prove that Micah did this," Detective Penance says, focusing his young protégé on the task at hand.

"Yeah," she whispers.

"I think the key here is this Ghost guy. Wanna hear my theory?" Detective Penance asks.

"Sure."

"I think Micah planned this. I think he hires this Ghost guy who sells Lennox drugs, then freaks out when the job's not done when he gets home. The company, having planted the camera in the living room, accidentally records the murder, watches the videos, and disposes of the hard drive it recorded to."

"Yeah, I get it. Thought about it, actually, then I checked a few key things. First, why would Micah hire someone to kill Lennox in their home with the same knife that he has in their home? Only to take the weapon from the scene? Plus, there's no missing knife from their set of eight knives, and all the knives are clean."

"To throw us off."

"It's working," she says, putting down the photo of Josh. She rubs her eyes with both hands and lets out an audible sigh.

"And second?" he asks.

"What?" she replies.

"You said 'first,' then talked about the knives. I was just assuming there was a second. Something about the camera maybe?"

"Probably." She continues to rub her eyes. "Yes, the camera is confusing to me. For the life of me, I don't understand why it was there."

"Hey, let's break for the night," Detective Penance says, recognizing her exhaustion. "I still think there's something there, though. We gotta stay vigilant. All eyes are on us to finish this thing. We have to get this right."

◆

"I thought you said, 'It won't go wrong.'"

Elaine Holcomb thrusts herself into Astrid Lerner's office, slamming the door in the same motion.

"How did you get in here?" Astrid asks, looking through the glass at everyone else in the department, who are all sitting in their cubicles looking at her with blank expressions.

"They know me. You don't." Elaine sits down. "If you did, you'd know that I don't do well with liars."

"Elaine, I don't have time for this."

"Really? You said there was more than enough evidence to prove that this monster killed my son. I believed you. I trusted you. You are losing."

For a brief moment Astrid thinks of matching Elaine's shrill tone, but the word *son* allows her to calm down and see Elaine not as a bitchy ex-ADA out for a win, but as a desperate mother out for justice.

"We've had some setbacks," Astrid says.

"Setbacks?" Elaine raises her voice.

"Tomorrow we bring the DNA evidence and the testimony from this girl, Jenna. Plus, we have the psychological exam results. It's enough, Elaine."

Elaine takes a deep breath.

Astrid sees the pain in her face and continues. "All of it will point to a willful motive, and we'll elaborate on Micah's propensity toward violence."

"I want to take the stand."

"No. Absolutely not."

"The jury needs to hear from me." She feels a lump in the back of her throat. She slows her pace, lowers her voice, and continues like she's sharing a testimony at church. "I know things about Micah, things I couldn't see clearly before, because he's a genius at manipulation. He had to stay on my good side, so he could keep his life with my wonderful boy. But now I can see it all. He puts on this smiling, naïve, Southern bullshit face, but he was out for Lennox's money, plain and simple. I mean, shit, the man would sit at home all day, working on God knows what in his barely six-figure freelance job, spending all of Lennox's money on extravagant vacations and interior designers. He used my Lenny. And when Lennox betrayed him, Micah threatened to murder him. And he did, I know it. I know it as much as I knew my boy. The jury needs someone they can sympathize with. They didn't know Lenny. They should hear from someone who did."

"It's not a good idea," Astrid says. The thought of anyone finding Elaine sympathetic almost makes her laugh out loud. "The jury may see all this emotion as a desire for vengeance."

"I can contain myself. You underestimate me."

"I think the feeling is mutual."

Elaine moves in closer to Astrid.

"Let me see your face," Elaine says. "Did we move too fast? Do we really have enough?"

"I believe in the process," Astrid says in a lowered voice, as if she's forcing the words. She knows Elaine's questions are actually threats. "I would not have agreed to proceed so quickly otherwise."

"Good." Elaine retreats. "Promise me one thing. If you feel like you have another day like today, or if anything threatens your resolve, you will offer him a plea for criminally negligent homicide. He can't walk away from this."

"I promise," Astrid says.

◆

"Shawn, swear to me you won't get too cocky." In the visiting room at the Tombs, Micah is sitting across from his lawyer and friend, who is beaming from his victories of the day. He looks at Shawn intently, studying his face.

Shawn snorts a curt giggle as he beats a stack of papers on his lap, pounding them into alignment. "Is there such a thing?"

"This is my life, Shawn. I wanna go home."

"You will. These people are recklessly pursuing a path that will only lead to acquittal, and they're too blind to see it."

"They seem pretty resolved."

"And that, my friend, will be their downfall. The jury is on our side, I can sense it. Now, about tomorrow, Jenna will be on the stand. You okay with me going after her?"

"What do you mean, *go after* Jenna?"

"Micah, listen. They are coming after us again tomorrow, so I just want you to be prepared for what you may experience. It'll be a rollercoaster."

"Go easy on Jenna, would you? I'm serious. I love that girl. She's the only friend I've got besides you."

"Hey, hey, hey. I've been really proud of you so far. You've held it together like a pro." Shawn scoots his chair closer to Micah. He places his hand on Micah's. "I just need you to trust me. We're good. I've got this."

CHAPTER 36

"The People call Jenna Ancelet," Astrid says.

Jenna enters through the large thick wooden doors and begins to walk toward the witness stand. To offset her anxiety, she is dressed in her self-proclaimed "courtroom power-suit," which means black Dior slacks and a white Gucci silk blouse, complemented by an orange-and-lilac-patterned Hermés scarf. Her brand-new Valentino stilettos click with a fearless purpose, and she walks in front of the jury to take the stand.

"Oh, Jesus," Shawn says under his breath to Micah. Micah smiles.

She weaves her way through the waist-high wooden railings to her place on the witness stand, confident that she has bruised both of her hips, and places her hand on the Bible.

"And who do we have here?" Judge Wilson asks, impressed and not annoyed by the entrance. "State your name for the record, please."

"Jenna Ancelet, that's A-N-C-E-L-E-T," says Jenna, remembering the previous night's online coaching by the prosecution.

"Raise your right hand. Do you promise that the testimony you shall give in the case before this court shall be the truth, the whole truth, and nothing but the truth, so help you God?" asks the clerk.

"I do."

"Ms. Ancelet, thank you for appearing before us today," Astrid Lerner addresses her latest witness. "Can you tell me the nature of your relationship with both Micah and Lennox?"

"Absolutely," Jenna says, noticing her French accent is a little more prominent than normal. She decides to run with it. "I first met Lennox at Élan Publishing when I began working as his executive assistant about four years ago, around the same time as he was dating Micah. We all hit it off immediately."

Astrid opens her mouth to ask a question of clarification, but Jenna continues before she can begin.

"I met Micah at an after-work cocktail reception. At first, I thought he was good-looking and single, of course. But soon I found out I was wrong. Turns out Micah also worked for Élan, so I got to see him all the time." She realizes she has been babbling.

"Ms. Ancelet, can you tell me about the relationship between you and Mr. Josh Harrison?"

"Sure! We are best friends. Super close. For like ten or twelve years. Josh is a freelancer too. We all saw each other a lot." She stops to rephrase, to make herself sound smarter. "We saw each other a great deal, a great deal."

"Since you guys saw each other a great deal, did it surprise you when Josh and Lennox started having an affair?"

"Not really."

"And why is that?"

"Well, Micah, and excuse me for saying so, Micah has always had a jealous streak. On several occasions, either at the office or out at a bar, Lenny always got a lot of attention. Micah would, too, but he was so wrapped up in Lennox that he never saw it. Micah would get jealous, sometimes give Lenny the ice shoulder, or sometimes just walk out of the bar and go home. Does that answer your question?"

"Sort of," Astrid says. "Specifically, Ms. Ancelet, can you tell me about the affair between Josh Harrison and Lennox Holcomb?"

"The affair. Yeah. Uh, that kinda started right under my foot. I saw the attraction between Josh and Lennox, and I think I may have stoked it. I mean, I always loved Micah, don't get me wrong, but Josh was my best friend, and I simply adored Lennox. It's not something I'm proud of, and Micah and I have talked about it. I had no idea it would turn into a thing."

"A thing?" Astrid hopes to focus her witness.

"Yes. It was definitely a thing. Micah found out about Josh and Lenny, I'm not sure how, but he also knew I was hiding it from him. We didn't hang out for months."

"Can you tell me about the confrontation between Josh and Micah? I understand you were there?"

"Yes, yes, I was. Micah and Josh were scheduled for the same meeting at Élan, a meeting that Lenny and I were to be at as well. It was a high-profile campaign that needed a lot of money, so that's why Lennox and I were there. Outside the conference room, Micah approached Josh and started screaming obscenities."

"Like what?"

"Homewrecker. Whore. Fuck this and fuck that. There was a look in his eyes I'd never seen from him before. From anyone really."

"Did he ever threaten Josh?"

"Yes. After he was screaming for a while, he looked at Josh right in the eyes, got all up in his face and said something like, 'If you ever get near him again, I will kill you both.' Josh didn't leave his apartment for weeks after that."

"Thank you, Ms. Ancelet. I have no further questions." Astrid Lerner nods in approval and walks back to her seat.

"Your witness, Mr. Connelly," the judge says.

"Ms. Ancelet, may I call you Jenna?" asks Shawn, injecting a sense of professionalism between two friends.

"Yes, you may." Jenna plays along.

"Jenna, you said you saw a look in Micah's eyes that you'd never seen before from anyone, is that correct?"

"Yes."

"What did Lennox look like when he fired you?"

"Objection! Assuming a fact not in evidence."

"Your Honor, prosecution has the same access to all the company files as we do. I'm simply asking about a fact that has relevance to this witness."

"Tread lightly, Mr. Connelly. Overruled."

Jenna is visibly shaken. *Ambushed by my friend*, she thinks.

"Jenna, you were fired by Lennox on March 21, 2016, is that correct? Remember you're under oath."

"I know I'm under oath, Shawn." She lowers her voice. "It's just hardly anyone knows that, and my current job could be in jeopardy now, thanks to you."

"Please answer the question."

"Yes, I was fired. They sent me off with a glowing recommendation, as long as I signed an NDA, which I did. But I did nothing wrong."

"Do you think lying to your current employer is wrong?"

"Objection."

"Sustained."

"Isn't it true that after Lennox found out that you were thinking of leaving Élan, even suspected of stealing company secrets, that he screamed at you and called you names in front of several people in your department?"

"Objection. The witness is not on trial here."

"Sustained. Mr. Connelly, you are on thin ice."

"Withdrawn. We have nothing further but retain our right to recall this witness in the future."

Jenna, not having the chance to defend herself, or right any misgivings about what was said, gets up out of her chair. Heavy-hearted and powerless, she looks at Micah and Shawn. Neither looks back. She leaves the room, her heels clonking and scraping against the rugged vinyl floors beneath her.

CHAPTER 37

"Stab number one scraped the spinal cord, slightly severing it," the witness begins.

A short, bald man with twenty-two years in criminal forensics, Dr. Eddy Frischell, dressed in a white lab coat, is on the stand offering expert testimony. He holds the remote control for the television monitor, clicking through a series of morbid photos of Lennox's naked body. Dr. Frischell is a favorite of Astrid Lerner's. With an attention to detail and an ability to address the jury in layman's terms, he still manages to convey the science without overdramatizing.

"This wound is the deepest, approximately two inches, directly in the victim's back. This MRI of the lumbar spine demonstrates a partial transection of the spinal cord at the L3/L4 spinal level, which we believe caused partial paralysis of the legs. Stab number two went directly into the abdomen and was thrust upward. However, this stab was not fatal, as it narrowly avoided both the stomach and the heart. Stabs three and four were to the victim's side, hitting two ribs and puncturing the right lung. Again, not fatal. We believe these were inflicted with the left hand due to the angle."

Micah fidgets in his seat, but he knows the afternoon will be like this. He is prepared but fears he will doubt his ability to hide his discomfort with each new witness.

"Stab wounds five through twenty-two are along the pectoral muscles and below, one scraping across the sternum downwards to the other lung but did not collapse it. Stab number twenty-three is through the side of the throat at a forty-degree angle, this time with the right hand. And, as you can see from this illustration, wounds twenty-four to thirty-three are in various places along the body, including wrists, arms and legs, some deep and some not. Wounds of note include these two along the Achilles tendon, which caused a muscular tear from here to here on the right leg, and one other wound from here to down here on the right foot, along the superior extensor retinaculum, partially severing the victim's right foot. And this one on the right wrist, which has all the indications of being a defense wound."

Micah watches in a fog-like state as Astrid and Shawn discuss the forensics with Dr. Frischell. He does not remember the doctor leaving the stand. He watches as the medical examiner takes his place. The scenes go by as if in a movie, with words reverberating like muted echoes in the background of his consciousness.

"We have concluded that the victim was still alive when the defendant came home."

"That this was a particularly savage crime, and the victim was lucky to still be alive at that point."

"With thirty-three stab wounds of a hunting knife, he would have been dead within the hour, especially with the precision of the cuts being mere millimeters from vital organs. However, in my expert opinion, the murder weapon is a simple kitchen knife, or what some would call a steak knife, one from the same maker as the knife set we found in the defendant's apartment."

"In my expert opinion, yes, if Lennox were found earlier he most certainly would have survived. Paralyzed from the neck down, but alive."

"The victim was mutilated and tortured in a crime of passion and left on the floor, clinging to life for over three hours."

Micah finally comes to and realizes the past two hours have been a blur.

"What are you doing," he whispers to Shawn. "You're not saying anything."

"What are you talking about? I've been objecting to a ton of things. But most are indisputable facts in evidence. Remember, you didn't do any of this. Not relevant 6tto our defense."

"And would you state for the record your name and title again, please?" Astrid addresses her next witness.

"Sure, I'm Dr. David Lynna, Director of the Crime Analysis Division at NYAFS, the New York Academy of Forensic Sciences."

"Dr. Lynna, how long have you been in your position?"

"I co-founded the crime analysis division about five-and-a-half years ago and have served as its director for the same amount of time."

"Were you personally involved in the analysis of the crime scene in this case?"

"Yes, I was."

"Now, from your analysis of the crime scene, what significant findings can you share with us today?" Astrid has been careful to not over-complicate things for the jury and does not want to start now.

"Well, since the victim was stabbed earlier in the evening yet remained alive, the blood found at the crime scene occurred in several stages. Based on the coagulation cascade, we determined initial blood splatter to be about three hours old by the time it was analyzed, placing the initial stabbing at around 7, 7:15pm. Since the victim was still alive and his heart was still pumping, several other blood samples show various times of coagulation throughout the evening, up until time of death, which is roughly 10:15pm."

"Is this coagulation cascade the same for the blood on both the victim and the defendant?"

"No, coagulation is relevant mostly to the victim, as the blood on the defendant was mostly from around 10pm until the time of the victim's death."

"I noticed you said 'mostly.'"

"Yes," Dr. Lynna uses a laser pointer to call attention to the closeup of Micah's face that Astrid has placed on the easel in front of the jury box. "We did find two spots of the victim's blood on the defendant, one on the face right here, just below the mandible to the right, and one here in the middle of his neck above his larynx."

Micah scratches his neck.

"I'm sorry, doctor. Are you saying that the victim's blood found on the defendant's neck was from earlier in the evening? How can you be sure?"

"It's two spots, which is not significant in comparison to how much blood there was on both the victim and the defendant, the whole living room really. But what is significant is the way it spattered. As you can tell from the photo of the defendant taken at the police station that night, attached here, the blood is a drop or a spatter. Had it been a smear or an irregular shape, one might argue that it was from the victim, or contact blood, due to the trauma of the defendant trying CPR on him and pounding his chest."

"Are you saying that based on your findings, you believe the defendant was spattered with the victim's blood earlier that evening?"

"That's the only explanation we have, yes."

Shawn looks in the direction of the jury. They are all looking at his client. For the first time, he senses he is in trouble. He has prepared for his cross-examination but feels unprepared for the reactions he is experiencing.

"And the DNA." Astrid walks in front of the jury. "The DNA and fingerprint analysis of the crime scene. Results came back threefold, the victim, the defendant, and the housekeeper. Is that correct?"

"That is correct."

"And the housekeeper was ruled out as a suspect because she was out of the country at the time."

"I have no idea."

"But to your knowledge, doctor, there was no one else there who left their DNA behind."

"To my knowledge, the crime scene contained only the DNA of the victim and the defendant."

"Thank you, doctor."

"Your witness, Mr. Connelly," the judge says. He looks at his watch. "This will be the final witness, the final redirect of the day."

"Thank you, your Honor. I'll try to make this quick." Shawn turns to the witness. "Regarding the two tiny blood spatters on the defendant's neck, you claim that they were from earlier in the evening, and that there's no other explanation. That's quite a statement." Shawn looks at him for longer than a moment.

"Is that a question?" Dr. Lynna asks.

"I was just thinking about all that blood, from several different parts of the night. Pools of it, both around the victim, on the victim. Now, I'm no expert, but if I'm desperately trying to save this person, with all that blood, some old and some new, I'm thinking during CPR, I'm gonna hit at least one of the pools from earlier in the evening, and it's gonna spatter on me. Is that logical?"

"You would think, but that's not how spatter works. As I said earlier, the two spots on the defendant's neck were clearly spatters, meaning circular splotches of liquid. If the blood came from an older pool that had already coagulated, it would have been more gel-like, and it probably would not have adhered to the skin at all, much less make a perfectly round spatter."

"*Probably*, hmm. Thank you, doctor. Are you familiar with visible wavelength hyperspectral imaging?"

"Yes," the doctor answers, his eyes moving back and forth like they're watching shells at a carnival.

"Can you tell me what that is?"

"Sure. It's a relatively new way to determine not only that a sample is in fact blood, but also how old that blood is."

Shawn pulls out a piece of paper from a folder. "So, this technology, which the crime scene analysts in this case did *not* use, takes photos at different wavelength bands using a liquid crystal tunable filter, and can pinpoint exactly what material is in fact blood, and how old that blood is based on its characteristics through these filters. Is that correct?"

"Yes," he replies.

"Now, allow me to read you the reason why this technology was created. This is from the Journal of Forensic Professionals for the Advancement of New Technology, of which you are a member. 'Today's standard practices for the determination of blood stain age is neither accurate or reliable, neither scientifically robust or ethically usable for crime scene analysis. Therefore, our highest recommendation is as follows: that standard practices of blood age determination be discarded immediately, and that visible wavelength hyperspectral imaging be the benchmark moving forward in any and all professional applications.'"

Shawn looks up from the paper. "Dr. Lynna, did you use this new technology that your professional affiliation highly recommended to determine the age of the spatter, or did you ignore the recommendation and rely on your current methods?"

"That technology is very expensive, so we relied on our current methods, which are actually tried and tr—"

"Thank you. Doctor, you mentioned there was no other DNA at the crime scene?"

"I'm sorry?" the doctor asks, reeling from another change in subject.

"Did you mean low-level DNA? Touch DNA? You mean to tell me there was nothing else in that entire living room that contained fingerprints or touch DNA?"

"No DNA or fingerprints other than the defendant's, the victim's, and the housekeeper's," Dr. Lynna says in a determined voice. He wants to redeem himself from the previous suggestion that he did not do all he could have or should have done. "No other fingerprints or DNA from the lamp, no other fingerprints or DNA from the coffee table, no other fingerprints or DNA from the camera, no other fingerprints or DNA from the television remote. Nothing."

Bingo, Shawn thinks.

"Objection! Move to strike the answer." Astrid yells.

"Counselors, approach the bench," the judge says, turning off his microphone. Shawn and Astrid approach the judge.

"I'm assuming you'll want the box with the camera in evidence now, counsel, is that correct?" the judge asks Shawn.

"Yes, sir."

"Your Honor," Astrid says, "there is absolutely no evidence it had anything to do with the murder, no fingerprints, no touch DNA, no hard drive with recorded videos. It has no bearing on this case, as you've already ruled."

"This will teach you to prepare your witnesses a little better, Ms. Lerner," says the judge, then looks at Shawn. "Somehow it's found its way into evidence."

"Thank you, your Honor," Shawn says.

"That wasn't even a clever move, Mr. Connelly, you got lucky," replies the judge, banging his gavel. "The jury is dismissed until tomorrow morning at 9:30am."

CHAPTER 38

"We'd like the court to know that my client has willfully and graciously allowed the prosecution access to these personal notes, as well as any and all testimony given by this witness," Shawn announces to the courtroom. The defense has nothing to hide. And Shawn will do whatever it takes for the jury to see it.

Micah's therapist, Dr. Amy Eisen, is a renowned therapist in psychiatric circles in New York. Small in stature, with dark brown hair and white-grey roots, Dr. Eisen has been Micah's therapist for well over six years. She had not wanted to take the stand because of patient/client privilege. After Micah agreed to waive the privilege and give complete access to the prosecution, the doctor had no choice but to respond to the subpoena and cooperate.

"Thank you for being with us today, Ms. Eisen," Astrid begins.

"My pleasure."

"Can you state your full name and describe the nature of your relationship to the defendant?"

"Yes, my name is Dr. Amy Eisen. I am a psychotherapist here in New York City, and Micah has been my client since early 2012."

"Can you describe why the defendant initially came to see you?"

"Yes, initially he came in because he'd been self-medicating. You see, Micah comes from an extremely religious household. His father was a pastor of a small church in Arkansas, and Micah, being gay, found the religion he grew up with was fundamentally flawed, as he could not connect the teachings of the Bible with what he experienced to be true and right in his soul. After he discarded the beliefs he was taught as a child, which many of us do along the path of spiritual evolution, Micah was ostracized by both parents. He was also denounced by his church. And having no foundation at home or within his spirit, he felt unsure of his footing in his own life. And thus, he began to self-medicate with drugs and alcohol."

"As a result of your counseling, he became sober, is that correct?"

"The credit goes to him for that. Very proud of him for recognizing it and seeking more outside help," Dr. Eisen says in a motherly tone, looking at Micah. He smiles back at her.

"Now, doctor, it says in your notes back in 2015 that you were concerned for Micah's well-being. Can you explain these notes right here, if you can read them out loud for us, please?" Astrid hands the doctor a bound set of pages.

The doctor pulls out her reading glasses that rest on a chain around her neck. A photo of the notes appears on the monitor. She reads them aloud.

> "May 18, 2015
> Anniversary of mother's death approaching
> Micah = incongruence
> 'Good Micah, Bad Micah'
> Intimacy absent
> Integration needed"

"Thank you, Dr. Eisen. Can you explain what you meant by these notes?"

"Yes, I believe so. First of all, these are essentially notes I take when listening to a client, in this case Micah. He mentioned growing up hearing from his mother that he is either 'Good Micah' or 'Bad

Micah,' depending on the actions he was taking or the emotions or reactions he was exhibiting. Throughout adolescence and adulthood, he had still been considering himself as two different entities, depending on what was happening in his life at the time."

"Could you please give us an example?"

"I remember he talked about an old boyfriend of his cheating on him, or he suspected of cheating on him. He mentioned having thoughts of hurting this person in some way. I asked him to tell me a little more, and he said they were just thoughts. He had no definitive plan of hurting this man. Remember, this was years ago."

"And Dr. Eisen, can you explain what you mean by incongruence?"

"Yes. It's the whole 'Good Micah, Bad Micah' thing. My job is to help, sorry, *was* to help Micah understand that we all live with both the good sides of ourselves and the bad sides of ourselves. Congruence is the ultimate goal, to be okay with all aspects of ourselves and to understand that there is no good Micah or bad Micah. Just simply Micah."

"Thank you. And what about intimacy, this note right here?" Astrid approaches the doctor and points to the line in her notes.

"Oh yes, I remember him saying something about not being able to feel true intimacy with someone like he used to when he was little. I think he was remembering his mother at the time."

"Why did you bother to write it down?"

The doctor hesitates.

"Well, my initial thinking, why I wrote that down, later proved to be—"

"But why did you write it in the first place, doctor?" Astrid interrupts before Dr. Eisen can qualify her statement.

"Because lack of intimacy is one of the clear signs of a sociopath. But as I was going to say, later—"

"Thank you, doctor. We have nothing more for this witness."

"Later … you were saying, doctor," Shawn says, picking up where Astrid had abruptly stopped.

"Later, my initial thinking proved to be false."

"And why is that?"

"Micah developed, I don't know, a transformative relationship with Lennox, I guess you'd say? Throughout his courtship and marriage, I saw major progress in Micah's capacity for intimacy."

"Such as?" Shawn asks.

"Such as a decrease in jealousy, an assumption of positive intent when it came to what Lennox was doing, where he was, who he was with."

"Thank you. Doctor, out of the 212 times you saw our client, how many times do you mention 'good Micah, bad Micah?'"

"Oh, I don't know the answer to that, sorry."

"Could it have been only twice? The second time was in December of 2016. Could you turn to that please and read it for us? Page 17, highlighted."

Dr. Eisen flips to page 17 and reads. Shawn grabs the remote and clicks to the photo of her notes for the jury to see.

"Micah okay
Refers to himself as Micah when talking about dark thoughts
Asked about Good Micah Bad Micah
Says no"

"Thank you, can you explain what you meant by that?"

"Yes, we had done a lot of work around being okay with his dark thoughts. We all have them. It was the first time I noticed that he was talking as if the two sides of him had been integrated. I asked him about it. He laughed and said he hadn't thought that way in quite some time. It was a good day for me. I felt I'd helped in some small way."

"Small way, indeed." Shawn looks at the jury, hoping to put a period on this Hail Mary from the prosecution. "Thank you. We have nothing further for this witness."

"Is there a redirect?" the judge asks.

"No, your Honor." Astrid shrugs.

Dr. Eisen removes her glasses and gets up. She walks past Micah and places her hand on his hand. Micah puts his hand on hers and smiles. She nods and walks out of the courtroom.

"The prosecution rests, your Honor," says Astrid.

"You're up, Mr. Connelly," says the judge.

"Thank you, your Honor," Shawn says. "We'd like to call our first witness, Ms. Jenna Ancelet, back to the stand."

Jenna enters the courtroom with little to no fanfare. She is dressed in a familiar black-slack-white-blouse combo, albeit different designers. But this time, there is no extravagant scarf, no swagger, no confidence.

She is there for Micah. *Shawn can go to hell.*

"Raise your right hand. Do you promise that the testimony you shall give in the case before this court shall be the truth, the whole truth, and nothing but the truth, so help you God?" asks the clerk.

"I do."

"Thank you for being here, Ms. Ancelet," Shawn says.

Jenna does not look at him.

"Ms. Ancelet, earlier you testified that you were friends with both the defendant and the victim. Could you elaborate on that friendship for the court?"

Jenna does not address Shawn. Instead, she looks at the jury.

"Lennox was my boss, also my good friend. Yes, I may have been fired, but we eventually came to an understanding that our business life and our professional life were not to be mixed ever again. Not on purpose, anyway. I loved that man."

"Lennox, you mean?"

"Yes."

"And your relationship with Micah? Please describe it."

"Micah and I hit it off too. He reminded me a lot of Josh. Still does. They're very similar. Both kind, tender-hearted, great listeners, funny. Lennox was super smart. Very literal. Micah was a good offset to Lenny, they balanced each other out. Anyway, we live very close to each other, so we hang out all the time. Hung out, I guess you'd say." She lets out a singular chuckle. "We'd laugh a lot, cook each other dinners, house-sit for each other, you name it. I like to think we were always there for each other."

"So, with both professional and personal affiliations with the deceased, Lennox Holcomb, you had access to a lot of information. There are areas that I'd like to discuss. One is the company you both worked for, and the second is his former drug dealer. Let's start with the company and why you were fired."

Jenna moves in her chair and wipes her nose. She is uncomfortable. Her fidgety demeanor is subtle but noticeable. She knows she is violating her NDA, but Shawn has assured her if they come after her, which they won't, he will make sure she is taken care of.

"We both worked for Élan International. I was asked to send through paperwork all the time. Usually I knew what it was for. But there was a period, right before I was fired, when I questioned some of it. Purchase orders and the like. It didn't have anything to do with anything else, but I was asked to keep my mouth shut."

"By whom?" Shawn asks.

"Lennox. He told me to just take care of the purchases and send them through a separate chain of accounting. So I did."

"Yet, of all the documents recovered from Élan's servers when they were seized by the police, none of those documents exist."

"I don't know what to tell you."

"I just find it interesting. Is that ultimately the reason you were fired, because of these lost documents?"

"Yes and no. Yes, I think that was the reason I was fired. But no, that's not the reason they said. They said I was fired because they thought I was giving this information to Cooper Harlow."

"That's the company you work for now, correct?"

"Correct. Élan's biggest competitor. Now, granted they had no proof because I hadn't been selling company secrets, but nevertheless I was fired. My guess is that I knew too much, and that's why they let me go, but not without signing an NDA."

"A non-disclosure agreement. Which you are violating right now."

"Yes."

"And why are you putting yourself at risk like this?"

"To help Micah."

"Why?"

"Because I believe in him."

"Thank you, Jenna. I know that was hard."

Jenna finally looks at him. "All of this is hard, Shawn."

Maybe it was her whispered response that only he could hear. Maybe it was her pointed, blank stare that seemed to mask a thousand emotions cutting right to his soul. Whatever the cause, it has made Shawn's throat swell, and he coughs aloud. Then coughs again.

"Excuse me." Shawn returns to his seat, grabs the stale coffee that has been resting on his desk all day, and takes a big sip.

"You okay, Mr. Connelly?" asks the judge.

Shawn grabs his chest, gives a thumbs-up to the judge, and returns to Jenna.

"Ms. Ancelet, do you have any knowledge of Lennox and his history with drugs?"

"Yes."

"Can you explain his relationship to a character you all refer to as 'Ghost'?"

Some of the jury members smile and look at Astrid, who raises her eyebrows, puckers her lips, and turns her head to the side in agreement.

"Oh yes," Jenna answers. "This guy's the real deal. Lennox was petrified. He tried to help this man, but he turned out to be bad news, threatened Lenny's life several times."

"Why did you refer to him as Ghost?"

"Well, he's not a ghost, obviously. Lennox described a tattoo that this man had on his arm, said it looked like a ghost, with some words underneath that he said looked like French, but I couldn't translate it. Some of the words were missing from the tattoo, he said, because of a bullet wound that had been scarred over." She takes her finger and draws a small imaginary circle on her shoulder.

"You're fluent in French, though, correct?"

"Yes. But these words were put together strangely. Like a mix between French … and Italian, maybe?"

"Do you remember any of the words?"

"Oh, no. In one ear, out the next. No, wait, I remember the French word for 'home,' which is maison. But I'm sorry, nothing else. What I do remember is that what Lenny was describing as far as what this man looked like and who he was, was terrifying."

"Terrifying, huh?" Shawn shows Jenna a picture of the heroin bag from evidence. "Is this similar to the ghost tattoo he was describing?"

"Yes! This is exactly what Lenny drew for me. Looks like a skinny house with a line through it. Where did you get this?"

"From bags of heroin in Lenny's bedroom, one of them half-empty."

"Impossible! Lennox was not dealing with that man again, trust me."

"Toxicology results showed no drugs in his system, which means he had not used in the past three months or so. But I'm curious, what makes you so sure he hadn't been buying drugs from this man again?" Shawn asks.

"Because of the letter," Jenna says.

"The letter? What do you know about the letter?"

"Objection!" Astrid appears to have reached her limit. "Counsel is trying again to introduce another red herring. There is no letter. No letter. It does not exist."

"The witness introduced it. And I'm curious to see where this is going," says the judge. "Proceed with caution, counselor."

"The letter about this Ghost guy, Lennox transcribed it to me," Jenna says. "I don't remember everything because after I printed it out, he told me to delete it, which I did."

"Can you paraphrase it at least?"

"The gist was that this guy, this Ghost character, had been Lenny's drug dealer during the time he was using. When Lenny started getting clean, he tried to shake this guy. Even tried to help him by suggesting recovery. The guy threatened Lenny several times, stalked him outside meetings, beat up some of his friends, even pulled a knife on him once." Jenna looks at the jury. "He was petrified, said if anything ever happened to him, to look for the guy. Even gave his address."

"Do you remember where this Ghost guy lives?"

"Somewhere in Alphabet City. Avenue C? D? I'm sorry, I don't remember."

"Thank you, that's all we have for this witness," Shawn says, followed by an immediate, "One more thing, Jenna. Did you know your Wi-Fi is accessible from Shawn and Lenny's apartment?"

"Objection!"

"Sustained! Mr. Connelly, would you like to lay a foundation for this shiny new narrative?"

"Not at this time, your Honor."

"Somehow I didn't think so. Your witness, Ms. Lerner."

"I have nothing for this witness."

"Court is adjourned until tomorrow at 9:00am," says Judge Wilson, banging his gavel. "Let's get an early start. If anyone comes across a Starbucks on their way, I'd like an almond milk latte."

CHAPTER 39

"You're coming across as kind of a dick," Micah says as soon as Shawn enters the visiting room.

The sunlight that normally beamed through the small opening in the top of Micah's visiting room is fading into a blurry illumination on the ceiling just outside. Micah is dressed in a white T-shirt and jeans, while Shawn is still in his tan tweed suit from court. Noticing the disparity, Shawn loosens his tie.

"I'm sure I was." Shawn changes the subject. "Now listen, even though Jenna just implicated James West's company, and we already talked about his voice message the night of Lenny's death, I am not bringing him in as a witness. The first rule of calling a witness is to know what they're going to say. If West simply denies everything, we look like complete idiots. If he brings up some angle about the phone call that lets him off the hook completely, we're fucked. And I think it's always better to just leave the question lingering in the jury's minds, which it already is, but I'll make sure of it in closing argument. Remember we don't have to prove the company did this, just simply argue that you didn't."

"Makes sense." Micah says with little affect. He stares at Shawn.

"Then why do you keep looking at me like that? What? That little outburst pointed at your girlfriend? Micah, I did that only to set up a very particular part of our defense."

"What? Pointing in the direction of Jenna? She was cleared, Shawn. Clear alibi, like Josh. Like me. All at the same event."

"Did *you* know her Wi-Fi is available from your condo?"

They both stand arms crossed, almost like funhouse-mirror reflections of each other. About the same height, same age, yet Micah is clearly bigger, and without the dad bod.

"So, you found a familiar Wi-Fi accessible from our home, and now you think Jenna recorded us in our living room? Why on earth would she do that?"

"Hey, my job is to defend you zealously, blah blah blah."

"Shawn, I'm serious. She's my friend, and I thought she was yours too."

Shawn knows he's walking a tightrope. He senses his strategy is coming to life, but he also feels like it's killing him.

"She *is* a friend." He buries the emotion. "A friend who got fired by your husband. A friend who lives close to you, who has access to your home, who used to work balls-deep for a corrupt company. Do I think she could do this to Lenny? No! Do I think I need to suggest that she could? Absolutely. You didn't stab your husband, so who did? The company, the jilted employee, the Ghost. They didn't follow through with anybody. So they're gonna get it all."

CHAPTER 40

((Bang bang bang.))

The judge hits the gavel on its stand, rattling the Starbucks cup resting next to it. He takes a sip.

"Okay, who's up?" asks the judge, wiping the froth from his lip with his robe. "Thanks for this ... whoever gave me ... anyway, okay, let's go."

Shawn recognizes his cue. "Defense would like to recall Officer Mateo Palino."

While Officer Palino takes the stand and is sworn in, Shawn takes a small white metal table from the side of the room and rolls it in front of the jury. On top of the table sits the small African box that houses the tiny camera that could have recorded the murder. Astrid feels her eyes begin to roll, but stops and blinks instead. Shawn puts on blue latex gloves, opens the plastic bag containing the hand-carved box, and removes the camera from inside.

"Thank you, officer. I just have a few questions about this box right here. First, can you tell me where you found it?"

"Yes, it was in the back left corner of the victim's living room, where the kitchen peninsula meets the back left wall, sitting on top of a side table."

"And which direction was it facing?"

"Toward the living room away from the wall."

"And what did this hand-carved box have inside of it?"

"A camera."

"What type of camera?"

"It was wireless."

The jury begins to move a little. Some look at others right next to them. Some move forward in their chairs as if they want to hear better.

"A wireless camera. And can you read me your notes about this wireless camera, please, officer, right there?" Shawn points downward.

Officer Palino has his notes on the witness stand right in front of him, courtesy of Shawn, who had placed them there earlier in anticipation of the day's events.

> "Wireless camera still warm. Possible recording of murder."

"So according to your own notes, this camera, which could have recorded everything, was still warm when you found it?"

"That's what it says."

"That's what you said, sir. These are your notes from the evening of August 17, 2018, are they not?"

"They are."

"Thank you. Your witness."

"Officer Palino," Astrid says in an exasperated tone. "In your opinion, does this camera have anything to do with this murder?"

"We have found no correlation. No evidence that there was a server or hard drive or anything that it recorded to."

"Thank you." Astrid dismisses the witness.

"Is there a redirect?" asks the judge.

"Yes." Shawn stands. "Officer Palino, in your professional opinion, do you believe a hidden camera in a living room would exist merely for decoration? For some interior design nuance?"

"Objection," says Astrid.

"I withdraw the question. We have nothing further for this witness."

Palino leaves the stand.

"The defense would like to recall Detective Bronson Penance," says Shawn.

Detective Penance enters and takes his place on the stand.

"Detective, you and I had a conversation the day my client was arrested, did we not?"

"I'm sorry." Detective Penance is confused at the line of questioning, which isn't what he thought he was there for. "I'm sorry, I don't remember."

"Let me refresh your memory. We were in that dreary brick building where you work, and you gave me a brief tip that might steer me in a better direction for my client."

"I wouldn't have done that." He remembers the conversation now.

"Well, you did, and you also said, *'Contrary to popular belief, we do our job here,'* do you remember that?"

"I do remember that."

"Do you think you did your job when it comes to this camera and what it may or may not have recorded?" Shawn asks.

"Objection! Detective Penance is not on trial here." Astrid stands to make her point. "There's simply no reason for this attack."

"Your Honor, I'm simply trying to show that the prosecution has not explored all obvious avenues of investigation, and therefore, my client has been unfairly rushed to judgment."

"I'll allow a rephrasing of the question," rules the judge. "Strike the first one from the record, and be careful, Mr. Connelly."

"Detective Penance, did you or any member of your department ever find the recordings from the wireless camera?"

"We did not. But not for lack—"

"That's all I needed to know."

"That's not all he has to say, Mr. Connelly," says the judge. "Detective, you may continue."

"We tried everything we could to find that recording, alleged recording," Detective Penance begins. "We logged over 250 man hours on this issue alone, issuing search warrants for residents in the Garfield Building, interrogating adjacent neighbors. Because of the location of their condo among many other large residential buildings, there are over seventy Wi-Fi accounts that are accessible to the living room in question; anyone within five hundred or a thousand feet could have had access to that camera, even a passerby on the street."

"Even a friend who lives close by?"

"Yes."

"Thank you, Detective," Shawn says, then looks at Astrid. "Your witness."

Astrid pauses, shuffling through papers as she thinks. She could bring up the African box that Detective Penance found in James West's office, she could talk about the company keeping tabs on conspirators in financial cover-ups, she could bring up the possibility of the camera accidentally recording the murder. But would the jury buy the idea of a camera *accidentally* recording a murder? *Too convoluted, too reasonable-doubty,* she concludes.

"No questions for Detective Penance, except to say thank you for your tireless service to this community."

"Defense would like to recall Jenna Ancelet."

"Again?" asks the judge.

"Final time, I swear."

Jenna takes her seat and looks directly at Shawn. Her eyes do not blink.

"Ms. Ancelet, did you know that your Wi-Fi is accessible from Micah and Lenny's condo?"

"No, I did not. I am not surprised, though. It's a pretty strong signal."

"Did anyone else have your password?"

"Everyone does. I mean, shit, my password is "password". You want access to my phone? It's 1-2-3-4-5-6. That's my phone's password. I have nothing to hide."

"Thank you, Ms. Ancelet. I have nothing further for this witness."

"Ms. Ancelet, apologies from the court," says Astrid. "Is it true that you have been cleared of any wrongdoing, and your alibi is unshakable for the entire evening of the victim's death?"

"Yes, so I've been told."

"Thank you."

"The witness is dismissed," says the judge. He smiles. "Thank you for coming again, Ms. Ancelet."

Jenna forces a grin and begins her exit from the courtroom.

This needs to be over, she thinks on her way out. Disappointed and betrayed, she is careful not to look directly at either of her friends. As the judge calls the next witness, she sees Shawn and Micah out of the corner of her eye, whispering between themselves.

Probably a fake conversation, she thinks. *Goddamn hypocrites*.

"Please state and spell your name for the record," says the court clerk.

"Talbot Lexington. That's T-A-L-B-O-T Lexington, L-E-X-I-N-G-T-O-N."

"Thank you for coming today, Talbot. Is it okay if I call you Talbot?" Shawn asks his young witness. Softer and gentler, Shawn's tone is noticeably different than the one he'd taken with the other witnesses.

Talbot is dressed in baggy jeans and a hoodie, with a crisp, white, button-up shirt underneath. With blondish-brown hair flattened by a cap he is no longer wearing, he sits with his back curved in a slight hunch, as if waiting to be punched from above.

"Sure thing," Talbot answers.

"Talbot, first of all, I'm sorry about your friend. He got hurt pretty bad, huh?"

"Yeah." A nervous, inappropriate laugh accompanies his response.

"You and your friend Frank were sponsees of Lennox Holcomb in Narcotics Anonymous, is that correct?"

"I'm not supposed to say." Talbot cowers under the fear of exposing his anonymity.

"It's okay, we can speak in a general sense." Shawn has dealt with people in recovery before. "You and Frank were in recovery together, and Lennox was helping you through it, is that correct?"

"Yes."

"And how long have you been off drugs?"

"Two days ago, I celebrated sixty days."

"Whoa! That's amazing. Sixty-two days clean. Congratulations."

"Thanks."

"You're welcome." He moves closer to his witness. "Talbot, for the purposes of today, can you tell me what happened to your friend Frank?"

"He overdosed on some shit he got from a friend of Lenny's."

"Okay, wait, let's back up. How do you know Frank got drugs from a friend of Lenny's?"

"Lenny always told us beware of this guy he called Ghost. He knew we was heroin addicts, like he was."

"What did he tell you to beware of?"

"Well, he said he was bad news. He described him as all freckly and shit, like an albino black guy or something. We had other friends who knew the guy, said he wasn't that bad. Said he had awesome heroin. We always thought of him as this badass superhero villain dude. He was kinda like one of those myths, ya know? Like somebody you heard about but never could see?"

"Like a ghost?"

"Psshht. Yeah." Talbot laughs again.

"So, what happened the other night. To your friend Frank?"

"Well, Frank, the dumbass, was thinking about using again. I tried to stop him. But he was jonesin' bad. He texted me all this shit about setting a deal up in the middle of the night."

"Can you read aloud for me the texts from that night? And can you read the times of these texts as well, so the jury has an idea of when all of this happened?"

"Sure." Talbot says. He begins to read in monotone.

"11:07pm, Frank:
Doing it. Made a new friend LOL
11:08pm, Talbot:
New friend? WTF?
11:37pm, Frank:
Dude says to meet him at 3am down by the river. Says he'll be in a fucking wheelchair.
11:40pm, Talbot:
No. Don't do it. Not worth it.
3:03am, Frank:
Got it. And get this. It was Ghost guy! Creepy AF dude, all freckly and shit. Iconic.
3:07am, Frank:
Swear to God, he had that heroin with the ghost thing on it. I've got some good shit.
3:08am, Frank:
Had to snap a pic of the Ghost before he vanished haha! I've got the shit baby. Come join me!

"Then he sent a blurry pic of the wheelchair dude," Talbot says.

Instead of using the monitor, Shawn pulls a giant cardboard-backed photo that had been leaning against the side wall, and proudly places it on the giant easel in front of the jury.

"Is this the photo that Frank texted you?" Shawn asks Talbot.

"Yes, sir, that's him, I guess. Fucking stupid what Frank did."

"Thank you, Talbot. Now I know this next part might be hard, but can you tell me what happened to Frank the very next morning?"

"It was all over the news."

"Yes, but can you tell the ladies and gentlemen of the jury what happened to Frank?"

"He was in the middle of OD'ing, roaming the streets, and got hit by a taxi and died."

"Yes. Wait—he died?"

"Yeah. Yesterday."

"Jesus," Shawn says. "Apologies to the court. I'm sorry, Talbot." Shawn sits back down.

Astrid stands up. "Mr. Lexington, I'm Astrid Lerner."

"Excuse me, I'm not done yet," Shawn interrupts. "Gimme a second, please."

Astrid sits back down.

Shawn takes a moment to compose himself, allowing the feelings of guilt to pass through him. First Jenna, now Talbot. He sees his single-mindedness of winning has infiltrated his core beliefs, slowly ripping them from the inside out. *How could I have missed the fact that Frank died?* He shakes his head.

"The bag was never found, so it couldn't be analyzed, but here are the toxicology results from his doctor." Shawn waves a sheet of paper at the jury. "Turns out he was poisoned. Poisoned with a fatal mix of heroin, crystal meth, and cyanide. And, according to the text exchange that Mr. Lexington just read to you and the photo you see here today, he was killed by the same man whose heroin was found inside Lennox's apartment."

Shawn remains seated.

"If that's all, then your witness, Ms. Lerner," says the judge.

Astrid approaches Talbot. "Hi, Mr. Lexington. I'm so, so sorry about your friend. I was talking with his parents this morning, and they were asking about you. Are you doing okay?"

"Yes, ma'am. Staying close to the program. Haven't done any drugs or drank or nothing."

"I'm so proud of you. That's awesome. I just have three questions for you. The first one is, can you tell me what other drugs that you and Frank would do together?"

"Yes, ma'am. We did crack, heroin, and crystal meth."

"Thank you. Next question. Do you know or do you suspect that Lenny was doing drugs in the weeks or months before his death?"

"Oh, absolutely not. I could tell if he was. Trust me. Lenny was clean."

"How can you be sure?"

"Ma'am, I may be young, but I've been around. I can tell if somebody's doing heroin. I woulda asked him for some if I thought he was using."

"Thank you, Talbot. Last question. How do you feel about that guy right there?" Astrid asks, pointing to Micah.

"Objection. Relevance."

"Goes to motive, if you will allow the witness to continue." Astrid crosses her fingers.

"I'll allow," rules Judge Wilson.

"Micah is a fucking jealous faggot," Talbot says.

The judge bangs his gavel. "Watch your language, young man."

Talbot swallows and hunches over even more. "Yes, sir."

Astrid walks toward him. "It's okay, Talbot, just tone it down a little. You were saying…"

"Yes, ma'am." He sits up in his chair. "I loved Lenny like a brother, but *that* guy, Micah? Fucking jealous, sorry, freaking jealous as hell. My friend Frank was one of them pretty boys, swung both ways. Whenever Lenny would hang out with Frank, Micah would be all up in their business. Asking where they'd been, fucking calling Lenny all the time."

239

"Objection," Shawn says. "Hearsay."

"I know what hearsay means," Talbot says, looking up at the judge. "And Frank didn't just tell me that shit, I was there."

"Overruled," says Judge Wilson.

"I have nothing more for this witness."

"Mr. Connelly, you may call your next witness," prompts the judge.

"The defense rests."

"Court is adjourned until tomorrow morning at 9:30am," says the judge.

"Thank you, Talbot." As Talbot walks by him, Shawn tries to make up for his lack of empathy and follow-through. "I'm so sorry about Frank. Hang in there. You got this."

Talbot leaves the room in silence as the jury completes their exit. Astrid begins packing up while the jail escort begins to take Micah back to the Tombs.

"Could I have just a quick moment?" Shawn asks the jail escort.

"Sure."

Shawn grabs Micah's arm and sits him down.

"Now, that last part didn't go quite as well as I'd hoped," Shawn says, "but most of these last few days have gone pretty well. I'm still confident you'll be acquitted. But I need to know if you are interested in a plea deal, to the lesser charge."

"Do you think it went that badly?"

Shawn makes a flat hand and moves it sideways left to right. "So-so."

"Whatever you think is best, Shawn, I trust you," Micah says, hoping that the situation won't come to that extreme. "Wait, what's the jail time for the what's-it-called?"

"We have to go," says the jail escort.

"Criminally negligent homicide. With no prior record, it could be anywhere from one to four years."

"Do it." Micah is halfway out the door.

Astrid watches him leave, then addresses Shawn.

"Ready to make a plea deal?" Astrid asks, with a post-eavesdrop snicker.

"Haha. Nice move making buddy-buddy with our witness's parents. And his friend's parents, geez. Too bad you didn't end up calling him as your witness, you could have knocked it outta the park."

"Ahh, you underestimate me, Mr. Connelly. Could have been my plan all along."

"So what about that deal? Criminally negligent homicide, two years."

Astrid laughs. "You know, you're pretty good, Shawn. Yesterday, I might have been inclined to take that deal. Today, mmm, not so much."

She grabs her bag and begins to saunter toward the door.

"See you tomorrow," she says.

"So that's a no?" Shawn replies.

CHAPTER 41

"Yes, baby?" Shawn asks.

Haylee has been giving her husband Shawn some space ever since he got home from the long, emotional day. Noticing that he has relaxed into a more peaceful state, she seizes the moment.

"I have something to tell you."

"You finally remembered where you saw the Ghost logo?" Shawn says, leaning upward in his chair. They'd talked about this so often, it had become a running joke.

"God no," she says, defeated, as if the wind had been knocked out of her gut.

Shawn, still reeling from his earlier self-observation with Talbot, recognizes his mindset is still exhibiting a need to win, this time with his own wife. He stands and walks toward her with both hands outstretched.

"Baby." He invites her to come closer to his arms.

She takes his hands.

"Funny that you call me baby right now." She pulls his hands and places them on her stomach.

Shawn looks at her. His mouth drops.

He begins to touch her belly, staring at it. He begins to weep. He falls to his knees, his hands dropping from her stomach to her thighs. He pulls her closer, pressing his face into her abdomen.

"Honey." She places her hands on his head. She plays with his hair. "It's gonna be okay. Shhh. It's gonna be beautiful. You're beautiful."

He continues to cry. *Objection*! he thinks, *I'm an awful human being who essentially accused Jenna of murder, who didn't know that Talbot's friend Frank had died, who doesn't deserve to be a father.*

"And you're going to be an awesome father," Haylee says, as if reading his mind.

He looks up at her and tries to smile. She smiles and continues rubbing his head, taking some of his hair in her finger and twirling it.

"Case closed," she says.

CHAPTER 42

"You may begin your closing argument, Ms. Lerner," Judge Wilson announces.

"Thank you, your Honor," Astrid says. "Ladies and gentlemen of the jury, thank you for your time and patience, and commitment to this community and its process for justice.

"The facts of this case are overwhelming and indisputable. Blood spatter results show definitively that the defendant was at the scene of the crime at the exact moment the victim was originally stabbed. DNA also places the defendant, and only the defendant, at the scene of the crime when the victim finally gave in to his thirty-three fatal wounds and his last breath was literally pounded out of his body by the defendant.

"Gaps in both the defendant's recollection of the evening and proven video and GPS surveillance of the night show clearly that the defendant had enough time to dispose of the murder weapon, which incidentally is the same type of knife found in their apartment, and any sort of other evidence that would link him to the crime. Testimony revealed a propensity toward violence, an actual threat of murder, an incongruence of a 'Good Micah, Bad Micah,' a questionable psychopathic tendency, and a frightening rage that could often be triggered by unrelenting jealousy.

245

"And keep in mind that we also have a confession. We have the exact moment, on video, of the defendant realizing what he had done."

She grabs the remote and pulls up an image of Lennox. He is smiling a crooked grin, with creased dimples engulfed by the perfect amount of scruff. His face is skinny, but his body is well defined even through his tight shirt and suit.

"Now, imagine with me for a moment. The defendant's husband, Lennox Holcomb, age 37, as you can tell quite a handsome man, a successful vice president of finance, a loving and giving partner, has just taken a shower. He is naked, walking around his home, as many of us do from time to time. He decides to fix some cereal, sit down at his desk, maybe read the paper, look at his phone. With not a care in the world, he is simply passing time before he meets his sponsee. He loves his recovery work. He has devoted his life to helping others through the addiction that he has overcome, just as others have helped him.

"Suddenly he feels a sharp pain in his back. Then another in his abdomen. Still fueled by rage over an affair, his money-obsessed, so-called loving husband begins to stab Lennox in his chair over and over, over and over, eventually dumping him on the living room carpet like a bag of trash. However, this strong young man is still alive, despite the attack from his partner of four years. After leaving his husband lying on the floor, bleeding out from thirty-three stab wounds and a collapsed lung, unable to move, unable to call for help for three agonizing hours, the defendant comes home from a party, turns on the lights, and realizes he has to finish what he started. Rather than call 9-1-1 immediately, he chooses to take matters into his own hands. He administers what he calls CPR, but in actuality was the continuation of a truly maniacal torture that ended in pounding on his husband's chest, over and over, over and over. Finally, it was done. He calls 9-1-1. Arguably, his affect is one of acting. He is replaying a scene from a play he was in months before.

That would be a horrible scenario, ladies and gentlemen, would it not?"

Some of them nod in agreement. Astrid walks in front of the jury, her voice widening to fill the entire room.

"Now, as promised, the defense tried to distract you with corrupt corporations and even his own friend of many years, Jenna, whom he threw under the bus to protect his client. And then there was this Ghost character. In a *wheelchair*. Did anyone stop to think how a man who is in a wheelchair could have allegedly attacked friends of Lennox, according to Jenna's testimony describing the alleged contents of the alleged letter, allegedly linking Ghost to the murder? Now, moves like these reek of desperation. And make no mistake, the defense was desperate. Mr. Connelly tried to tarnish the reputation of an esteemed detective by suggesting he did not do his job, and Mr. Connelly also tried to discredit decades of blood spatter analysis techniques, simply to try—and the key word here is *try*—to plant a reasonable doubt in your mind."

Astrid is almost back at her table. She turns around.

"Oh, Micah Breuer killed his husband. There's no doubt about that. The evidence is indisputable and overwhelming. And let's not forget the motives: the jealousy over the affair with Josh Harrison and the one-point-five-million-dollar insurance policy and seven-million–dollar condo he stands to gain if you acquit him.

"Lennox Holcomb was a young man. He was a good man. He was giving back to his recovery community, making living amends with his husband after a brief affair, and being a loving and caring friend and son. He didn't deserve to be tortured, left for dead, and brutally murdered. I ask that you find the defendant, Micah James Breuer, guilty on all counts so we can keep this diabolical and sadistic man from ever doing this again."

Sitting in the back of the courtroom, Elaine Holcomb has been grabbing her husband's hand while listening to Astrid's closing arguments. The grip becomes so strong that Wallace tries to remove his hand.

"Sorry," Elaine whispers, removing her hand from his.

Wallace then places his hand on top of hers. "It's okay, sweetie."

"Counselor?" Judge Wilson motions for Shawn to begin.

"Thank you, your Honor," Shawn replies.

He stands up, buttons the top button of his suit jacket, and begins his closing argument.

"This case should have never come to trial. The prosecutor knows it. We know it. And the real killer who is still out there definitely knows it.

"There's no murder weapon. There's no motive. There's no indisputable evidence. There's no real confession. But you know what there is? A multitude of suspects and angles that the prosecutor and police never fully explored. Why? Because they were getting pressure from the mother of the victim's son. That's right. Elaine Holcomb, Lennox Holcomb's own mother, who used to have that job right there."

He points to Astrid, who does not give him the satisfaction of looking back at him. Shawn grabs his remote and turns on the monitors. He reveals his first slide, a close-up of the heroin bag sticker with the ghost emblem.

"That's why they ignored the half-used heroin that was found in the victim's possession."

His next three bullet points begin to pop onto the same PowerPoint slide, the first bullet point above the ghost logo, the second one to the bottom left, the third one to the bottom right.

"That's why they ignored the drug dealer's past of violence, threats toward the victim, and the possible poisoning of one of the victim's sponsees."

Red arrows appear connecting the three bullet points, encasing the ghost logo in a triangle.

From the audience, Jenna squints. Her eyes widen. She pulls out her phone and does a quick Internet search for "European intersection signs." Up pops a photo of a red triangle encasing a pointy silhouette of what looks like a skinny house, with a thick line through it.

"That's why they ignored the corruption of a corporation that was using Lennox for God-knows-what." Shawn clicks through the slides one by one. "That's why they ignored the motion-sensor camera hidden in a carved box in the victim's living room."

Jenna looks up from her phone and is about to wave her hand to get Shawn's attention, but is distracted by her own face on the screen.

"They even ignored the jilted employee living right across the street," Shawn says, "whose Wi-Fi access is available from the victim's home. Is this all coincidence? I mean, that's a lot of coincidence, don't you think?

Jenna puts down her half-raised hand, turns off her screen, and rests the phone in her lap.

"Desperation, plain and simple," Shawn says. "The prosecution needed a win, to uphold some sort of high esteem of the office, to prove a new reputation with a new regime. Something."

He remains perfectly still. He does not walk the floor. He stays standing in front of his table, facing the jury.

"There is no murder weapon. None. It was from the same type of knife set that was found at Micah and Lennox's apartment, but that set was complete, tested, and found clean.

"There is no motive. Micah has a jealous streak. So what? So do I sometimes. So do many of the people in this courtroom. The good thing about Micah is that he was in therapy, even dealing with the repercussions of the spiritual abuse he was subjected to as a child. Hey, he's used to it, right? People abusing him, ganging up on him, the church, the prosecution. He's tough. He can take it. He's a strong man, resilient, as evidenced by that fact that his own therapist was happy with his progress. He had made amends to Josh Harrison, even after the alleged threatening confrontation, enough to where Josh and Micah were laughing and hanging out arm-in-arm at the beach just a few short months ago.

"Plus, I was the one who suggested the life insurance to Lenny. Me. Their lawyer. Because I knew they were continuing to travel and to take part in all these crazy adventures like hiking and bungee jumping and falling out of airplanes. They needed to protect each other, in case something happened. And one-point-five is nothing in relation to their lifestyle.

"There is no indisputable evidence. The blood on Micah's neck that their DNA expert claims is from the time of the stabbing could have easily been spattered during the life-saving measures Micah took that evening. And contrary to what the prosecution would have you believe, the older methods of blood analysis are inferior to the more current ones. The professional association, of which the prosecution's expert witness is an active member, highly recommends discarding the practices that he himself used to analyze this crime scene. Plus, Micah was at a party that evening, dressed in a tuxedo, white shirt, no blood anywhere. He saw plenty of people, and no one reported him acting strangely or mysteriously.

"There are no gaps in the timeline. There was an unusual amount of activity in the city that night, and the so-called gaps are no more than twenty-five minutes each way. Less time than a sitcom on TV when you bypass the commercials on your DVR." Some of the jury members laugh.

"Lastly, there is no confession. My client was distraught. He saw his best friend, his traveling partner, his husband of two years, gasping for his last breath and did the first thing that popped into his mind. He tried to save him the only way he knew how. And when he realized that what he did to help his husband actually harmed him further, he was distressed about his choices. As any of us would have been.

"That's all this case is about. A devoted husband wanting to save the love of his life. Save him from whatever, and whoever, happened to him earlier that night.

"I ask you to find Micah Breuer not guilty on all counts and force the prosecution to explore the many other leads they ignored. Thank you."

Shawn sits back in his chair next to Micah.

"Is there a rebuttal, Ms. Lerner?" Judge Wilson asks.

"No, your Honor."

As the judge issues his instructions for the jury, Shawn turns to Micah, who is shaking.

"Hey, buddy, what's wrong? You gotta hold it together. We got this," he says.

"You keep saying that, but it's gonna be"—his breath gets the best of him—"be bad, I can feel it."

Micah continues shaking, beginning to spiral out of control. Out of the side of his eyes, he sees one of the jurors do a double-take, and the adrenaline rush calms the episode.

"You good?" Shawn asks.

"No."

CHAPTER 43

"I know you may have felt pressure from us, but we wanted to tell you, no matter what happens, we appreciate you and all you have done for our son."

Elaine and her husband are standing in the doorway of Astrid Lerner's office, but do not bother to come in.

"I appreciate that, Elaine," Astrid replies, setting aside some case notes on the Union Square murder. "I really do."

The phone rings.

"We'll let you get that," Elaine says, pulling her husband's hand.

"Astrid Lerner," she says into her iPhone.

She pauses.

"You've got to be kidding me."

CHAPTER 44

"All rise, court is now in session," announces the court clerk. "The honorable Judge Christopher K. Wilson presiding."

Micah is dressed in his white T-shirt and jeans. Shawn is dressed in his suit from earlier in the day, but his tie is gone, and he is a bit drunk. He grabs Micah's hand in nervous, excited anticipation.

Astrid has situated herself at her table, tapping her phone with her fingernails. She has experienced a quick jury before, and the result is never good news.

Having never gone home, Mr. and Mrs. Holcomb are standing next to the door. Jenna is sitting in front of them. Micah turns around to see who is in the courtroom.

"You called Jenna?" he asks Shawn.

"I texted her that there was a verdict. She didn't text back. Is she here?"

"Yes!"

"Thank you," Judge Wilson begins. "I know it's late, so let's move through this. Ladies and gentlemen of the jury, it has been less than ten hours since I gave you instructions and sent you into deliberation. You have considered four counts, including second-degree murder, first- and second-degree manslaughter, and criminally negligent homicide. These are all very serious charges. Have you reached a verdict?"

The jury foreperson, the same one who had performed the sign of the cross after saying that child-abusing priests should be hung by their testicles, stands up.

"We have, your Honor," he announces.

"What say ye?"

"We, the jury, in the case of *The People versus Micah Breuer*, in reference to the count of murder in the second degree, find the defendant, Micah James Breuer, not guilty."

Astrid flinches.

"On the count of first-degree manslaughter, we, the jury, find the defendant, Micah James Breuer, not guilty."

"On the count of second-degree manslaughter, we, the jury, find the defendant, Micah James Breuer, not guilty."

As if she were hanging on these next words as if they were her last hope, Astrid looks behind her, searching for Elaine and Wallace Holcomb. They are nowhere to be found.

"On the count of criminally negligent homicide, we, the jury, find the defendant, Micah James Breuer, not guilty."

Shawn grabs Micah's hand even tighter, flings it around, and the two friends embrace each other.

"Thank you, ladies and gentlemen of the jury for your service. You are excused." says the judge. "This court is dismissed."

"Shawn, thank you, thank you, thank you," Micah says into Shawn's ear as they linger in their embrace.

"It's what we do," Shawn says. "I'll come see you in a few and take you home. Well, actually, you can spend the night with Haylee and me tonight. You shouldn't be alone your first night back as a free man."

"Okay." Micah smiles through his tears. "I think that's a good idea."

They let go of each other, and Micah is taken away by the prison escort.

"Well done, Mr. Connelly," says a voice to his left. Astrid is still sitting, the arch in her back a bit more pronounced than before. Her folders and notes are in the same places as they were during the verdicts. "Not sure how that happened, but that's justice for you."

"Thank you, Ms. Lerner."

"Do you really think he's innocent?"

"I've known him a long time. Yes, yes, I do."

"I don't."

"Well," he says, with a guttural chuckle. "Good thing you weren't on that jury. Come on, Ms. Lerner, I'll walk you out. You've got a killer to find."

They both pack up their things and leave out the side entrance.

Jenna is still sitting. Aside from the bailiff, she is the last one there. She gets up, walks to the back of the courtroom, and turns around. The bailiff turns out the lights. Jenna remains silhouetted in the doorway.

CHAPTER 45

The room is dark, though it is 7:20am. Again, Ghost finds himself huddled at a desk in front of a cracked, mustard-yellow wall interrupted only by a single tiny window, haphazardly covered by black velvet curtains. Light trickles in above and below, revealing only the slightest details of his workspace.

He turns to his laptop and jostles it awake. He sees a new email from a familiar address. He opens it.

Confess. I have the letter.

The man, the father, heads toward his son. He watches his own shadow, cast by the computer screen, become smaller and clearer as he walks down the hall.

"*Mon cœur,* Daddy has to go to work, but can you do something for me while I'm gone?" he asks, announcing himself. He enters the room and pulls a small suitcase from underneath the bed.

"Yes, Daddy?" the child says, pulling back the covers, revealing pajamas with a repeating pattern of "I Heart NY."

"Can you pack yourself some of your favorite clothes and your toothbrush and toothpaste, and a couple of your favorite dump trucks?" He stretches out the word *favorite* as only a father can.

"Sure! We going on a trip?"

"It's a surprise. I will tell you all about it when I get home. Make sure you pack everything neat like Daddy."

"Okay!"

"Thank you, sweet boy," Ghost says. "When I leave, make sure you lock the doors like I taught you. If someone knocks, don't answer, you hear? Make sure you don't let nobody know you're here."

He kisses his son on the forehead and exits the apartment, leaving his filthy computer to continue casting its eerie glow.

CHAPTER 46

"My car is filthy, baby, I'm gonna head out to the car wash, you need anything?" Haylee asks her husband, who is sitting on their avocado-green mid-century sofa, reading the paper and drinking coffee. "The birds shit all over the hood again."

"Birds? It's the dead of winter." Shawn says.

"I don't know what to tell you. Either it was birds or those neighborhood kids." She laughs at her own ridiculousness. "Last chance, do you need anything?

"Nah, I'm good," Shawn says, making a slurping noise. "So good."

"Have fun basking in your victory," she says.

"Wait, don't leave just yet, come over here a second."

Shawn pats the couch. Haylee accepts the invitation.

"My firm just got word that the jury selection was key in acquitting Micah, and I wanted to thank you for that."

"I don't understand," she says leaning into his chest. Shawn lifts his arm and places it around her shoulder.

"Well, I don't know if you remember this, but we were getting ready together one morning a few weeks ago, and you mentioned something about several clients of yours experiencing spiritual abuse. You had a theory that people who are ultra-religious usually move to the city to escape the abuse. You remember that?"

"You listen to me!" Haylee says, pounding her husband's knee.

"Of course I do, honey. Turns out you were right. All I had to do was find people who were fairly new to the city, with extreme religious views, which is mostly what the prosecution was looking for too. For entirely different reasons of course. I think they thought they'd secured a pool of homophobes, and that was that."

"I don't completely understand," Haylee says, almost following his thought process. "But from what I understand, well, that was a pretty risky move."

"Seems like some sort of unconscious empathy," Shawn says, proud of the phrase he'd just coined. "According to post-trial interviews, some of the jury thought Micah was being ganged up on. With the addition of the fact that nobody else was even fully considered, they all felt they had no choice but to acquit for one reason or another."

"Wow, that's kind of incredible," she replies, getting up.

"*You're* incredible. You should eat something and take it easy," Shawn says. "Want me to fix you some French toast?"

"Baby, I'm pregnant, not dead. And I'm going to get the car washed, not running a half-marathon."

Shawn raises his left eyebrow as if to say "good point" and continues drinking his coffee.

"Hey, I thought Micah was spending the night last night." Haylee looks around.

"Oh yeah, you missed him. God, baby, he was so happy to be in a normal space, he conked out as soon as his head hit this couch."

"You didn't give him one of the spare bedrooms? Honey, it's Micah."

"Baby, he was exhausted. He fell asleep right there, I think in mid-sentence."

She opens the front door to leave, turns back around and looks at the couch. She sees a folded blanket with two pillows on top on the far side of the sectional.

"He said he was gonna head back to his place," Shawn explains, then looks at his watch. "But Lord, he must've left early. I got up at six, and he was already gone."

Shawn's phone rings.

"That's my cue," Haylee says. "I'll see you soon. French toast would be nice when I get back."

She blows a kiss to him and shuts the door behind her.

CHAPTER 47

Opening the clear floor-to-ceiling doors to his building for the first time in months, Micah can still hear the glass breaking from the night of the murder. Everything in his building's foyer has been replaced, yet he can still feel the crunching of broken pieces underneath his feet.

He enters the elevator and presses 7. The floor does not illuminate. He resituates a folded newspaper he is cradling underneath his arm, takes the key from his pocket, and turns it in the lock on the elevator panel, then presses the button again. The number 7 lights up.

The ride up feels long. He hears the voices from that night in the back of his mind.

> *"Baby, please! Don't. Please, God help me, PLEASE!"*
> *"Stay with me! Please, God."*

((Ding.))

The elevator opens. He walks inside and turns on the light. The voices continue.

> *"So, you must've turned on these can lights above us here after you tried to save him?"*
> *"And that's your husband right there?"*

The shades are all drawn, courtesy of Jenna, he assumes. Micah flips the paddle switch on the wall next to the elevator, and the can lights in the ceiling illuminate the familiar space. He looks at the corner of the living room and walks toward the spot where his husband breathed his last breath. He sees a photo of Lennox and himself on the console table behind the sofa. They are in front of Machu Picchu, smiling, arms around each other. He turns the photo upside down. He cannot move any further. He collapses into the cushions, noticing the smeared dried bloodstains on the arms of the couch. He throws the folded newspaper onto the pillows beside him. A huge headline "KILLER STILL FREE?" looms above a photo of him exiting the detention center.

He pulls out his phone and summons the courage to call Jenna. He waits for her to answer.

"Micah!" Jenna exclaims. "Is that you?"

"Yes," he replies. "I just got home. Jenna, I can't do this."

"Oh, sweet Micah, I know how hard this must be. Want me to come over? I'm in Soho right now, my regular Friday night nanny gig for those godawful children, but it's almost over. I was gonna go over to Josh's, but I can be there in, like, thirty."

"No, no, no, it's okay," Micah says.

"Seriously, it's no big deal, I want to come over."

He fights back tears. "Jenna, I didn't know Shawn was gonna do that. I tried to stop him."

Jenna is silent.

"He went too far," Micah says. "Are you okay?"

"He *did* go too far. He doesn't really believe that, does he?"

"No! He was just too wrapped up in trying to help me." Micah tries to comfort her. "I hope it doesn't hurt you in any way. Please know how much I love you and appreciate everything, *everything* you have done for me."

Another call beeps in Micah's ear. It's Shawn.

"Oh, my pleasure," Jenna says. "We're gonna get through this. I'll let you have some time at home, but I'll check in on you later, okay?"

"Okay. Thank you!"

"Bye, sweetheart."

Micah presses to answer the other call.

"Hey, Shawn, sorry I left so early, I just needed some air."

"No worries, buddy. How's it going there?"

"It's okay," Micah checks his soul to make sure his comment is true. "Yes, I think I'm going to be okay."

"Well, that's good."

Micah can tell by Shawn's tone that something's not right. "It sounds like there's something else you want to tell me."

"Elaine and Wallace Holcomb are suing you in civil court," Shawn blurts.

CHAPTER 48

A deluge of water flops over Haylee's windshield. The sound startles her.

She laughs and pulls out her phone. She types in the words "When to expect morning sickness" into the search bar.

She is sitting inside her black Mercedes ML 350, which is gliding through the car wash.

Atlantic Car Wash is an easy-in-easy-out, old school auto detailing establishment at the corner of Vanderbilt and Atlantic in Brooklyn. One of the two turquoise-painted brick buildings houses the service and repair garage, the other the track system that carries vehicles through suds, rinse, and dry.

While her SUV moves down tracks to the rinse cycle, two employees dressed in heavy black raincoats and thick gloves are waiting just beyond the cement walls. Both are jumping up and down to keep their blood flowing while they wait to hand-dry her SUV in the middle of winter.

At the top of the dark, cavernous room, a hose breaks free from the ceiling, and the metal nozzle crashes down on Haylee's windshield, cracking it with a loud thud. She drops her phone and looks up to watch the hose dance around like a snake, spewing its icy venom across the space, dousing one of the two employees waiting outside. Completely soaked, the man takes control of the serpent and wrestles it to the ground, while the other man pushes a button on a side console to stop the water.

Haylee takes control of her breath and picks up the phone that had fallen just beneath her feet. She watches the drenched man begin to take his vinyl jacket off. As if in slow motion, he takes off his coat and reveals his thin, freckly arms, covered only by a dirty white tank top.

Haylee's eyes grow wider as she sees the ghost tattoo on his shoulder. She tries to catch her breath, letting out a quick, heavy snort, releasing a tiny bit of mucous onto her upper lip. She reaches for a Kleenex in her purse, while at the same time moving her phone into camera mode. She wipes her lips with her tissue and positions the camera.

((Flash.))

"Shit," she says, dropping her phone again.

Ghost looks through the windshield, directly into her eyes. He puts his coat back on and walks out of view.

Haylee starts her car and moves it forward off the tracks. Once free, she presses the gas, and the car barrels through pools of water, splashing the second man. The tires screech as she bolts right on Atlantic and hits the interstate to go back home.

"Heeeyyy," says the other man, waving a white towel at the Mercedes SUV, surrendering to what has just happened.

◆

Ghost bursts through the door to his boss's office.

"Sir, sorry, but I need to go home to change. Hose broke off in the rinse bay. Got soaked and I'm cold as fuck." He takes off his drenched vinyl coat, throws it on the floor. He begins to scrunch up his wet tank top to wring out the water.

The boss looks up. He is a big man with a moustache and failing hair.

"You have twenty minutes."

Ghost looks at his boss's desk. A multitude of checks are laid neatly in front of the man.

"I suppose you want your check?" The boss is annoyed by the staring.

"If it's not a problem." Ghost is composed, trying not to reveal that's the only reason why he came into work in the first place.

"Here." His boss holds out a check. "You have twenty minutes to make it back."

Ghosts grabs the check and runs out of the office to his right. He takes a left at Clinton and runs toward the C train, folding the check carefully so that both corners line up. He sticks the check in the back of his jeans as he picks up his pace.

Twenty minutes, he thinks, doing the math in his head, *Fuck that.*

His home is at least twelve minutes by subway across the East River to Jay Street, then a transfer to the F train to 2nd Avenue, and he still has to run about ten blocks to his apartment.

And besides, that's not the reason I'm leaving, he thinks. *Somebody has recognized me.*

He sees an unchained bike resting on a stone wall beneath a huge rosette window and a sign that reads Church of St. Luke and St. Matthew. He grabs the bike, hops on, and races in the direction of his apartment.

The wind is cold on his bare arms and shoulders. His son could be in danger. He needs to wrap up loose ends. He has nowhere else to turn.

CHAPTER 49

Ghost puts the key in his front door lock and turns.

"Don't worry, it's me," Ghost says, teeth chattering, in a volume just loud enough for his son to hear. "Can you open the other lock for Daddy?"

A series of clicks reverberate through the hallway, and the door opens.

Ghost grabs the boy, flings him up into his arms. He wraps himself in his son, relishing the warmth and safety. They move down the hallway to the bedroom. Ghost sees the suitcase neatly packed.

"Good job," he says.

Ghost flips through the suitcase, then opens the dresser drawers, pulls out underwear and socks, throws them into the luggage. He opens the bottom drawer, pulls out 10,000 dollars in stacks of 100's, throws it in and closes it. He pulls an old corduroy coat from the closet and wrestles it onto his thawing body.

"What's wrong, Daddy?"

"I need you to be a man today, okay? We're leaving a little sooner than we planned." Ghost knows it's a half-truth. "Now, come with Daddy."

Ghost grabs the boy's suitcase and rushes to the living room. His son follows closely behind, still dressed in his "I Heart NY" pajamas.

Ghost stops at the computer table and opens the drawer. The jostle of the commotion wakes the computer from its sleep. The words *Confess, I have the letter* are still visible, taunting him. He feels a pressure that he's never felt before, like a vice crushing his soul, his future, his son. He pulls out two plane tickets, takes one, leaves the second one in the drawer.

I can get an earlier flight at the airport, he thinks, shoving the ticket in his corduroy jacket.

Ghost grabs his son in one hand and the suitcase in the other and heads out of the apartment, pulling the door closed with his foot. They run down the stairs and out the front door.

He places the boy down on solid ground and places the suitcase in front of him. He hails a nearby taxi.

"Daddy, I'm scared."

"Oh, *mon cœur*, all will be okay soon."

The taxi pulls up. The passenger window is down.

"Where to?" asks the taxi driver.

Ghost and his son enter the cab.

"JFK!" he replies, as if his son's life depended on it.

CHAPTER 50

"Micah, I'd like you to meet the private investigator to whom you owe your life," Shawn motions in the direction of the other man who had just arrived at Shawn's home.

"Allen Pinchot," the man says. "Glad to finally meet you."

They are all seated on the back patio area of the Connellys' brownstone in Cobble Hill. A nine-foot wall of horizontal teak slats stretches along the back of the outdoor space, with a smooth concrete floor surrounded by manicured grass. Micah sees an empty chair next to the detective.

"I can't thank you enough." Micah almost bows as he shakes Allen's hand.

"Not a problem at all. It's what we do."

"Allen's the one who found out about Jenna's Wi-Fi," Shawn explains as they all take their seats in wire-mesh chairs with light green oversize cushions. "Ultimately not our proudest moment, but I think it helped give us an edge."

Micah isn't sure what to say, so he remains silent.

"Thanks to both of you for rushing over here on a Saturday. Elaine Holcomb works fast, so we all need to plan our attack on this silly civil suit she's concocted," Shawn begins. "This is about the life insurance, plain and simple."

"I don't care about that," Micah says. "Can't we just give her the money?"

"Not so fast," Shawn says, thinking about some of the proceeds from the life insurance paying his legal fees. *And I'm about to be a father.* "We have to fight it. It's bullshit. This is going to be a long day, so let's just hunker down, all of us."

Haylee enters through the front door, gasping for breath. Shawn senses something is wrong and rushes through the open sliding glass doors toward her, frantic that something has happened to her or the baby. The others follow quickly behind.

"Honey, what's wrong?"

"I saw him. At the car wash." She sits down on the nearest chair she could find, which is the entry bench next to the door. "Ghost."

"What?" Shawn says. "Did he hurt you?"

"No, baby, I'm okay." She grabs his arm, gives him a curt glance. She doesn't want him to ask about the pregnancy in front of the others. "But this Ghost guy. He works there! That's where I remember him from. Last time I washed my car there, it was summer. And I remembered his tattoo because it was so strange. It had a bullet hole through it, which scared me. I remembered his look. But I didn't put it together until today." She gets out her phone. "There was an accident at the car wash and this man, this really pale black man got soaked and took off his jacket, and there it was." She pulls up the photo of the man. "He saw me taking this picture, I'm sure of it."

Shawn grabs the phone. The photo has a glare from the cracked windshield, but overall, it is clear and focused. When Shawn zooms in, he can see most of the tattoo, and the side of the man's face. "Holy shit."

Shawn pulls out his phone and begins searching for a number.

"What are you doing?" asks Allen Pinchot.

"Calling Detective Penance," says Shawn. "If we nail this guy, the civil suit may drop before it even gets started."

CHAPTER 51

"Detective Bronson Penance's office, this is Lilith McGuire, how can I help you?"

"Lily, this is Shawn Connelly. I represented Micah Br—"

"Yes, I know who you are, Mr. Connelly," Lily says with an accidental snark. "Detective Penance took the weekend off, as you can imagine. But if there's anything I can help you with, I'd be happy to."

"My wife just found the Ghost guy that killed that young boy Frank, and most likely killed Lennox Holcomb. After she recognized him, he bolted quickly and you gotta find him. He works at Atlantic Car Wash, 800 Atlantic, in Brooklyn. And the phone number is 718-555-0045."

Lily writes down the information on a scrap piece of paper on Detective Penance's desk.

"I'll give him the message," she says.

"Is your department going to follow through this time?" Shawn urges. "Please don't let him get away."

"We got this." She matches his severe tone. "Thank you, Mr. Connelly."

Lily hangs up the phone and looks at the piece of paper. After five seconds of thought, she takes the note, grabs her purse and leaves.

CHAPTER 52

Lily McGuire stands in front of a Lower East Side apartment building, staring up at the fourth floor. She double-checks the address she had scribbled in the cab. The angry car wash owner had also given her a detailed description of his missing employee that matched everything she already knew about the illusive Ghost. Now she's standing in front of his home, with both his name and his address literally in the palm of her hand.

Bastien Morrell
152 Avenue D, Building C, Unit C-412

So, Ghost's real name is Bastien, she thinks. *A beautiful name for a killer.*

Several buildings of differing heights surround Building C, each in a taupey-brown brick with white windowpanes. The brick has been patched several times over the housing unit's half-century existence with newer brick that does not match. The result is a cold, forgotten veneer hiding hundreds of forgotten stories.

What am I doing here? she wonders. She wants to prove something to herself, to her boss. She is armed, confident in her ability to take care of herself and wants to follow through, no matter the circumstances. She calls the precinct but has every intention of proceeding on her own.

"Unit 7-28. Approaching suspect at 152 Avenue D, number 412, requesting backup."

"All units respond, officer at 152 Avenue D, number 412, requesting backup."

"10-4. Unit 12-42 on our way."

She enters the five-story building through a metal and glass grid-like entrance with a huge rectangular fluorescent lamp above the doorway. She walks up four flights of stairs. A foul stench, a rancid mixture of marijuana and cleaning supplies, wafts through her nostrils, causing her to cough out loud. The noise echoes as it bounces off the concrete walls. The sun squeezes through a tiny row of windows along each floor, and the lights above flicker as if emitting a warning to stay away.

She approaches the apartment door marked 412, and knocks. The door creaks open. She draws her gun, nudging the door open further.

"Mr. Morrell?" She opens the door even more. "I'm Detective Lily McGuire. I just need to talk with you a moment, if I can."

No one answers. She creeps into the room, pointing the gun toward any blind spots, just as she was taught in training. She leaves the door open to let the intermittent light from the hallway shine through into the dark apartment.

She walks down the short hallway and checks the bedroom and closet, observing the open drawers and the indentations on the bed.

Somebody was in a hurry.

Confident she is alone, she puts her gun away.

Walking back through the living room, she notices a row of three framed photos, all at 45-degree angles, each spaced from the other with equidistant precision, all in the exact same frame: A beautiful blonde woman, probably Italian, holding a newborn baby in her arms; two men in foreign uniform in front of a military base, under a sign written in a language she didn't recognize; a pale, snaggle-toothed toddler with curly reddish-brown hair, smiling against a light-gray studio backdrop.

She takes the bottom part of her sleeve and pulls it down over her hand, picking up the photo of Ghost's son. She smiles. She places it back on the table, then moves to the kitchen. A pile of dirty dishes rests in the sink. Next to the messy kitchen is a small table with two place settings, each arranged as if an elegant dinner were about to be served. A bright yellow-and-black book titled "Home-Schooling for Dummies" rests on the chair just next to the table.

She turns around and walks to the desk next to the window. The computer is open but asleep. Again, she pulls her sleeve out to cover her hand and she clicks on one of the keys. It awakens.

Confess. I have the letter, she reads on the open Internet window.

She glances above the body of the email to see the address of the sender.

Frenchy228@hotmail.com.

She moves the mouse to the "sent folder" and clicks. A bevy of emails sent to Frenchy228 appear, one after the other.

Just as she's about to click on the first email, she hears footsteps climbing stairs echoing through the hallway outside. Lily moves the mouse over the top of the screen to put the computer to sleep. The screen does not fade. She stands up and walks out the door and into the hall. She peeks out over the stairwell just in time to see the wiry hair of the man she had come here to confront, making his way up the steps very quickly. Too quickly.

She goes back to the door, almost closes it and knocks on it, as if she's just arrived.

"Mr. Morrell? Are you there?" She begins to enter again just as Ghost arrives at the door.

"Can I help you, ma'am?" He barges in, switching places with her in the process.

"Yes. Are you Mr. Morrell?"

"Yes."

"Hi, I'm Lilith McGuire of the Seventh Precinct," she says, flashing her badge. "I'm sorry to bother you. We were just doing some follow-up on a Mr. Lennox Holcomb and wanted to ask you a few questions."

"Lenny? Of course, come on in." Ghost turns on the single ceiling light. "I'm just in and out today, I only have a few minutes."

"Oh, this won't take long. I really appreciate it."

Lily enters and looks over at the computer. It is still glowing. She looks for Ghost and finds him in the kitchen, washing dishes in the sink.

"I'm sorry. We're not used to guests," he says, turning on the kitchen faucet.

She walks away from the sightline of the computer, so when Ghost looks at her, he will not see the evidence that she has already been in his apartment.

"We?" She plays dumb.

"Yes, my son and I live here. He's at school right now."

Lie, she thinks, remembering the yellow-and-black book.

"Oh? How old is he?"

"He's ten."

She looks at the computer, which has gone black. She exhales.

"Ten. That's such a precocious age, isn't it?"

She sees three bags of heroin on the bookcase. She recognizes the logo, walks over and picks one up with her sleeve-covered hand.

"Yes, it is," Ghost says, chuckling. "Very much so."

"And how about his mother?" She runs the bag along the edge of the bookcase.

Ghost doesn't answer. He turns off the faucet and turns around to find Lily holding the bag of heroin with a ghost emblem on it. He drops a dishtowel in the sink with such force that it knocks over a small pile of plates. "Why did you come here, Ms. McGuire?"

Lily jumps, but continues to hold the bag of heroin. "Where is your son, Mr. Morrell?"

"I took him to the airport to fly him to my brother overseas."

"Overseas?"

"It's none of your business where I took my son, bitch."

Lily moves her hand to her gun. A loud voice from her belt echoes through the room.

"12-42 for 7-28. Requesting 10-7. Repeat 10-7."

Fuck, she thinks. *They can't find me.* She realizes her mistake.

"Actually, sir, let's calm down," she says, turning down her radio. In the same motion, she clicks her call button three times, hoping dispatch will figure out she means Building C. She then reaches to make sure she has quick access to the gun if she needs it. "I only want to know about your relationship with Lennox Holcomb."

Still dressed in damp clothes, Ghost tries to make himself look comfortable by picking up the dishtowel and wiping his hands. He gently places it on the counter.

"Ah, the saga of Bastien and Lennox." He yanks a chair out from underneath the kitchen table and sits. He interlocks his hands and pounds them on the table. He takes a breath to calm himself down. "Well, Lenny was an addict. A whore of an addict. One of my best customers, if not the best. When he stopped using, hell, *dealing* and using, it kinda fucked me. I mean, I got a son to support."

Armed with little knowledge of what may or may not be happening in this moment, Ghost begins to think through his responses. "I may have overreacted a bit, threatened him, scared him and his friends a little. It was a hard time for me. Shit. He threatened me back, told me he'd written a letter identifying me, saying if anything happened to him, he'd hidden the letter someplace secure, and it would lead everyone directly to me."

"So when something did happen to him, why didn't you run?"

"That's where the saga takes an interesting turn. You see, I got clean. I mean, really clean. I got a whole year under my belt. No drugs, no dealing, no nothing. That's when Lenny and I became friends."

Lily laughs and plays with the bag, almost taunting Ghost to tell her the complete truth. With her other hand, she clicks her radio three times again.

"Yeah, I know. It looks bad. But I'm serious. I didn't think anything, cuz Lenny was my man. He was there for me. And my son. Lenny knew I wanted to move back home. Even invited him to come stay with me and my family some time." He pauses and looks up at the ceiling, as if transported somewhere else. He whispers, *"Rue de Sylvere Bohn et Strada di Scogliere Blanches. Sempre ma amore. Sempre ma maison."*

Lily hears him and recognizes the word *maison* from Jenna's testimony about the tattoo. *Maybe he's quoting what the tattoo says?* She palms her jacket for a pen.

"I wanted to go back home," Ghost continues. "Buy a place for me and my boy. Just the two of us. Lenny knew I needed the money. He's the one who suggested I start dealing again. Make some quick cash. Told me I should brand this shit, make it seem better than it was."

Lily gives up on looking for a pen and puts the bag of heroin down on the table. She wants to focus.

"Lady, shit is going down all over the place, and I didn't do fuck. I don't trust nobody right now. It's like somebody's out to get me. You gotta help me."

Lily looks over at the computer. She knows the answers are there. She knows backup cannot find her. She decides to stall so she can figure out her next move.

"Listen, if what you're saying is true, here's my card," she says, reaching into her shirt pocket. "Give me a call on Monday and we can talk about this at my office, maybe work something out. We'll help you, Mr. Morrell. We'll help you."

He takes the card, looks at it, and laughs. As he watches her move toward the door, he notices the framed photo of his son out of place.

Lily reaches for the door knob and feels a sharp pain in her right hand as the door slams shut. She looks down to see a large knife embedded through her hand and into the door. She cannot move it.

She reaches for her gun with her left hand, but feels cold fingers already wrapped around her holster.

"I can't let you go," Ghost says.

He grabs her other hand and forces it against the thick wooden door, thrusting another knife through her hand deep into the wood. She lets out a grisly scream. Ghost grabs her radio and presses his body against hers. "I'm gonna press this button, and I need you to say these words as calmly as possible. 'Unit 7-28. 10-80, repeat, 10-80.'"

"What?" She knows what he's asking. To cancel her backup.

"Don't fuck with me. I know they can't find you." He jostles the knife in her left hand. She wails. "Now let me hear it."

"Unit 7…" She can't say the rest.

"Take a deep breath." His mouth is warm against her ear.

She puckers her lips and lets out a shaky breath, followed by two involuntary inhales. She tries to calm herself down. She thinks it's the only way to save her own life. Through sheer will, she soothes her breathing.

"Okay."

"There you go. I'm pressing the button now."

"Unit 7-28. 10-80. Repeat. 10-80."

He lets go of the button. "Good girl." He places the radio back in her belt and rushes to the kitchen. He grabs the dishrag, opens a drawer, pulls out duct tape, then places them both on the table next to the computer. He heads to the bedroom, changes into his blue LES overalls, then pulls out what is left of his cash from the bottom drawer of his dresser. *There's no time to pack. Only one more loose end and I can leave this wretched place.*

He shoves two small stacks of $100 bills in his overalls and heads back down the hall, opens the drawer that holds his plane ticket, tucks it in his pocket, grabs the rag and tape, and heads toward Lily.

"Mr. Morrell, I don't think you killed Lenny."

"Of course I didn't."

"But this, this is something else. There's no coming back from this. I can help you. Please."

He grabs the rag. "No one can help me."

"Sir, please don't. Think about your son."

Her comment only adds fire to his rage. He shoves the rag in her mouth, overcoming her struggling. He wraps duct tape over her mouth and all the way around her head three times, making sure each round of tape lines up with the previous one. His precision is unsuccessful.

"This is gonna hurt." He opens the door on which both of her bloody hands are impaled. Lily lets out a muffled scream, shuffling her legs to ease the pain to make sure she doesn't fall to the floor and rip her hands in two. Then he closes the door, causing Lily to whimper in agony. She lays her head against the door, shoulders shrugging. He locks the deadbolt.

CHAPTER 53

The white door reads 228 in aluminum sans-serif numbers. Freckled hands unlock the front door with a key. They are careful to use the key only, leaving no fingerprints on the handle.

"Hello?" he says in a loud voice. No answer.

He's been here before.

Dressed in his navy coveralls, Ghost begins to ransack the apartment, desperate for the letter. He enters the room where he'd made the laptop exchange in the closet. Everything is just as it was months earlier. He runs back into the living room. He sees photos on a table behind the sofa and begins tearing into them one by one: Jenna with Josh, Jenna with Lennox and Micah, Jenna with James West. He doesn't find the letter.

He rushes to the bedroom on the other side of the apartment, just past the kitchen. He opens the closet and rifles through the designer blouses, pants, and gowns. Nothing. He opens each drawer of the dresser. T-shirts, panties, socks. Nothing.

He stops at the third drawer. He sees a black-and-white carved box. It looks familiar, only much larger. He opens the box. A cell phone rests on the left. Tucked beside it is the letter he's gone to great lengths to find, the one with his signature logo on the front of the envelope, the one his friend Lenny wrote years ago implicating him as the murderer. To the right of the letter is a small note on folded yellow paper, with the words "GHOSTS DON'T EXIST" written in block letters. The yellow note sits atop a homemade bomb, complete with a timer.

((5-4-3-2-1... BOOM!))

As the explosion fills the room, the letter shoots across the room, tossing and turning with each heaving flame. Plumes of fire, smoke, and ash push past the letter and through the windows, littering debris onto the street below. The unopened letter is engulfed by the flames and reduces to ash.

Ghost's broken and charred body lies paralyzed in the corner of Jenna's room. He opens his eyes. He cannot move. He can barely see. Partially aflame, the folded yellow note, the only evidence that can potentially prove that someone is framing Ghost for the murder, continues to glide through Jenna's bedroom. Out of the corner of his eye, Ghost spots the flittering object floating through the air, a yellow butterfly soaring with majestic beauty, dancing and flapping in a beautiful display of unfettered joy. Everything within him cheers for the creature as it flies out the window to freedom only to float back inside the room, landing beside him just outside his view. He closes his eyes and lets out a long breath. The flame on the yellow note reduces to a flicker, eventually dying next to Bastien Morrell himself, the words "GHOSTS DON'T EXIST" still visible.

Pedestrians at the corner of Henry and Rutgers gather to watch the blaze shooting out of the second-floor apartment at 10 Rutgers, the six-story building just north of the church with the bell tower. The tai chi class in the park across the street pauses their peaceful meditation and watches through the iron fence.

Other windows begin to buckle and burst as the flames begin to engulf the building. Small sections of brick continue to drop to the pavement as onlookers begin to scream and run, fearful their peaceful neighborhood is under attack.

Minutes later, firemen arrive and burst into Jenna's apartment, number 228. They go room by room until they reach the fire's point of origination. Opening Jenna's bedroom door blows a small ember onto the yellow note, sparking new life in the charred edges, consuming the note in a rapid flash of hungry fire. The black lacy remains fly out the window and disintegrate into nothingness.

CHAPTER 54

"We found what was left of Bastien Morrell, the man we refer to as Ghost, identified by the tattoo you see here."

Detective Bronson Penance shows Astrid Lerner a gruesome photo of a bloody and burned torso lying face down, arms missing to the elbow. His remaining clothes are burned away, scorched, or melted into what is left of his body. A partial shoulder tattoo of the Ghost logo is blackened and barely visible.

They are sitting in the work area just outside of Astrid's office, surrounded by paralegals, police officers and detective teams, all brought in from their weekends to ascertain what has happened.

"Was he wearing coveralls?" Astrid asks Detective Penance, trying to make out the bits and pieces of the scene. "And it's burned to a crisp, but does that part right there have an iron-on that says 'LES'?"

"Maybe, I can't really tell," says the detective.

"We thought about this guy early on," she says. "Couldn't find him."

"We also found some tiny fragments of what we think is a wooden box strewn around the room," Detective Penance continues. "Some fragments were unburnt and had black-and-white markings similar to the African box that housed the camera. We think it's the box that held the bomb."

"Christ," Astrid says, putting it all together. "He was pinning it on Jenna. How could we have been so wrong?"

"We think he came there to kill her, plant a bomb," Detective Penance reasons out loud. "It was a homemade device, but it was powerful. We think his plan blew up, so to speak."

"Jesus, Bron," Astrid says.

"Jenna's safe. She's with Josh, has been since around noon."

"That's good. Have you heard from Lily?"

"The police are still searching the apartment complex where she was last seen, somewhere in Alphabet City," Detective Penance answers. "She canceled her backup request, so hopefully she's okay, maybe took the rest of the day off. I was supposed to be off today, too, but look what you made me do."

Astrid laughs. A policeman holding a laptop and a plastic bag comes toward her.

Officer Mateo Palino enters the room.

"We didn't find much left of Jenna's condo," offers Palino. "But there was a closet on the opposite side of the apartment, and the contents were mostly safe. We found this plastic bag and a laptop. Melted a bit outside, as you can see, but it powers on. Wanted to get these to you immediately."

"Let's check it," says Astrid. "Copy the drive and get some people on it."

She takes the plastic bag and looks inside.

"My God." She reels backward from the smell.

"One more thing," Palino says. "The kitchen was mostly destroyed, but we did find a set of Jenna's knives that match the exact same knives that belonged to Micah and Lennox. We are testing to see if any DNA can be recovered from any of them."

"Well, test these bloody clothes as well." Astrid hands the black plastic bag to Officer Palino.

CHAPTER 55

Astrid, Detective Penance, and Offer Palino watch with their eyes and mouths wide open. The screen they are viewing is filled with hours of silent movie images that pass by in a dreamlike succession. All are from the same view: the corner of Micah and Lennox's apartment. Each are triggered by movement in front of the camera:

> Ghost setting up the camera, his face distorted in the middle of the scene. He taps the lens as if to make sure it's working.

> Lennox and Micah setting up dinner in front of the television, eating and laughing at an episode of *Will & Grace*.

> Micah walking across the room and looking out the window.

> Lennox straightening his tie, getting ready for work, checking the weather outside.

> Lennox drinking coffee on the couch, Micah hugging him from behind.

Micah and Lennox pulling the shades. Night vision comes on. The couple begins making out on the couch.

Lennox grabbing the remote from the coffee table.

A naked body being dumped on the floor into view of the camera.

"Hold on, here's something," Astrid says, pausing the video. "I knew it! He was dumped outta that chair like a bag of trash."

"And you can't see who dumped him. Ever." Detective Penance is noting the details. "That's interesting, like the killer's avoiding the camera."

"But why? We've already seen Ghost's face at the beginning of these videos," Astrid says.

"Dunno," Detective Penance responds, then looks at Officer Palino. "Look, though. The camera's night vision is triggered. That means the lights are off. Palino, let's watch and see when it switches back to normal."

"Will do," he replies.

"We're sure that's Lenny on the floor now, right?" Astrid asks.

"From the skinny build and the lack of clothes, probably. That's approximately where we found him," says Officer Palino.

Astrid hits play. Every time the body moves or heaves, the camera comes on for a few seconds. The body convulses in a series of twelve different scenes with time stamps covering a period of almost three hours.

In the final scene, another figure runs to the body and begins to pound on Lennox. Over and over. Over and over.

"Jesus," Astrid says. "This is amazing."

"That's one word for it," says Detective Penance. "Night vision is still triggered. The lights are definitely off, so we were wrong on that."

"I concur," says Officer Palino.

"So much for our Perry Mason moment about the light switches," says Astrid.

"And that's Micah pounding on Lennox's body, I can tell by the hair and the build," adds Detective Penance.

In the continuation of the final video, Micah stops pounding on Lennox and sits beside the limp body. He tries to get up and slips onto his husband. He pulls his husband's arm around him.

"That's all the video, there are no more files." Astrid pauses the video.

A hush covers the entire room. Everyone is frozen, soaking in the enormity of seeing the videos that had evaded them for so long.

"I don't know about you, but I see a distraught husband trying to save the love of his life." Detective Penance breaks the silence.

Astrid contemplates. "I think I agree. And given all of the absolute shit that happened today, I might be up all night making amends to these people."

"You're not going to believe this," says a twenty-one-year-old intern who's been hacking into the emails of the computer's owner. "I combed the drive for email addresses, accounts, passwords, and unlocked everything. Looks like some things are missing forever, but I recovered what I could.

"First of all," she continues. "I know our initial thought was that this laptop was planted in Jenna's closet by the Ghost man person thingie. But it actually *belongs* to Jenna. Jenna Ancelet. It's Jenna's old laptop from her Élan days. I cross-referenced the serial numbers with an equipment list we had from the company. This email address also belongs to Jenna Ancelet, a Frenchy228 from hotmail. I printed this email exchange, so you could see them. I think she's talking with Ghost."

"Frenchy228," Astrid repeats aloud.

"228 is the number of Jenna's apartment," says Officer Palino.

"Jenna's father is French, and she lived in France until she was 15 before they moved to the States," Detective Penance adds.

The intern lays out twelve emails and their responses in order of date. Each are short and succinct.

> From: Frenchy228@hotmail.com
> Subject: Job
> Date: December 14, 2017
> To: YouNeedaHero@yahoo.com
>
> I'm a friend of Lenny's, and I have a quick job for you. $10,000 upon completion. Interested?
>
> ＊＊＊＊＊＊＊＊＊＊＊＊＊
>
> From: YouNeedaHero@yahoo.com
> Subject: Re: Job
> Date: January 6, 2018
> To: Frenchy228@hotmail.com
>
> Sorry, I don't check this email often. Depends.
>
> ＊＊＊＊＊＊＊＊＊＊＊＊＊
>
> From: Frenchy228@hotmail.com
> Subject: Re: Re: Job
> Date: January 8, 2018
> To: YouNeedaHero@yahoo.com
>
> Need a camera set up in a condo on the LES. No breaking and entering, I have the key. I will give a phone number to send further instructions.

* * * * * * * * * * * *

From: YouNeedaHero@yahoo.com
Subject: Re: Re: Re: Job
Date: January 10, 2018
To: Frenchy228@hotmail.com

Gimme the number.

* * * * * * * * * * * *

From: Frenchy228@hotmail.com
Subject: Re: Re: Re: Re: Job
Date: January 10, 2018
To: YouNeedaHero@yahoo.com

555.921.5569

* * * * * * * * * * * *

From: YouNeedaHero@yahoo.com
Subject: Re: Re: Re: Re: Re: Job
Date: March 9, 2018
To: Frenchy228@hotmail.com

IT'S DONE

* * * * * * * * * * * *

"What's done? Setting up the camera?" Astrid asks.

"Yes, look at the date," replies Detective Penance. "Must be Ghost taking a job to set up a camera for Jenna. It's about five months before the murder."

297

"That phone number looks like a burner," says Officer Palino. "Might be the phone we found in pieces at Jenna's apartment. We'll check it out, find out what we can."

"Okay, look at these next emails." Astrid shuffles a small pile. "They start about six weeks before the murder."

From: Frenchy228@hotmail.com
Subject: One more
Date: July 5, 2018
To: YouNeedaHero@yahoo.com

Got one more small job. $5K upon completion. Lemme know.

****

From: YouNeedaHero@yahoo.com
Subject: Re: One more
Date: July 11, 2018
To: Frenchy228@hotmail.com

I'll do it.

****

From: Frenchy228@hotmail.com
Subject: Re: Re: One more
Date: July 18, 2018
To: YouNeedaHero@yahoo.com

There's a laptop in the boiler room of the building where you set up the camera. There's a key taped to the top of it. The key is to 10 Rutgers,

apartment 228. Once inside, go to the
right bedroom closet and place the
laptop underneath the stack of papers.
Payment will be taped to the ceiling of
the closet.
Don't do this until I tell you to. Call
me.

****

From: YouNeedaHero@yahoo.com
Subject: Re: Re: Re: One more
Date: July 22, 2018
To: Frenchy228@hotmail.com

When?

****

From: Frenchy228@hotmail.com
Subject: Re: Re: Re: Re: One more
Date: August 16, 2018
To: YouNeedaHero@yahoo.com

Call me.

****

From: YouNeedaHero@yahoo.com
Subject: Re: Re: Re: Re: Re: One more
Date: August 22, 2018
To: Frenchy228@hotmail.com

Finished.

* * * * * * * * * * * *

"So it *was* Jenna. She sent him to break into her own apartment," Astrid says.

"Brilliant," Detective Penance says, with a hint of sarcasm.

"Diabolical would be another word," Astrid replies. "I mean, look at the last date. He must've gotten the laptop right after she murdered Lennox, or right after *he* did, and taken it back a few days later."

"Seems like a lot of trouble," Officer Palino interjects.

"Yeah." Astrid squints as she scans the email exchange again. "She must've been in over her head. I mean, why videotape her friends, kill one of them, then try to frame someone else?"

"The fucking company, that's what I think," offers Detective Penance. "What I wanna know is, where's the letter? The one that Lennox supposedly wrote pointing to …"

Anticipating someone would ask, the intern lays a single page on top of the emails they've been reading.

Date: August 2, 2015
To Whom It May Concern:

My name is Lennox Holcomb, Jr. Currently I reside at 142 Henry Street, Apt 7, in New York, New York.

If you are reading this, then something has happened to me, and I've needed to take this precaution to point you in the direction of someone who has threatened my life, inflicted pain on my friends, and has even shared my heroin addiction with my supervisor at my workplace, which almost resulted in my termination.

Though I am grateful for the wake-up call of almost being fired, I write this letter to lead you directly to this man, this terrorist, this monster.

On March 21 of 2010, I began a program of recovery. The fact that I had a heroin problem is one that I do not hide any longer, I am not ashamed of, nor has any bearing on this letter. As of this letter, I have been clean and sober for over four years.

The man's name is Mr. Bastien Morrell. People call him Ghost. He was my heroin dealer for over four years. I was the source of much business for him, as I not only pointed high-profile clients in his direction, but I also dealt for him on occasion. When I left his growing operation to become sober, his business all but dried up. His resentment of me and my friends resulted in threats, encounters at my workplace, and the harming of two of my close friends, each stabbed several times and left for dead. Thankfully, both have recovered, although they are not the same. Neither am I.

Again, this monster's name is Bastien Morrell. He lives at 152 Avenue D, Building C, Unit C-412, here in the city. He has a son. Whatever you do, make sure the boy's okay.

```
Please make him pay for what he has
done.
Respectfully,

Lennox Holcomb, Jr.
```

"Well, we took care of that," Detective Penance jokes. "Hold on, look at that address! That's where Lily was, but they didn't have the building number. Hopefully they've found her. I'll be right back."

"My God, Bron, please keep me posted. Hopefully the boy is okay too."

Astrid thumbs through the pages on the table in front of her and looks at the computer. The still of Micah hugging his dead husband lingers on the screen. She turns away and looks out a window. "It's getting dark," she says.

CHAPTER 56

Darkness surrounds the Brooklyn suburban home of Shawn and Haylee Connelly. Shawn's private investigator Allen Pinchot is on the back patio, talking on his cell phone, breathing in the brisk, late winter air. Shawn is in the guest bathroom across from the kitchen, relieving himself of the long day.

Micah is enjoying the break from talking about the civil case, relaxing on the couch while Haylee pours them all drinks. She pours a glass of water for herself. Micah notices.

Allen Pinchot comes in from the cold.

"Guys!" Allen is barely able to contain his excitement, and looks at Haylee and Micah. "And gals, sorry. Where's Shawn?"

"Here." Shawn comes out of the bathroom, wiping his hands on his pants.

"Just got off the phone with my contact at the station. They just arrested Jenna for the murder of Lennox." Allen opens his mouth as if to scream, but no words come out.

Micah stands but doesn't move. Haylee stops handing out the shots of whiskey she's poured.

"Jenna. Sweet Jenna. For real?" Haylee asks.

"Yes. Apparently, there was an explosion at her place today. If we'd been watching the news, I'm sure we would've seen it."

"I would've heard it," Micah says. "She lives just around the corner from me."

"That's the thing," replies Allen. "Apparently, the laptop that recorded the videos from that fucking camera were found in her place. All those videos are still on the laptop. Jenna's laptop."

"No!" Shawn says.

"Ghost set the camera up. There are email exchanges back and forth from Jenna to Ghost. Jenna was the mastermind behind it all. Tried to set Ghost up, then planted a bomb to kill him. That's their theory for now, but obviously they are still looking into it. So, Micah, you were found innocent by a jury, but now the whole city will know it for a fact."

The room is silent. Everyone is hanging on to every word Allen is saying. Haylee continues handing out shots.

"As a result of all this malicious nonsense, I have no doubt the civil case will be dropped." Shawn shifts his gaze to Micah.

Micah forces a smile and looks around the room.

Haylee is uncomfortable with the lack of response. "Cheers!" She offers up her water. Everyone holds up their glasses.

"Cheers!" Shawn and Allen reply.

Haylee motions for Shawn to join her on the back patio. Shawn shrugs and follows her.

They walk in silence, each taking a seat on the wire mesh chairs with the green cushions. Shawn senses something is wrong and scoots his chair closer to her.

"Does this mean you'll be defending Jenna?" Haylee is shaking.

Shawn stands up and closes the glass patio door. Micah watches. Shawn gives him a *Don't worry, I got this wink* and turns back to Haylee.

"If she asks me, I will." Shawn returns to his chair.

"Even after all of this? What you did to her?"

"Turns out I was right."

"Jesus, Shawn, that's not the point."

"I get the point, baby. She's not going to ask, mostly because of exactly what you said … what I did to her during the trial."

"But if she does ask, you said you'd defend her. That's concerning."

"You don't think the company was behind this? Listen, Jenna didn't do this alone."

"Not the point."

"I mean, come on. Jenna Ancelet, a murderer by *choice*?"

"You still don't get it. Another trial like that could go on for months. And if you're personally involved again, well, I saw what this one did to you. Now we have the baby to think about, Shawn."

"Honey, I know I got wrapped up in this trial. In winning. But now? Baby. Sweetheart. Something changed in me, I can feel it. I just haven't gotten the chance to show you. And it has everything to do with this baby we are having." Shawn puts his hand to her face. "I love you. If I have anything to do with Jenna's defense, I promise it'll be different."

Haylee looks down. She just needed reassurance, but now she's embarrassed. She nods in agreement. "We got this."

Allen taps on the glass and mouths, "That's not all."

Shawn opens the door. "Yes, Allen?"

"Just had another call from my contact. Get this. They also found many, many email exchanges between her and Ghost about setting up the camera and shit. Plus, Jenna's emails show receipts for a wireless camera and African wooden boxes. Internet search history shows that she researched how to build a bomb, how to frame someone, everything she needed to know about stab wounds and paralysis so that someone would suffer before dying, some serious fucked-up shit. Plus, she has the same set of knives that Micah and Lennox have! They're testing them right now. She's been planning this for a very long time, and was pinning it all on Ghost."

"Dear God," Shawn says, turning to Haylee.

"Coulda snapped. Psychotic breakdown?" Haylee offers.

"And the final blow?" Allen continues. "A red gown, black overcoat, and long black gloves were found in a plastic bag in Jenna's closet with blood *all* over them. They're testing to see if the blood is Lenny's."

"A red gown?" Micah asks. "Maybe it was— Shit. I was wondering why she didn't wear that one. She was supposed to wear it the night of the event. A big red oversized Halston gown with these ridiculous flared sleeves. But she didn't wear it. I even asked her where it was. She said she couldn't find it."

"Dear God." Shawn's phone rings. "Hold on, guys, I need to take this." He walks back outside and closes the glass door. Micah takes advantage of the interlude to pull Haylee aside.

"Congratulations," he says.

"Congratulations?" Haylee's voice is hushed. She pulls him away from Allen. They move to the corner of the living room while Allen walks to the kitchen and pours himself another shot.

"Don't worry," Micah says after a few moments of silence. "I won't say anything. But given all this, I'm really happy for some good news."

"Micah, this is all good news. I know you loved Jenna, but it really looks like she did this. We finally know who killed Lenny now, and your name will be cleared completely."

"But at what cost?"

Haylee places her hand on top of Micah's. "Thank you for the wishes. I'm more than happy to be the bearer of some good news. That is, for about seven more months."

She laughs. Micah smiles.

The glass door opens and slams shut.

"So that was Detective Penance," Shawn announces. "They found the letter, a digital version of *the* letter that Lennox wrote, which led them directly to Ghost's place. Remember Lily, Detective Bronson's right-hand gal? She was basically crucified and left for dead right inside Ghost's front door."

Everyone stands aghast.

"Crucified?" Micah asks after a moment of silence, remembering how good Lily was to him that horrible night at the police station.

"Yes," Shawn says. "Turns out she took the information I gave her and found out where he lived. Stupidly, she went there before backup arrived. Ghost surprised her, ended up putting a knife through each of her hands—she was literally pinned to the back of the door. It would've been too painful to move, and she was gagged so she couldn't scream, much less warn the police when they finally arrived. The door was thick, so they had to burst through with a battering ram. She's banged up pretty bad, lost a lot of blood and is in and out of unconscious. But she's alive. They think she's going to recover. Haylee, baby, the main reason for the call is that Lily told him about you seeing Ghost at the carwash, so we gotta go down and make a statement tomorrow, show them the photo you took of Ghost."

Haylee nods.

"I don't understand," says Micah. "What would make Jenna do this? Put this in motion? Why would she do this to us? To Lennox?"

He looks around the room.

Shawn steps up. "Everyone's still reeling from this convoluted mess she made. Framing you, framing Ghost, using company tactics to throw off the scent. Detective Penance still seems to think the company is behind this. In fact, they're combing Ghost's apartment as we speak to see if they can find that missing hard drive. Remember? The one stolen from evidence?"

Micah shrugs.

"They're still looking for that goddamn hard drive," Shawn says. "And I bet it's with Ghost, or got blown to hell with Jenna's apartment. I agree with the detective. My guess is that Jenna hired Ghost to help carry out some sort of financial cover-up for Élan, which might explain why she did all this. Why she killed Lenny. And trust me, if any of that's true, that company will feel my wrath." He winks at Haylee.

Shawn turns to Micah. "Buddy, nobody is forgetting about this, about Lenny. Justice is coming. Finally."

"Cheers to Lennox!" Haylee raises her glass.

Shawn and Allen lift their glasses. "To Lennox!"

"If you'll excuse me." Micah places his drink on the counter and walks to the bathroom. He closes the door, muting the celebration from the other room. He can still hear them.

"Poor Micah," Haylee says.

"This is a lot to take in. Fucking Jenna, putting Micah through all this," Shawn says.

"Imagine losing the love of your life, going through what he went through, and now all of this," Haylee replies.

"He made it through, though," Allen adds.

Micah, still listening from the bathroom, puts his hands on the vanity, holds his head down and cries, his shoulders heaving. The sounds grow softer.

"Can you believe how many suspects there were?" Micah hears someone say.

"I know!" someone else adds. "We were seriously on the edge there, going who did it, who did it?"

"Not once but like five different times, we were like, 'He did it.'"

"She did it."

"No, they did it."

"No, he did it."

"Oh, no, SHE did it."

They chuckle.

"Hey, guys, it's over now. We know who did it."

As the laughing from the other room fades to deafening silence, Micah takes a deep breath and closes his eyes.

> The affair.
> The day he threatened Josh.
> The fight.
> The secrets he collected.

The last time he saw Lennox alive.
The knife he shoved into his husband's back.

He rattles his head as if he's shaking the whole disturbing, awful, exasperating experience off, pulls back his shoulders, and looks in the mirror.

"You did it."

ABOUT THE AUTHOR

"When you think back to your original passions, the ones you had when you were a child, remember those passions are the ones that are God-given. Innate. Soul-born. They fill you up, they never tear you down."

—paraphrased from Pete Wilson,
former pastor of Crosspoint Church

Those words. I can't tell you what they did for me. I was at a crossroads, a place where monotony met discontentment, struggling with what was next for me. About that same time, a friend of mine Kelly Oechslin released her first book. I saw the light in her eyes, the pure unadulterated joy of presenting what she'd accomplished. Evidently the universe was trying to guide me. It was like my childhood was whispering, "Hey, remember me?"

Ever since I was little, I can remember writing. I wrote my first book when I was ten. Well, "book" is a bit of an overstatement. It's roughly 20 pages about a little girl with cancer, with the title "In Other Words, You're Dying" in huge adolescent cursive on the front cover. I don't remember what was happening at the time, but clearly I was trying to work through something. I devoured hundreds of books as a child and well into high school. Essays were always my favorite test-taking form. Creative writing courses in college led to me being fashion editor of our university newspaper. In the early nineties, I wrote a lost episode of "Friends," thinking that somehow NBC would pick it up, and I could play Chandler's long lost brother. I also wrote an original script about a struggling record company called "Off The Record," a vehicle for Kirstie Alley because I couldn't bear thinking that "Cheers" would never return.

Then it stopped. Life happened. I stopped writing. I listened to other people tell me who I was, I moved from city to city following pursuits on whims. My mom passed away. I drank. I did drugs. I did manage to start a novel in the midst of a drug binge, but I didn't finish it. You can imagine why.

I got sober. I began coming back to myself. I moved back "home" to Nashville.

That's when it happened. Pastor Pete. Kelly Oechslin. I dusted off the novel I began years ago during the drug binge. The memories of where I was and who I was at the time came flooding back. I wanted to give up immediately, but I noticed that the story itself had legs. I shifted the narrative to another perspective and began mapping out the new book. Character by character, chapter by chapter, the ideas started flowing. Then I took a long trip to Italy to help celebrate my two best friends and their milestone birthdays *(photo on previous page was taken by my friend Ruben during the trip)*. It was there that I finally typed the first chapters of this novel. That was 2016. It has been a roller coaster of pure unadulterated joy ever since.

Now as I am writing this letter to you, it is two weeks before I release my first novel to the world. I am nervous. Excited. Sometimes I struggle with getting caught up in the whirlwind, in thoughts of success. But then I have these moments, like right now talking with you. *These* are the moments I love... the ones of centeredness, of gratitude, of peace, of KNOWING that I am doing what I'm supposed to be doing. It's all the success I need.

If you are struggling with passion, or perhaps wondering "what's next," try listening to that childhood whisper. It might just be waiting for you to give it a voice.

AN EXCERPT FROM
TRANSPARENT
Coming Winter 2020

"Why, Josh Harrison, you son of a gun," Josh hears someone behind him, mimicking a Southern accent.

Josh turns around. "Why, Miss Hillary Gordon, as I live and breathe." Josh overtly mocks her mocking him.

'This is all your doing, right, you handsome Southern devil? 1 knew tonight was going to be amazing when I got this lovely invitation in the mail."

She reaches into her purse to find it.

"You should see the gift bag," Josh replies, anticipating Hillary's "Ooh, aah" moment over the invitation.

Hillary is the 57-year-old wife of Walter Gordon, one of the pioneers of the recent Internet commerce re-emersion. *Time* had recently awarded him the title "Man of the Future." In most business circles, he is considered one of the smartest men in the world, a former think tank member under Obama, respected, rich, and indispensable to many Fortune 500 clients who have benefited from his revolutionary tactics that consistently stayed ahead of consumer trends. Whenever Gordon announces a new method or product, it makes headlines, people flock around it, and his clients make money. And Hillary is his perfect wife. The constant, loyal, and proud companion. Poised, graceful, and personable, she is one of Josh's biggest fans. And vice versa.

"Oh, lookey here," Hillary says, pulling out her phone instead of the invitation. "You know, my husband Walter is running late, and I bet I just missed his call. Will you excuse me, please?"

Josh nods, turns around, and begins walking through the enormous crowd at the event. He allows himself to be proud of his accomplishment, this extraordinary event he has created for Élan. *So many celebrities, so much media*, he thinks. *Damn, this is good.*

Not paying attention to where he is walking, he bumps into a returning Jenna standing perfectly still. All the blood has drained from her face. She is pale, disengaged.

"Jenna, what's wrong? Is Tracy okay? Michael? What?" Josh has never seen her like this. "Talk to me, please."

She slowly scrunches her brow, trying to make sense of what she is about to say. She takes a deep breath.

"They're at Union Square. Michael just picked up Tracy at her apartment. They were waiting for a cab, just... talking to me." Jenna's face has no expression.

"What happened? Jenna, you're scaring me." Josh moves closer to her and rests his hand on her shoulder.

"Then Tracy started screaming and handed the phone to Michael. Michael told me a man in a tux just fell down dead, practically in front of Tracy. He'd been shot in the back." She begins to speak in whispered disbelief. "Michael said there was blood on Tracy's shoes."

"What? Oh, Jesus." Josh takes Jenna's hand. "Are they okay?"

"Josh... they said they recognized him, the man in the tux," Jenna continues, finally looking at Josh directly in the eyes. "It was Walter Gordon."

Josh pauses, looks down, then with widening eyes turns around to Hillary. At the same moment, Hillary drops her cell phone and falls to the ground.

They rush to her side and hold her. Barely coherent, Hillary begins to mutter, "My husband, my husband" over and over.

"I think I just heard him die."

---

*Visit Royce.co for more on the author,
and for more information on upcoming titles*

CPSIA information can be obtained
at www.ICGtesting.com
Printed in the USA
LVHW081138080921
697319LV00019B/372

9 781734 335705